SORRY NOT SORRY

JAIME REED

POINT

Copyright © 2019 by Jaime Reed

All rights reserved. Published by Point, an imprint of Scholastic Inc., *Publishers since 1920.* SCHOLASTIC, POINT, and associated logos are trademarks and/or registered trademarks of Scholastic Inc.

The publisher does not have any control over and does not assume any responsibility for author or third-party websites or their content.

This book is a work of fiction. Names, characters, places, and incidents are either the product of the author's imagination or are used fictitiously, and any resemblance to actual persons, living or dead, business establishments, events, or locales is entirely coincidental.

Library of Congress Cataloging-in-Publication Data available

ISBN 978-1-338-14900-5

10 9 8 7 6 5 4 3 2 1   19 20 21 22 23

Printed in the U.S.A.   23

First edition, March 2019

Book design by Yaffa Jaskoll

SORRY NOT SORRY

ALSO BY JAIME REED

Keep Me in Mind

PART 1

CAUSE

CHAPTER 1

It's for a good cause.

If I had a dollar for every time someone said that this week, I could rebuild the town myself from the ground up. No need for charity events or pledge drives—the money would come solely from uninspired platitudes. What did people mean by a good cause anyway? As opposed to a bad one?

I should've asked the old lady who'd said it, but she'd already walked off, and she probably didn't know the answer, either. She was one of those pinch-lipped, cardigan-wearing schoolmarms who'd play the church organ on Sunday, then gossip and gamble the rest of the week. She'd rolled up to my booth, all grins and holy conviction, and handed me a box of expired relics from a cellar pantry.

"Oh them poor, unfortunate souls!" she'd cried out in a breathy Scarlett O'Hara drawl, clutching the pearls around her neck. "So many people, completely destitute in a matter of hours—can you believe it? My prayers are with the victims and their loved ones during these trying times."

Going by the state of her donation, the question was who needed prayer more: the hurricane victims or whoever ate from this E. coli care package. It was a good thing that all the volunteers were required to wear rubber gloves, because dealing with this much rust had me wondering: *When was my last tetanus shot?*

Clipboard in hand, I inspected each dented and dusty tin: chicken soup, string beans, corned beef hash, and some janky preserves with peeling homemade labels. Out of two dozen contestants, eight cans made it to the finals. Could it be that "a good cause" had nothing to do with generosity but with the downsizing of one's cupboard space? Or maybe the weather was making me cranky. Who knows?

We were a month into the school year, and the sun had hooked the state of Virginia on a rotisserie spit. Thanks to the mother of all storms ravaging half the East Coast, the air was so thick and sticky you had to breathe in sips. I was the color of a bronze statue; I'd traveled to countries literally sitting on the equator and not once in all my eighteen years had I needed sunscreen until now. No hairstyle could survive this steam bath, which was why I kept my micro braids pinned in a high bun and off my neck.

I turned to deposit the cans in the box labeled FOOD. I'd organized six separate boxes for my booth: clothing, food, hygiene products, baby paraphernalia, bedding, and miscellaneous. Cases of bottled water, first-aid kits, and blankets were popular items today, as requested by the local news bulletin. The less imaginative givers slipped a few dollar bills in the water jug on the counter. Nothing wrong with that—at least they were honest.

My friend Sera had been helping me all morning but was now dozing in the folding chair next to me. Her head and limbs drooped like a wilted flower; her mouth gaped open in a gurgled snore. Even in sleep, Sera Kimura was over the top.

A bullhorn dangled from one hand and a portable fan whirred on full blast in the other. Since sophomore year, Sera had been by my side at every organized walkout, boycott, hunger strike, fundraiser, and picketing protest rally at our school, but even she was losing her pep today.

I bent down to the red cooler by my feet, dipped my hand in the slushy water, and flicked droplets at her face.

Sera returned to the conscious world with a start, hopped to her feet, and cranked the horn.

"Leave your donations here, people!" she shouted. "Come right over and give to the hurricane relief! Every little bit helps!"

"Good save," I muttered, fighting a case of the giggles.

"Show your support for your fellow citizens! White Chapel needs your help!" She targeted a student filming the action on his phone. "Hey, you, Neckbeard! This ain't the Coachella Music Festival, bro! Either go big or go home! That is, if you still have a home left. Not many do around here!"

Sera had a scratchy, I've-got-strep-throat voice that put you in mind of tobacco, whiskey, and a spittoon. It was a jarring combination with her five-foot height and long black pigtails that made her look like a twelve-year-old.

"Our town is in ruins, so roll up your sleeves and lend a hand!" Sera continued. "If not you, then who? If not now, when? Ask not what White Chapel can do for you, but what you can do for White Chapel!"

I snatched the bullhorn from her, its feedback screeching in the air. "Any more famous speeches you wanna steal?"

"Hook or crook, I'm gettin' the crowd riled up!" Sera replied and made a grab for the horn, but I held it out of her reach. One of the perks of being five nine.

"Oh, I think they're riled up just fine. They wouldn't be here otherwise." I dropped the horn into a crate under the table, then swept a glance around the school parking lot.

The lot resembled a county fair, crowded from end to end with tents and folding tables. Colorful banners divided each station by its purpose. The kiosk to my left sold I SURVIVED BIG LORETTA T-shirts and coffee mugs for ten dollars. The battle of the baked goods kicked off to my right: homemade vs. store-bought. Blue-haired grannies manned their booths in opposition to the soccer moms across the lane.

My heart swelled with pride at what we'd accomplished in so little time. People were coming out in droves to help, neighbors who'd never spoken before joining together for a common goal. This was the beauty of humanity, and it was a real shame a tragedy had to strike for it to happen. Better late than never.

Before that thought could settle, a disruptive vibe contaminated the air. It wasn't smoke, though that had been common lately, due to the recent spike in barbecues. The power had been out last week, so people were grilling up their refrigerated food before it spoiled.

But no. What now alerted me to the approach of evil was a Valley girl croon, followed by an all-too-familiar fake laugh.

"I know, right? It's *boiling* out here. Weather is so disrespectful."

The mean-girl posse of White Chapel High School approached our tent in a strut that looked choreographed. Leading the march was Alyssa Weaver: patron saint of the backhanded compliment, homecoming queen two years running, and voted by the student poll as most likely to star in her own reality show.

Alyssa sported the same yellow disaster relief T-shirt that all the volunteers had to wear. Mine hung past my shorts and made me look like a bruised banana. Hers had been bedazzled to death and was cropped, revealing flat abs and a belly button ring. An effective, albeit tacky, route to rally up supporters, but we'd take what we could get in a crisis.

The other girls in Alyssa's crew had followed suit, as was standard operation within the Borg, as Sera called them. There was a fine line between copying a style and falling under collective mind control. Kristen, Jenna, Liz, and Destiny had yet to find that distinction, so the *Star Trek* reference fit.

Alyssa stopped at my booth and pulled her sunglasses to the bridge of her nose. "Oh, there you are, Janelle! We've been looking for you all morning."

7

"I don't see how, since you didn't get here until noon," Sera replied with a snarl.

"Yeah, well, it's Saturday," Alyssa pointed out, as if that were a legit reason for tardiness. "Plus, I had to grab a few things around the house to donate." Standing on her tiptoes, she peered over heads in the crowd and waved someone over.

Sera's brother, Ryon Kimura, broke through the mob, towing a wagon full of bloated trash bags. He'd worked up a sweat pulling the load, yet maintained the effortless cool of a K-pop cover boy. Ryon had done a lot of volunteer work with us in the past, but unlike Sera, he kept his enthusiasm at a lower volume.

Each member of the Borg took a bag from Ryon and carried it to our booth. Arms folded, Alyssa oversaw the labor with the superiority of a queen.

My gaze flitted from the jumbo bags, the worker bees, and then to her royal highness herself. "Somebody's been spring cleaning," I told her.

Alyssa tossed her head back and stared at me. She was delicately pale with an athletic build and long, strawberry-blond waves that made her look like a mermaid on dry land.

In a tone ripe with exhaustion, she said, "You. Would. Not. Believe the stuff my mom had lying around."

"Oh, I believe it." I recalled her mom's frequent wholesale shopping sprees. Their living room and kitchen were loaded with so much crap in bulk, Alyssa was often embarrassed to bring friends home.

I hadn't been there in ages, but the memory was burned into my brain.

I dove into the first bag, and every household item you could think of spilled onto the counter. Twelve-pack cases of shampoo and body wash. Bedding sealed in its original packaging. Did the folks at Costco know that half their inventory was missing?

Sera opened a second bag full of clothes. "You sure you wanna let these go?" she asked Alyssa. "They still have the tags on them."

Alyssa finger-combed her hair and examined the ends in an attitude of boredom. "Nah. Half the stuff is so last season, and since I lost eight pounds, they don't fit anyway. I'm sure someone else needs them more than I do. Just because they're homeless doesn't mean they have to look the part."

And just like that, the new and not-at-all-improved Alyssa came out to play. It served to remind me why we were ex-besties, just barely on speaking terms. She hadn't always been like this, but it was the state of affairs nowadays.

I noticed that her loyal subjects had abandoned their unloading task and were currently checking out the soft-pretzel vendor two tents over.

"You think he's a college student?" Liz asked.

"Who cares? Pretzel guy is bae goals for real!" As always, Destiny sounded clipped and corny, like an exchange student who had no black friends. Her family was from Trinidad and yet she'd had the nerve to tell me—on several occasions—that *I* talked like a white girl. Priceless.

No goon squad would be complete without an enforcer, and Destiny Howell, my light-skinned clone, was the real MVP. This designer knockoff had been trying to rust the link between Alyssa and me since freshman year. We hadn't really needed Destiny's help on that front—our friendship chain had fallen apart on its own.

Ryon shuffled forward and set the final bag on the ground by the counter. "Okay, that's the last of it. You really outdid yourself, babe. All I brought was water and toilet paper." He stood up straight, cracked his back, and rotated his broad shoulders. Sweat clumped his short black hair into spikes and formed a dark stain on the back of his yellow T-shirt. "I think I might have pulled something," he groaned.

Alyssa wrapped her arms around his neck and planted kisses on his sweaty face. "Thank you so much, Sugar Booger. You didn't have to carry all that stuff for me."

There went that fake laugh again. It was an artificially sweetened giggle that grated my ears and caused my left eye to twitch. Nobody laughed like that in real life, and Alyssa's *true* laugh was a loud series of snorts and croaks.

Wait, did she say Sugar Booger? *Seriously? That's a new one.*

"No problem," Ryon mumbled between kisses. "I don't think you would've gotten all that stuff here by yourself."

Alyssa stroked his biceps. "I know. But it's still sweet of you to do that. I can't believe how strong you are."

Nuzzling noses, they stared dreamily into each other's eyes as Ryon replied, "You know I'd do anything for you."

The sad part was he actually meant that, and his cultlike devotion had baffled me and leading scientists for the last two years. I never would've shipped those two together. I'd read fan fiction with more plausibility.

And Sera? She didn't even try to hide her disapproval of this sickening rom-com. She grabbed the bullhorn from under the table and yelled into her brother's face, "No PDA on school property!"

Ryon leapt back and cupped his left ear. "God, Sera! What is wrong with you?"

"Give me that!" I snatched the bullhorn before one of the teachers confiscated it. Again. As seniors, we'd been entrusted to operate the booth by ourselves.

"Sera, you're just jealous. Maybe one day—when you stop dressing like a cartoon character—someone will love you the same way," Alyssa taunted, still holding on to Ryon's neck.

"I hope not, 'cause what you guys got going on looks highly unsanitary. You should probably get vaccinated. Besides, I don't have to change who I am to get a dude to like me. That's more your speed, pumpkin." Flipping her pigtails, Sera sauntered to the back of the tent, proud of the first-class shade she'd thrown Alyssa's way. Truth be told, so was I.

Alyssa's eyes darted from me to Sera's back, and I could almost smell the jealousy in the air. My question was why. The Borg were Alyssa's new partners in crime, so she shouldn't be that pressed over who I hung out with.

11

Those same eyes suddenly went droopy and dim as Alyssa tilted to the left. I reached over the counter to catch her, but Ryon beat me to it.

"Whoa! Easy, babe. You okay?" he asked as she gripped the front of his shirt.

Alyssa stood straight but kept her head bowed. Out of earshot of her entourage, she said, "Yeah. I just skipped breakfast and got a little dizzy. Sorry, hon."

Ryon cupped her face in his hands. "You need to eat something, especially in this heat," he said. "You test your blood sugar?"

"Yes, Dad," she teased. Pouty bottom lip: protruded. Puppy-dog eyes: activated.

Like a punk, Ryon crumbled. "You won't do anyone any good if you faint from low blood sugar," he told her.

Swaying a little, Alyssa touched the back of her hand to her forehead like a Southern belle who'd caught the vapors. "I know, but I was in such a rush to get here. I just wanna help. We have to put the needs of others before ourselves."

It took every ounce of willpower not to blurt out, "Since when?" I'd seen this girl park in the handicap spot at the mall on more than one occasion. She once knocked down an old lady in a scooter to get to the head of the line at the Apple Store. My guess would be she was trying to score cool points with her boyfriend, who was a Nobel Peace Prize winner by comparison.

"Tell you what. We'll grab some food, test your blood again, and then finish up here," Ryon suggested. When Alyssa started to protest, he added, "Nothing too heavy—just something sweet to tide you over. Humor me, okay?"

Alyssa conceded with a nod, and Ryon scooped her into his arms, practically carrying her away.

Oh, for God's sake! This was a family-friendly event and they needed to take that mess elsewhere. Mark me absent, because I was not here for it.

Sera emerged from the tent, and the sight of the happy couple heading off made her dry heave. "Dude needs to spray some starch on that static cling. Secondhand embarrassment is real." Then she looked at me. "What happened? Did she break a nail? It'd be just like her to play the weak damsel to get out of working."

I had to disagree. Then again, I had a lot more experience with the incomparable Alyssa Weaver to know all the faces she wore by name. I also knew not to overlook any sudden dizzy spells from her. Even though we weren't tight anymore, old habits die hard. Whenever she was around, I found myself keeping watch for any warning signs of hypoglycemia. Alyssa had been diagnosed with type 1 diabetes when she was five years old. The condition hadn't come from making poor life choices, but a losing ticket in the genetic lottery.

But I didn't say any of this to Sera. Only Ryon and I knew about Alyssa's health issues, and according to her, that was one person too many.

POLICY 1.2: PREEXISTING CONDITION

FIVE YEARS AGO

"Okay, sweetheart, I need you to keep still while I put this on."
Mrs. Weaver pressed the adhesive onto Alyssa's arm. If you
squinted, the two of them looked more like sisters than
mother and daughter—same reddish hair, same hazel eyes,
same dire need of a tan. The only distinction was Mrs. Weaver's
constant fretting, but then all moms were like that.

Alyssa sat at her kitchen table, watching the installation of
her new monitor with her bottom lip poked out. I sat at the far
end of the table with my head down, my chin resting on my
folded arms. Her mom said that the pod thingy had a timer so
it would prick Alyssa's arm whenever she needed insulin. It
seemed simple enough. Saved a lot of guesswork.

"Looks like an iPod for runners and stuff, but without an
arm strap," I told her.

Alyssa's brows furrowed deep, her lips tightened into a
button when she murmured, "I'm a freak!"

Mrs. Weaver stroked the top of her daughter's head.
"Honey, don't say that. Ain't nothin' wrong with you."

"Nothing wrong? Nothing wrong?" Alyssa shrieked.

"I have a garage door opener on my arm. People are going to see it! Why can't we go back to the pen, Mama?"

"'Cause you've proven that you ain't responsible enough to take your medicine on time," Mrs. Weaver replied. "Be a real shame to have to wrangle you to the floor like you're six years old again."

Like a toddler falling out in the grocery store, Alyssa pounded her fists on the table and screamed, "I'm not a baby anymore! I'm thirteen! This is so unfair!"

"Life ain't fair, Lyssa. You think I wanted this for you? We gotta do the best we can with what we have and play the hand we've been dealt."

"This is all your fault!" Alyssa hissed. "Yours and Grandma's! Why have kids if you know they might get sick? You're both selfish!"

Now, if I'd said that to my mom or—heaven forbid—Grandma Trina, my bottom jaw would be sitting in the mailbox. But that was none of my business. What was my business was making sure my best friend stayed healthy and still kept her dignity.

"I've got an idea!" I sprang up from the table and headed into the living room.

On the outside, the Weaver house matched everyone else's in the neighborhood: trimmed lawn, pruned shrubs, spotless windows, and shutters. The inside, however, was a mini wholesale emporium. No membership needed. The only place in the house you didn't have to shimmy and Harlem Shake through was Alyssa's room.

Not even my grandma would cross the threshold. A fearless woman, who in her heyday counseled abused women and children and forged a clinic inside an abandoned school in Uganda, she had once taken one peek into Mrs. Weaver's living room and said, "Uh-uh. No, ma'am. The Devil is a lie," then walked out.

"That house—heck, the block—ain't big enough to fill the hole in that woman's heart. That husband of hers done ran off and did her wrong, and she thinks she can fix it with some hole-sale hoarding. Not 'whole' sale, but 'hole,'" my grandma had explained to me during the drive home that day.

But again, that was none of my business.

Now I found Velcro, a purple headband, a glue gun, and some sparkles from a craft kit. After a few minutes of tinkering, I created the coolest armband this side of Claire's.

I returned to the dining room and modeled my new invention on my arm. "See?"

Alyssa's eyes lit up as if it were Christmas morning. "That's so cute!"

"It is. The kids in school are gonna be so jelly," Mrs. Weaver added in her attempt to be cool.

Alyssa rolled her eyes, then asked me, "Can you make one in red? And blue? Oh, and lime green to go with my sneakers?"

That sounded like homework, a practice that I viewed as a form of fascism. I decided to meet her halfway. "Sure. But I'll show you how so you can make more on your own."

She agreed with a firm nod. "Deal! Ooh! We can make a bunch of these and sell them at school. Kids can place orders—"

"And have their names put on it," I added. "Or even their initials written in—"

"Gold and glitter! Omigod! Twinsies!" we said at the same time, pointing to each other.

"You're a genius! We're gonna make so much bank." Alyssa threw her arms around my neck and squeezed. "Thank you, Janelle."

"It's okay, really." I peered over Alyssa's shoulder to where her mom stood by the patio door.

Mrs. Weaver smiled back at me, hands clasped together in prayer, as she mouthed the words, "Thank you."

CHAPTER 2

Set about sixty miles south of DC, White Chapel was an idyllic Christmas card of a town, littered with houses and farms dating back to the Redcoat and Patriot days. Pickup trucks and John Deere hats reigned supreme. Everything was closed on Sunday, and citizens awoke every morning to the airy perfume of wood chips, fertilizer, and dead skunk. Home, sweet home.

I lived in the historical district, and my street was one of the first to get power after the storm. But the trash in the road turned my commute into an obstacle course. Moldy sofas and tables waited at the curb for the city to collect. Neighbors aired out their houses and patched up walls covered by tarp. Ancient trees had been pulled from their roots; toppled-over rooftops and power lines stretched across side streets like casualties of war. Chainsaws buzzed and branches snapped, a recurring melody that would carry well into the night.

To think, we had Big Loretta to thank for this extreme make-over. Not Hurricane Loretta, as the news stations called her, but

Category 4, board-up-your-windows-and-pray-your-house-doesn't-land-in-Oz Loretta. For a town that saw maybe two inches of snow three weeks out of the year, we'd taken no heed of the evacuation notice, but left all the shelves at Walmart bare. Suffice it to say that we. Were. Not. Prepared.

Behind the wheel of my sister's beat-up RAV4, I parked in front of the redbrick Victorian house that took up the corner of the block. In a movie, my house would either be haunted or overrun by orphans and a quirky caretaker. The latter wasn't a stretch since the home had been in my family since Prohibition and now served as a pit stop for the traveling members of the Pruitt clan. No matter where my parents and sister traveled around the world, 288 Pennington Lane was our home base.

Aside from a few missing roof shingles and a flooded basement, the house survived the storm unscathed, probably for the same reason Grandma Trina had. They were both old and built to last, and too stubborn to keel over.

Her maroon minivan sat in the driveway. Normally, Grandma Trina would've been at First Baptist helping out with whatever church activity was going on that week. She spent more time there than at home, so being here before dark was odd for her.

I entered my house and air conditioning, spicy food, and the whiff of wet dog hit me immediately. I heard tapping claws and jingling collars before the stampede. Soon, five dogs greeted me at the door. The black German shepherd and black-and-white border collie stood on their hind legs, begging for affection, their large paws tugging at my shirt. A brown terrier and a foxhound circled my legs, nearly tripping me, while their half-breed pup performed acrobatics to get my attention.

If anyone asked, I couldn't tell them how we came to acquire so many dogs or why. The animals were just strays that kept coming back when we fed them. I dropped my bag and picked up the happy pup. She was a flirty one, always licking my face and burrowing under my shirt and popping her little brown head through the collar. That's how she'd gotten the name Peekaboo. Never one to disappoint, she gave my neck and chin a good tongue bath while I sifted through the mail by the door.

Wedged in the middle of the stack was a postcard from Mama and Dad. It was a picture of an African shoreline, the sand bleached white, the water clear blue against a cloudless sky. The postage was dated three weeks ago, and I figured the storm had caused the delay.

If I called them now, the time difference would send me straight to voice mail. Mom and Dad would be working in the field and wouldn't get to their phones until nightfall.

I heard the lady of the house clattering around in the kitchen, and if my nose wasn't deceiving me, she was cooking. That alone was worthy of investigation. I strolled in that direction, reading Mama's silly message on the back of the card.

Enjoy the sun for as long as you can, it read. Whatever that meant.

Grandma Trina stood at the kitchen island, poking at the pork chops and greens simmering on the stove. She was a tall, busty woman whose height and dark complexion I'd inherited. Though the woman rocked a silver afro, her true age remained a mystery to this day, and she had more agility than most twenty-year-olds.

Her huge brown eyes lifted from the pan and she flashed me a bright, gap-toothed smile. "Hey, baby. I thought you'd be back later. You hungry? You look hungry."

I was starving and willing to eat anything that wasn't char-grilled, but I had more pressing concerns. Grandma Trina could throw down on any given occasion—she just didn't. Outside of holiday meals or church functions, the woman never cooked. So my next question came with good reason. "What's going on?"

She stirred mashed potatoes bubbling in the pot. "What's it look like? I'm cookin' dinner."

"But why though?"

"We're havin' company over." She tipped her head toward the bay window behind me. "Mateo, guess who's here? You remember my grandbaby Janelle, right?"

The postcard slipped from my fingers and fluttered to the floor. My knees buckled and my arm muscles clenched, causing Peekaboo to yelp and tunnel inside my shirt collar to safety. I fumbled and caught her with both hands before she fell through the bottom of my shirt.

At just the sound of his name, I underwent a freak astral projection where my soul left my body for two seconds.

"Yeah, I see her around at school all the time." The reply came from behind me and managed to extend my out-of-body experience to about a year.

Slowly, I pulled a 180 clockwise and observed the boy sitting at my kitchen table. Not just any boy, but Mateo Alvarez: six feet and 170 pounds of male perfection, Scorpio, professional introvert, and wanted in all fifty states for first-degree hotness.

He faced away from me, his back hunched over his phone, but I'd know those broad shoulders anywhere. The shape of his head, his black curls, and the way his ears poked out had been ingrained in my memory since the seventh grade. For fear of gossip and the all-seeing Borg, his side and rear profile were all I'd dared to admire on school property.

He set his phone on the table and slung his arm over the back of the chair as he turned around. "Hey, Janelle. *¿Qué pasa?*"

Of all the responses running through my head, panic gave voice to the rudest one. "What are you doing here?"

"Your *abuela* invited me over for dinner. I saw her earlier today and she brought me here. She said I looked hungry." His gaze lowered to my chest. "Something's moving in your shirt."

I glanced down at the wiggling lump in my arms. "Yeah, that's my puppy. She's needy like that."

His full lips curled into a sly smirk. "Looks like that dinner scene from *Alien.*"

It did, and yet I was too bugged-out to remove her. The whole situation felt unreal, so if Peekaboo burst out of my chest and started eating people, I wouldn't be any less surprised.

"Janelle, put down that mutt and go wash your hands. Dinner's almost ready." Grandma Trina then aimed her wooden spoon at Mateo. "Young man, get that dirty phone off my table and wash your hands, too."

As Mateo rose from his seat to do her bidding, she went on to say, "So, I get to church today and Bishop Campbell had us crammed in a hot van, droppin' off supplies to the shelters on the Southside. Four old black women, one van, no AC for six hours in the heart of Redneck County. But I ain't complainin'. We get to the last stop at Herrington Middle School and they've got generators and cots set up in the gym." She paused to look at me. "You used to go there, remember, baby?"

"How can I forget?" I muttered, then fished out the pup from my shirt and set her on the floor. Junior high was an awkward time in my life that I wished I could block from memory—the main cause being the boy walking toward me.

Looking away would've been smart, but I couldn't bring myself to do so. His scuffed black boots had no laces, with a gray bald spot on the toes where they'd been worn to death. His blue jeans and long-sleeve shirt were wrinkled as if thrown on in a hurry. Scrolling up, I caught the light dusting of stubble and a black scab on his chin. Red scratches marked his right cheekbone and eyebrow, but his eyes were what held the most turmoil. They shimmered in a kaleidoscope pattern of green, brown, and gold, framed by thick black lashes that shadowed his cheeks when he blinked.

Somewhere on the other side of the planet, Grandma kept talking. "So there I am, handin' out water and blankets at the school, and guess who I see up in there on one of the cots, lookin' hungry?"

I rolled my eyes. Everybody looked hungry to Grandma Trina.

"I'm searchin' the place, wonderin' why this baby's sittin' by himself. See, I know his mama—"

"You know everybody's mama, Grandma—"

"She'd come to church every Sunday draggin' this little runt with her." She held a hand at her mid-thigh. "He was about this high, runnin' around the aisles in his little suit, head full of curls like a wet poodle. Now, Anita ain't about to let her child starve in no shelter. She would've called me first, so I knew somethin' was up."

The last part of her rant caught my attention. "Wait. You were at a shelter? Why? What happened?" I asked Mateo.

"Loretta happened." He scrunched up his sleeves and moved to the sink.

I closed my eyes and allowed my imagination to reenact the fallout. He lived in the lower portion of White Chapel where the storm did the most damage. From what I saw on the news, blocks of that area had been leveled. The rural parts were now a wetland and they still had no electricity.

I joined him at the sink, then whispered, "I'm so sorry. Are you okay?"

"Not exactly" was his only reply as he handed me the soap. I didn't press the issue.

Side by side, we lathered and rinsed under the faucet in silence. This was the closest I'd ever been to Mateo, so I savored the sandalwood cologne and faint trace of sweat drifting from his direction. I snuck a glance at his hands: rough, and tracked with even more scratches.

"I tell ya, baby, that storm did a job on them people down there." Grandma swung the wooden spoon like a conductor's wand, sending gravy flying everywhere. "The campgrounds are flooded. All them RVs and trailer parks—ain't nothin' left but matchsticks. And this one here barely got out alive. The roof done caved in and fell on him and his mama. Had to pull her out of all that rubble."

"What?" I turned to Mateo. "Is your mom all right?"

He reached across me and snatched paper towels from the rack. "Yeah. She broke four fingers, two ribs, one leg, has a minor concussion, a punctured lung, and had her spleen removed, but she'll survive. Can't say the same for the house, though."

"House's flat as a pancake," Grandma added, and slapped scoops of mashed potatoes onto plates. "He told me what happened to Anita and how the hospital sent him to the shelter. I said, 'Lord, this baby's been by himself this whole time? I gotta take him home with me.'"

"Don't you have relatives you can call?" I asked Mateo.

"If I did, you think I wouldn't have done that already?"

I reared back and shook off the frostbite from his answer. "I was just asking."

Grandma Trina came from behind the counter and set three plates of comfort food on the table. "Y'all better come on here and eat this food. I don't cook like this 'less a man's here. Since my son's in Nigeria or wherever, I'm off the clock."

Right on cue, the German shepherd and the collie circled the table and jumped on their hind legs to reach the food.

"Ah-ah-ah! Corner. Now!" Her command cracked a whip through the room, making me and Mateo jump. The dogs whined and retreated to the doggy beds by the pantry door, their tails tucked between their legs. The woman had everybody under this roof trained, humans included.

We took a seat, mumbled a quick prayer, and dove into the meal. I couldn't describe what the food tasted like; I was too distracted by the boy by my side. I must have spent ten minutes staring at his lips alone.

Halfway through dinner, Mateo asked me, "So, your dad's from Africa?"

"No. We're American. He and my mom are there for a humanitarian project." I showed him the postcard they'd sent me. "My sister and I used to travel with them when we were little, but they wanted us somewhere stable for school," I explained.

"That sorta thing runs in our family, Mateo." Grandma spoke up. "My late husband and I did mission work in Africa. I did social work for forty years before I retired. My oldest grandbaby is off buildin' houses in Haiti and there ain't no tellin' what this one's gonna do." She jabbed her fork in my direction.

I sank lower in my seat, ducking the spotlight she put me under. I hadn't picked a college yet, but I wanted my future to involve something political: maybe becoming a public official or a diplomat. My family was more hands-on in their approach, but I craved enacting change on a broader scale. In the meantime, I'd make any small difference in my own backyard, even if it was collecting canned goods in the school parking lot.

"What you tryin' to do, sweetie?" Grandma asked Mateo. "You're a senior, right? You've got plans for the future?"

"Nothing that big, but I like to bake. I wanted to go to culinary school, but I'm more set on making sure my mom's okay."

"Cookin', huh?" Her dark eyes narrowed as she sucked loudly at something in her teeth. "Great. You can start by fixin' pancakes for breakfast tomorrow."

His brows knit together in a scowl. "And . . . why would I do that?"

"You gonna need somethin' to eat in the mornin'. I ain't gonna cook for you. Y'all old enough to fend for yourselves 'round here."

He looked just as confused as I felt. "I'm sorry—did I miss something? I thought this was just dinner."

She gave him a dismissive wave. "Boy, you knew good 'n' well you weren't sleepin' in that musty gym another night. You need a place to stay till your mama gets out of the hospital. By the look of things, that's gonna be a while."

At some point, I knew I should draw a breath, and it took a minute to remember how. I heard the words, understood what each one meant, but their sequence had me grasping for clarity. "You're gonna— Why would you— What are you saying right now? You mean he's staying? Right here, in this house? With us? Here?"

Grandma's reply was a lethal gaze, a quick scan up and down my frame, and a veiled threat in the form of a question. "Is there a problem, Janelle Lynn?"

Yeah, a big freaking problem. Mateo Alvarez, the guy I'd been crushing on for five years, would be sleeping under my roof. Eating my food. Using my shower. But I wasn't trying to die by this woman's hands, so I was like, "Nah, I'm cool with that."

"Mrs. Trina, it's nice what you're doing, but I'm fine on my own." Mateo tried to put her down gently, but he was messing with the wrong one.

"I don't recall askin' you if it was okay or not. This is my house and I already called Anita and she agreed that you'd stay here till she gets out the hospital. Lord knows you need somebody watchin' over you."

He dropped his fork, then pushed away his empty plate. "I'll be eighteen in another month. I don't need a babysitter."

"You need a hot shower, that's what you need. Runnin' 'round in dirty clothes, livin' out of a duffel bag, and sleepin' on cots around a bunch of strangers. But you're grown, right?" When no reply came, she turned to me. "Janelle, make yourself useful and show him to his room."

"Sure." I waved for him to follow, then exited the kitchen.

28

Mateo gathered his duffel bag from the living room and joined me up the stairs. My eyes remained forward the whole time and I centered all my conscious will on not freaking out. I considered putting him in the first room, but my parents slept there whenever they came home. The second room was cluttered with stuff that should've been in storage. The only available space was my sister's room. Right across the hall from mine.

I opened the door and clicked on the light. The room still carried Sheree's scent of vanilla and tea tree oil. Her yellow quilt stretched across the bed with that crisp military precision Dad taught us. Boy band posters and beach scenery hung on the walls. All that was missing were her clothes and, of course, her.

"Here we are. Sheree won't be back until Christmas, so it's all yours." I spread my arms and spun around. "It's not much, but you have a bed and plenty of dresser space."

"It's good. I don't have a lot of clothes." He dropped the duffel bag on the bed and observed the walls. "So it's just you and your *abuela*?"

"Yeah. We're used to it."

He nodded. "Same here. It's just me and my mom."

"Cool." Hands tucked in the pockets of my jean shorts, I rocked on my heels and searched the wall posters for a clever topic. I was never good at small talk. It usually came off intrusive and inappropriate. Case in point: "Where's your dad?" I asked him.

"Good question. I'll let you know when I find out."

My stare dropped to my feet. "Oh. It's like that."

"Like what?" His body language told me that I needed to come correct and do so quickly.

"Um, nothing, never mind. Do you need a towel or extra blankets?" I pointed to the door. "We have some in the hall closet."

He watched me carefully. "Are you always this jumpy? I know we don't hang out in school, but I've never seen you this wired."

"Sorry. This whole thing just caught me off guard. I didn't expect to see you here."

"Didn't expect a two-ton oak to bulldoze my house, but here we are." He rose to his feet and went for the door. "Look, if you have a problem with me being here—"

I blocked his path and pushed out my hands to stop him. "No, no! Stay! Stay!"

Mateo crossed his arms over his chest and sized me up. "I'm not one of your dogs."

"You know what? You're right. My bad. But you're more than welcome to stay. I'm across the hall if you need anything."

He kept staring at me. "Can I be alone?"

"Yup." I shot out of the room, closed the door behind me, and raced to my room.

Eyes shut, I pressed my back against my closed door and waited for my heart to slow. Puking posed a real threat, though that might help me remember what we'd eaten for dinner. From my end, the menu had been a hot plate of weird with a double helping of cringe. And I'd have to endure this on a daily basis? *For real?*

My first course of action was to call Sera, maybe even sleep over at her house for the weekend, but I'd left my phone in my bag downstairs. I didn't care if my bladder exploded—I wasn't leaving my room for the rest of the night. Besides, Sera would demand a full autobiography, and waterboard torture couldn't make me rehash that tale. No one, not Sera, not even my sister, knew about my obsession with Mateo. No one except, of course, Alyssa Weaver.

POLICY 2.2: PERSONAL HISTORY

FIVE YEARS AGO

"I don't know about this spot. Do you think we should move?" I asked Alyssa for the third time in the past hour.

"No way!" she replied. "This is prime real estate. We're gonna be out here all summer, so we need to stake our claim before some copycat steals our idea." Hands braced behind her head, Alyssa reclined in a lawn chair as though catching a tan.

At Alyssa's urging, we both wore frilly white Easter dresses and angel wings she'd repurposed from an old Halloween costume. Together, we looked like we were ready for a ballet recital. But Alyssa was insistent; this was all part of the sales pitch.

I wasn't worried so much about our wardrobe as our poster display. We sat behind a small refreshment stand framed by white balloons and a top banner in the shape of angel wings. A large sign hanging in front of the booth read:

PEOPLE IN HELL WANT ICE WATER.

HEAVEN OFFERS LEMONADE.

$2 PER CUP.

I had to admit, it was catchy, although it didn't feel quite appropriate for selling drinks in front of First Baptist Church. My grandparents were still in the building, and I wasn't trying to get yelled at, or worse, get dragged back inside for another sermon. One was enough for the day.

"Are you sure about the sign?" I asked the angel sitting beside me.

Alyssa fanned herself with a napkin, unbothered by the low-key blasphemy. "It's perfect. They've got services at nine, noon, and two o'clock. It's a bajillion degrees outside and probably ten times hotter indoors. And we just so happen to be sitting out front with ice-cold pitchers of the best drinks in town." She rubbed her hands together and belted a cartoon villain laugh. "I'm a marketing genius!"

That much was true. And we needed her genius if we were going to raise enough money to afford tickets to the water park this summer.

However, the quality of her products had needed a reboot. When she first came up with the lemonade stand idea, she'd given me a sample cup of what could only be described as Lemon Pledge on ice. I wasn't at all surprised. Alyssa wasn't allowed to have much sugar or carbs, and the stuff she could eat was measured out into daily portions. That was where *my* creativity and an old family recipe came into play.

Grandma Trina's lime coolers were about 80 percent

syrup and 20 percent fruit—a big hit at all the local functions. I could tell Alyssa wanted to try out the new batch right now, but three good sips could make her really sick.

Soon enough, the front doors opened. Organ music poured from the church as members filed out of the building.

"This is it! The big haul." Alyssa leapt from her chair and adjusted the straps of her angel wings. "Get ready, Janelle! Fix your wings and look cute! They're coming!"

In seconds, the walkway was a mob of big hats, suit jackets, and waving paper fans. I couldn't focus on anyone, though, because the lone figure heading our way had stolen my attention. And my breath.

Pushing a lawn mower across the grass, Mateo Alvarez trudged toward our booth. I distinctly recalled him looking swole in his PE uniform at school, but now his muscles were even more defined beneath a black undershirt and khaki shorts. Without thinking, I stepped from behind the folding table to greet him. The world around me began to move in slow motion as smooth R&B played in my head.

My pop-pop would say, *The heart is a lot like God. People only remember it's there when they're in trouble.* There was some truth to that, because my heart had been in trouble since Mateo transferred to Harrington Middle School that spring. Mystery automatically made any new kid cooler than the usual riffraff, but Mateo was something special.

I'd thought the summer would keep us apart, yet fate had brought us together—in front of my family's church, no less!

Mateo parked the mower at our drink stand, wiped the sweaty curls from his forehead, and smiled at me. "Hey, you were in my homeroom this year, weren't you? Jennet, right?" he asked.

Whoa! He knew my name! Sure, he was off by a few letters, but it was still recognition. "It's Janelle," I corrected him. "Um, so, you're mowing lawns today?"

"Yeah, I've been at it since six this morning. I'm saving up for tickets to the water park."

Wait a second. Both of us were broke this summer and we both liked swimming in water? We were *so* married!

"Really? We're working for that, too," I told him, feeling hyped over our new bond.

"*I'm* working. I don't know what *you're* doing," Alyssa mumbled behind me, then continued serving a customer in a suit.

"This is a cool setup you got here. I never would have thought of selling drinks in this spot." Mateo's gaze danced around our balloons and then settled on my outfit. "There're no restaurants or shops around, so no competition. Pretty clever."

My brain was mystery meat at that point, and all I caught was the word *pretty*. I gestured to the array of beverages on display. "Y-you want something to drink? We have iced tea,

lemonade, limeade, tea-lemonade, and red Kool-Aid. I rec-
ommend the lime. It's my grandma's famous recipe. It's really
good." I scooped up the glass pitcher. "Here, try some. It's on
the house."

Alyssa pulled a double take, then asked, "On the what?"

"You sure? I can pay for it." Mateo reached in his back
pocket for his wallet, but I waved him off.

"Don't worry about it," I said, filling a plastic cup. "You've
been working hard and could use some cooling off. Here you
go." I turned around, cold sugary beverage in hand.

"I've got cash right here. *No hay*—" Mateo jumped back
and tried to avoid a direct hit, but he wasn't quick enough.
Stunned stiff, he looked down at the dark stain growing on his
tan cargo shorts, then finished his statement. "... *problema.*"

Oh. My. God. I hadn't known he was standing right behind
me, ready to be bumped into.

"That's one way to cool him off. Real smooth, *Jennet.* Now
he looks like he peed his pants," Alyssa commented from the
sidelines.

"I am so sorry. Are you okay?" I grabbed a wad of paper
towels from the table and approached him.

Mateo stepped away. "*¡Oye! ¡Cuidado!* I'll wipe it myself."

I froze and waited for the ground to open up and swallow
me whole. Wasn't that what happened in freak disasters?
"Omigod! I'm sorry. I didn't mean to."

From the corner of my eye, I caught Alyssa shaking her head at me.

I glared at her, then turned back to Mateo. "Are you okay?"

"Yeah, it's fine. It'll dry in no time in this heat."

"Okay. Well, at least have a drink on me. No, not 'on me,' like spilling it or anything, but—here. Take it. It's free." I grabbed a fresh cup from Alyssa's hand, then passed it carefully to Mateo.

"Hey! That was for a customer!" Alyssa called behind me, but I couldn't be bothered. Mateo's fingers had brushed against mine when I gave him the cup, and I needed a minute to recover.

After taking a sip, he stared at the drink in amazement. "Wow. It *is* good. Thanks."

Feeling confident, I decided to show off more of my charms. Mateo needed to see that I wasn't some ordinary eighth grader. I was a mature, well-traveled woman with culture. Bowing at the waist, I replied, "*De nada*. And sorry about the mess. *Yo soy muy, muy embarazada*."

Mateo's mouth fell open and his eyebrows lifted high on his forehead. He was clearly blown away by my worldliness. "Uh . . . *yeah*. I hope that's not the case, but take care of yourself. See ya," he said, then backed away toward his mower.

"Okay. I'll see you at the water park." I kept waving until he disappeared around the corner. He kept looking back at me with a strange expression, as if he was trying to figure me out. Oh yeah, I'd definitely left an impression on him.

The drink stand was a success. Thirsty masses kept wandering over, sweaty and tired from the heat.

By dinnertime, Alyssa and I had earned two hundred dollars, enough for three trips to the water park for each of us. That meant three more opportunities to see Mateo in swimming trunks. Three more times to work up the nerve to talk to him without stammering.

"You have a crush on Mateo Alvarez?" Alyssa's voice crashed through my thoughts. She stood on her tiptoes, taking down the balloon banner. "Wow. I didn't see that coming."

My arm knocked over the folded lawn chairs and I rushed to pick them up again. "No, I—"

"It's okay, Janelle. I'm not judging you. He's kinda scrawny for my taste, but definitely cute."

I was relieved and outraged at the same time. "Scrawny? You didn't see those biceps?"

The slow shake of Alyssa's head told me that she wasn't following. "You must have some strong love-vision goggles on, 'cause all I saw were twig arms. What I wanna know is: Why didn't you tell me? We tell each other everything," she pointed out, sounding offended and betrayed by the secrecy.

I knew she'd be upset, but it was pretty much a nonissue. Speaking my feelings out loud would make them real. It would also make the rejection real, and I wasn't ready to face that. "It's no big deal." I packed up the extra cups and straws from the table.

Alyssa dropped the balloons and turned to me with wild eyes. "It *is* a big deal. A very big deal. You're coming out of your shell and experiencing love in all its gooey goodness." She grabbed me and pulled me to her with a firm squeeze. "My little girl is finally growing up. I'm so proud! Don't worry. With me coaching you, Mateo will be eating out of the palm of your hand."

Her tone was light and full of pep, but the words had a ring of certain doom. There was no telling what crackpot scheme Alyssa would cook up on my behalf. But it wouldn't hurt to hear her out. Just for curiosity's sake.

Still hugging me, she picked that particular time to tell me, "By the way, *embarazada* means you're having a baby."

And just like that, all my plans of going to the water park were officially off the table. In fact, I had no intention of leaving the house for the rest of the summer.

CHAPTER 3

Politics have always fascinated me, whether on TV or in real life. The plotting, maneuvering, alliances, and overthrows reminded me of how my pop-pop used to play chess—straight greasy. On rare occasions, I'd catch a news clip of foreign officials throwing hands (and sometimes chairs) while their colleagues rushed in to intervene or to participate. That, in a nutshell, was the White Chapel High School student government meeting.

Every Tuesday and Thursday before first block, I'd take a ringside seat and wait for the upheaval to begin. Sera and I were the fund-raising officers, but all final decisions required approval from the class president, aka Sera's brother, Ryon. Having bitter siblings in positions of power was an assault charge waiting to happen, but great entertainment.

I arrived at the Tuesday meeting before the other members. Room 108 was a US History class, and its lecture-hall seating formed a C-shape around the center podium. Pictures of all the presidents lined the top wall, and the national and state flags hung behind the teacher's desk. I took my usual spot in the first row, gathered my notes, and jotted a few last-minute ideas to share with the group. I'd stayed up until after midnight organizing my plans and writing a detailed proposal. If nothing else, I was thorough.

One by one, the senior members made their grand entrance. Ryon Kimura lumbered into the room, coffee in hand and a military-standard backpack strapped to his torso. We had block scheduling, yet he hauled sixty pounds of mandatory reading to all four classes like a nomad trekking through Europe.

Next on the roll call was Tabatha Morehouse, class secretary, and White Chapel's self-appointed PC police. To her, everything was racist, sexist, or some form of oppression, despite her being one of the richest white kids in school. Her penchant for doing the most on every occasion also transferred to her hair. This week, her shoulder bob was dyed sky blue with purple bangs.

Then entered Joel Metcalf: class historian, head of the yearbook committee, and all-around creeper. After that incident in the faculty lounge last year, I could never view him (or cheese fondue) the same way again.

Next was Devon Shapiro, class treasurer and Sera's secret crush that was a secret to no one. He was one of those band kid geniuses who played every instrument and was the only white guy who looked hotter *with* dreadlocks than without. Devon was partly the reason Sera joined student government and the *entire* reason she'd just followed him into the classroom like a lovestruck groupie. Boy, did I know that feeling, but no amount of money would get me to say that out loud.

Once everyone was seated, Ryon stood behind the lectern and called the assembly to order with a crack of the gavel. "All right, guys, the WCHS student government meeting is now in session. The community food drive was a success. We collected five thousand dollars and twelve thousand items from Saturday's fund-raiser."

The room erupted in hoots and cheers.

"This is a great start, but we can do a lot more. Now, we all agreed that a cleanup project would be our next volunteer activity. So, who's ready to present their suggestions?" Ryon searched the group.

My hand shot into the air and I was on my feet before he granted me the floor. Passing folders to each member, my nerve endings hummed with excitement and propelled me forward with vision and purpose. I moved behind the lectern and imagined the bored, sleep-deprived, and acne-prone faces before me were proud heads of state. What we decided here would affect our children and many generations to come, at least in my mind.

"I believe the park in Aberdeen Square needs the most attention," I began. "The place looks like a war zone, but the city is more focused on damage on the Southside. Aberdeen Square is our town's landmark, with plenty of shops and eateries that could grant us access to restrooms and food. The area is huge, so we'll need to assemble a cleanup party of at least twenty kids. That means we have to recruit extra volunteer—"

"Sorry I'm late! The alarm on my phone didn't go off, then I couldn't find my notes for the meeting and I've been racing to catch up ever since." With a power smoothie in hand and her backpack sliding off her left shoulder, Alyssa Weaver tore into the class like Loretta's wrath on the Eastern Seaboard.

The room fell quiet, the note-taking stopped, heads turned in her direction while I cursed the universe for its jacked-up timing. Did I forget to mention that Alyssa was our class vice president?

Alyssa was class vice president.

"I made more disaster relief T-shirts and bracelets for whoever donates." She crossed the room and slid into the seat next to Ryon. "I had a few designs drawn up, but I'm not sure which style to go with just yet—"

"Excuse you! I'm in the middle of a presentation. I have the floor." I gestured to the area surrounding the lectern to stress my point. "This whole thing right here."

She looked up in surprise. "Oh! Hey, Janelle. I didn't see you there. Actually, I did, but on GP, I choose to ignore you." Then she continued to talk right over me. "I have an idea for the disaster relief project."

"That's nice, but we already have a plan in motion. Thanks for playing, though," I told her.

"You mean that snooze-worthy strategy you mentioned last week?" Alyssa let out a haughty snort. "That's real cute, but that's not gonna get people to contribute. People need incentive and market appeal. That's where I come in." She pulled sketches from her bag and presented them to Ryon. "Along with the T-shirts, Kristen, Jenna, Destiny, Liz, and I are creating our own web series about charity work. It will show us helping out around town and giving makeup tips along the way. We're calling the show *Active Beauty*. You know, like 'active duty' with—"

"Soldiers. Yeah, we get it," I told her. "There's already a ton of YouTube videos about that sort of thing. What would they need you for?"

"Because it's *us*," Alyssa answered with perfect enunciation. The "duh" was silent. "We're not some strangers on the internet. We're the real deal, we're local, and we're popular. Naturally, people will want to join us and be seen in the video."

"We can post it on the school website," Devon suggested, while dreamy-eyed Sera nodded at him. "We could get other schools to participate."

"It'll have to look professional," Joel added. "I know a few guys in media class that could help. I've got all the film equipment you'd need. Sound, editing—the works. Maybe we could combine all the episodes later on and turn them into a documentary."

The group agreed and Joel grinned in triumph.

Alyssa's upper lip curled. "Make sure you keep it tasteful, fondue boy."

"Funny," Joel returned with a sneer.

"Hold on! You expect us to sit back and watch you and the Borg hijack the disaster relief project?" Sera piped up. "Tell me, just how inoperable is that brain tumor of yours?"

"Not nearly as dangerous as the laser treatment for your mustache," Alyssa clapped back. "You should really get that thing looked at. For a minute there, I thought you were Ryon."

"Omigod, that is so racist," Tabatha informed the group. "Just because they're Asian doesn't mean they all look the same."

Joel consulted the ceiling as if in search of divine patience. "Tabatha, no one mentioned anything about race. Siblings resemble each other."

With a hiked chin and a flip of her blue hair, Tabatha looked away from him. "How about you check your privilege before speaking for other cultures, okay, fondue boy?"

Ryon brought the meeting to order with another crack of the gavel. "All right, I admit that the web series would be a creative addition to raise awareness, and Alyssa's proven her ability to pull in the numbers."

"Thank you, Sugar Booger." Alyssa blew him air kisses, then took a dainty sip from her smoothie.

Fighting a blush, Ryon continued. "I also agree with Janelle. Aberdeen Park is the perfect spot to begin volunteer work. So we'll combine ideas and have a cleanup and fund-raising party. We can sell T-shirts and food; maybe have a live band play." Ryon looked to the treasurer.

"On it. I'll bring my guitar," Devon affirmed, rubbing the soul patch on his chin.

"And on that note, we conclude our morning meeting," Ryon announced. "We will convene again on Thursday."

At the sound of the bell, everyone collected their bags and filed out of the room. In her rush to gain as much distance from her brother as possible, Sera promised to meet up with me later, then bounced. As usual, Ryon and Alyssa were the last to leave. They held each other at the door, storing up enough melodrama to fill those cold, lonely hours between now and lunch.

But what I found strange—and by strange, I meant suspect— was Alyssa's sudden interest in charity work. A quick meeting was in order.

"Hey, Lyssa? Sidebar?" I pointed to a corner of the room.

Looking very much annoyed, Alyssa dislodged from her other half and strolled forward.

I waited for Ryon to leave before asking, "What are you doing? We had a system going here. You handled the prom committee and all the other party events in school, and I did the charity events. You're not trying to pick up litter and pass out water, so what's really going on?"

She leaned away from me, fake-appalled by my accusation. "Wow, Janelle, you want some pepper to go with that salt?"

"I'm not salty, bitter, sweet, or none of them flavors. I just wanna know what your end game is, 'cause I know you have one," I replied. "Your track record is public knowledge and consistent. If money isn't on your agenda, then recognition is next in line. I don't know what this new scheme is, but you're not coming up in here late, thinking you're running something."

She stood perfectly still until I finished my rant. "Can I go now?"

I blinked. "You think this is funny?"

She folded her arms, looking bored by the whole conversation. "No, I think it's sad. You keep thinking you're on my level when you don't even live in my building. You've got good ideas but no PR strategy. That's *my* department." She pointed to her chest. "*I* pull in the numbers, because—news flash: People don't volunteer or give money out of the goodness of their hearts. They do it out of guilt, for bragging rights, to follow a trend, to get into heaven— whatever. In the real world, *everything* is business and *everybody* has an end game. Not my fault that I'm a better player than you are."

"No. But stepping on people's toes in your pursuit to be basic *is* your fault. Question: Did you sell your soul retail or at factory price?"

Ooh, I'd definitely struck a nerve. Good.

She stepped forward, her face set in hard, angry lines. "Watch it, Janelle. We've been civil up until this point. You don't want me as an enemy."

"Yeah. Because with friends like you . . ." The sentence went unfinished as I marched out of the room, not looking back.

The weird thing about being frenemies was that you were still kind of friends. No matter how complicated or unhealthy the relationship, there remained a part of you that cared to a certain extent. Sometimes, caring meant walking away before things led to some sort of felony.

Turning the corner, I collided with a random bystander who smelled like sandalwood. Rough hands caught my arms and held me in place.

"Whoa! Careful. You okay?"

After a few blinks, I stepped back. "Sorry about that. I didn't see you there."

"That seems to be a popular thing this morning," the boy replied.

Slowly, my gaze lifted to meet Mateo's and I considered keeling over. A fresh batch of embarrassment hit me square in the chest at the mention of this morning's debacle.

It hadn't been my intention to walk in on Mateo while he was in the shower. It was just an unfortunate product of little sleep and habit. My parents showed up twice a year, so it had been us girls in the house since I was fourteen. Walking around half-dressed or brushing your teeth while the other showered went with the territory. It wasn't that kind of party anymore, evident by all the screaming on Mateo's end.

So yeah, this morning was an L, and I wasn't the only one catching awkward vibes, either. Right now, Mateo's stare remained floor-bound as he rubbed the back of his neck. "Soo . . . yeah, I saw you go this way and I wanted to ask you for a favor."

Yes! Yes! I will marry you and have as many bilingual babies as you want! my mind screamed.

"Can you take me to the hospital after school?" he asked. "I wanna visit my mom, but my truck's messed up from the storm and it's still in the shop."

Or we could just go with that idea.

I played off the disappointment with a nonchalant, "Sure. No problem."

A small smile curved his lips so quickly, I almost missed it. "You sure? I know you're busy doing . . . whatever it is you do. You won't have to stay. Just drop me off and I can get my boy Chris to pick me up."

"I don't mind waiting for you." I'd waited for five years—what was a measly few hours?

"Cool. Thanks. I'll see you later." Mateo walked away, leaving me watching his head grow small from the back. My usual viewpoint.

God, he had a beautiful head, perfectly round and full of springy curls. When he was talking to me, one of the ringlets had fallen over his forehead, and my fingers had itched to brush it away, but any public show of affection could lead to—

"And what was that about, Janelle Lynn?" Alyssa's voice rang behind me.

Trouble. Big, big trouble.

I kept my posture straight and my expression neutral while facing my nemesis standing outside the classroom door. Alyssa watched Mateo's retreating form with a calculated gleam normally found in eight-legged creatures. Then her predatory stare slid in my direction.

"You and Mateo together at last! Oh my goodness!" She flung her head back and howled in maniacal laughter. "This is so delicious; it's *gotta* be fattening."

Someone kill me now and put me out of my misery.

CHAPTER 4

I sat on my bed, Skyping with Sheree, like I did every Saturday morning. I'd get up around ten a.m., fire up the old laptop, and rehash the week's dumbness to a nonjudgmental ear. Even during the storm's blackout, my sister and I spoke over the phone for an hour before my battery called it quits.

Peekaboo sat on my lap, her tail tapping a beat against my thigh. Sheree's sweaty, exhausted face smiled back at me from fourteen hundred miles away. She and her team were staying in a hotel outside of Port-au-Prince. They were on a construction project where they'd build twelve houses and a church in six months. By comparison, collecting trash and repainting the gazebo in the town square sounded mad corny. But my sister listened as if my woes were the most fascinating thing she'd heard all week.

I told her about the group cleanup that was taking place that day at noon. We'd recruited fifty volunteers, including teachers and students. Fliers hung in every hall, T-shirts were sold during lunch, and the event was even publicized on the Borg's vlog channel. *Active Beauty*, as they called it, had gotten the green light from the principal and reached 30,000 subs in under a week. Against my better judgment, I'd snuck a peek at the first two episodes. Shameless self-promotion, unskippable ads, and twenty-six minutes of my life I could never get back.

"Well, it could be worse," Sheree said. "You could be in the middle of a refugee camp with no drinking water. And dysentery."

I removed the coffee mug from my lips, my desire for caffeine officially gone. "Ew."

"Yeah, the kids here have it bad and the team's trying to help as many as we can."

"Sorry," I said sheepishly, then placed the mug on the nightstand. "Where are their parents?"

"Most of them are orphans from the earthquake. We're heading to the hospital in a bit to help with supplies."

Trust big sis to make me feel bad about my first world problems. She was the optimist of the family, one of those upbeat, bubbly sprites you sometimes wanted to trip down a flight of stairs. Her philosophy was to see the good in people and believe that everything worked out for the best. Bump that! You had to recognize the problem in order to fix it. Of course, Sheree was proud of my humanitarian efforts, but her praise could never penetrate the brain, the same way when your parents told you that you were pretty. It didn't really count.

"Stop stressing, girl. This whole thing will blow over, trust me," Sheree declared in a way that not only understood the situation but had foreseen the outcome. She could find the bright side of midnight. "Anyway, I gotta go. I'll call you next week."

"Okay. Love you."

"Love you, too, kid." She winked at me and with a wave, the screen went black.

I closed the laptop and got up, searching my closet for something to wear. This had become a time-consuming addition to my daily schedule. An attractive male inhabited my house, and female law dictated I slay 24/7 without appearing like I tried. Rain or shine, my makeup stayed flawless, my braids glossy, my edges laid, and my legs hairless. Since manual labor was on the agenda today, I settled for my yellow volunteer T-shirt and jeans that flattered my shape while allowing me to breathe.

In the hallway, I found the door to Mateo's room open. He was still in a funk over the living arrangements, needing to bum a ride everywhere, and being appointed house chef. He'd barely looked at me during breakfast, just mumbled stuff in Spanish that sounded like cuss words. If Grandma Trina noticed, she'd kept it hidden behind a neutral stare and the morning paper.

Over the course of the week he'd progressed from pancakes and waffles to crepes and quiche, all of which were slapped onto my plate with contempt. All the food was five-star gourmet quality, but the cook was a little too salty for my taste. Outside of meals, he'd hide in his room or brood in the living room and watch the Food Network with the dogs.

He now sat on the edge of the bed, elbows resting on his knees, his head bent over an opened steamer trunk. It was covered in faded stickers and postage stamps, from back when people traveled by cruise ship.

"Where'd that come from?" I asked from the door.

"My house. It's all I could salvage from the storm. My dad left it to me before he went back to Reynosa. I keep all my important stuff in here: pictures, ID, documents, souvenirs." He closed the lid of the trunk and locked it. "You need something? Room service? A cup of tea, m'lady?" he asked with cheek-sucking bitterness.

That's it! Crush or no crush, he needed to be checked. I crossed the threshold. "Mateo, you're nobody's servant. Grandma Trina just wants you to practice your cooking skills. You're really good at—"

"Is that why you keep avoiding me? You barely say a word to me in school." A note of sadness broke his voice. "You're afraid folks might find out you've got a poor immigrant living in your house? Guess what? People see us riding to school together. Everyone knows."

Whoa! That wasn't why I was avoiding him. He was so off base, and I would've paid hard cash to have this conversation elsewhere. Like on a deserted beach. Or on our honeymoon. Now wasn't the time or the place to discuss feelings, and all I could say was "Weren't you born in Virginia?"

"Who cares!" He leapt to his feet so quickly, the motion made

53

me jump. "Nobody in school does, not students, teachers, nobody. That's the point. They just assume whatever they want."

"Maybe if you talked more, people wouldn't have to wonder about you." I took a step back and then another, until my feet landed in the hallway.

"Forget it. I don't care. I've got real issues to deal with besides you." He kept coming, his hand reaching for the door, ready to slam it in my face, when Grandma Trina's voice rang out.

"Janelle Lynn! What in the world are you up to now?"

Mateo and I exchanged glances, then turned to the old lady clocking us from her bedroom. Her fuzzy yellow bathrobe was older than I was and made the woman look like the sun, but there was nothing bright about the scowl on her face. "You not in here peepin' on that boy again, are you?" she asked.

Like a criminal caught in the act, I raised my hands and backed away from the door. "Grandma, it's not—"

"That boy's been through enough. He ain't got time for your foolishness." She wagged a finger at me. "And you better not be tryin' to sneak in his room at night. We ain't havin' none of that mess under my roof, you hear me?"

I swear, Grandma couldn't find a chill in the North Pole.

"As for you, young man—why don't you go and help Janelle at the park today?" she asked Mateo.

The smug grin he'd worn vanished. "Other than me not wanting to? No reason," he replied.

"Good, because you're goin'. So hurry up and change. It might

54

help you end this lil pity party you're throwin' for yourself. Seeing other people worse off than you makes you see clearer and count your blessin's."

"Which are?" he asked.

After a brief moment of reflection, I answered, "Well, you have a roof over your head and indoor plumbing. And you don't have dysentery."

His upper lip curled and he backpedaled into his room. "I'll grab my shoes."

"Great! I'll wait in the car." I moved to the stairs with an extra spring in my step.

Aberdeen Square was where all the parades and festivals were held, and where farmers sold their goods every weekend. The locals took pride in preserving the historical landmarks: the old courthouse, the clock tower, and the Protestant church that lent the town its name. Meanwhile, my peers' main concern was if the indie bookstore had free Wi-Fi.

I hopped the curb and crossed the street, following the signs pointing to the brick path at the lip of Aberdeen Park. White Christmas lights dotted the trees that lined the park's main path. They hung all year round and created a magical atmosphere. Perfect for a first date. Those trees now looked naked and eerie with wires dangling from branches like Spanish moss. Relighting the path was just one of many repairs needed, and I was all in.

Mateo, on the other hand, still looked annoyed and ready to swing. With hands stuffed in his jeans pockets, he sped up his pace and grumbled in Spanish the whole time. His long legs tore down the brick walkway, forcing me to jog to keep up.

"I've got a chisel you can borrow if you need help getting that chip off your shoulder," I told him.

He glared at me. "You don't think I deserve to have one?"

"No. But no one deserves a whiff of your funky attitude. You're not the only one who fell on hard times. Look around. This whole place is a hard time."

Mateo regarded the debris and fallen wires with indifference. "Meh. I've seen worse."

At the path's end lay a wide patch of grass where the day's activities would take place. A half-naked guy on a scooter came from that direction and was heading right for us.

"Block party! Woo! It's about to be lit!" scooter guy hooted, and pumped his fist in the air, his shirt hanging around his neck like a scarf.

"Watch out!" Mateo pulled me out of the way at the last minute, then spat curses at the kid's back. "You okay?" he asked me, and released his hold around my waist.

I didn't get a chance to enjoy Mateo's nearness or cop a quick feel of his biceps—I was too riled up. We were in a local park, so getting mowed down by skaters came with the territory. But after the third, fifth, and eighth scooter zipped by, I knew some foolery was in play.

"I'll get back to you on that." I quickened my steps toward the lawn.

My theory became fact on sight of the flash mob that covered the entire field. Kids from my school and a few other districts had arrived in full force. Some wore fatigue T-shirts with the words ACTIVE BEAUTY REPORTING FOR CIVIL DUTY spelled out in rhinestones. Other girls were dressed like it was the club and flirted with the male volunteers. One crying girl stormed off and begged her friend to take her home because she *just couldn't deal.* It was basically every school football game I'd attended, minus the bleachers.

The Borg's fingerprints were all over this crime scene, and the string of giggles and "omigods" told me that the suspects were still on the premises. I saw Joel Metcalf and two kids from media class filming the crowds entering through the wooded path.

I caught sight of Alyssa at one of the activity tables, taking group selfies with the student volunteers. I considered going over there, but that would just lead to a shouting match, wasted time, and a decline of IQ points.

"Janelle! Janelle!" Across the green, Sera jumped over heads to get my attention. Her waving hands and black ponytail flew in the air, then sank into the crowd. "Janelle! Janelle!"

"I'm coming, girl! Dang!" I scooted and slipped between bodies and met her halfway.

"Where did all these people come from?" she asked. "It was supposed to be twenty, thirty kids max."

"I don't know." I shook my head, feeling helpless and over-whelmed by the body count.

Devon Shapiro strolled past me with a guitar case strapped to his shoulder. Two band kids tagged along, carrying crates of equipment.

I grabbed his arm and pulled him aside. "So tell me, Devon, at what point did you guys think turning a cleanup party into *Project X* was a good idea? What was that thought process like? Walk me through it."

"Don't look at me. You've got *Active Beauty* to thank for this." He showed us his phone. "They're livestreaming the event. There's supposed to be some scavenger hunt. Whoever collects the most trash will get a prize or a guest spot on the vlog."

"They're gonna film us playing live." A band kid pointed to the makeshift stage behind him. "Might turn it into a music video."

Why was I not surprised? *It wasn't what you sold; it was how you sold it.* That was Alyssa's motto and the key to all our business endeavors in the past. But applying that tactic to a charity event didn't sit well with me. Not even a little bit.

"The guys and I gotta set up, but Ryon wants us to meet in an hour. Keep your phones on." Devon headed on through the crowd, and Sera tried to follow him toward the stage.

I pulled out my phone with one hand and yanked Sera by the collar with the other.

She stumbled back, then righted herself. "What? I just wanted to see if Devon needed help setting up."

"Oh, no, you don't. We still need to sign in. Focus, girl. This is a humanitarian project, not a dating app."

"Have you told the rest of these people that?" She swept a hand toward the crowd.

Lord knows, somebody needed to. The park was turnt up and loaded with party-scene angst that I could've watched from the comfort of my living room.

I turned around and tore through the crowd, my need to do bodily harm unsatisfied. Sera kept pace alongside me.

"Come on, don't let it get to you, Janelle. The Borg's just trying to create drama wherever they can." Sera tried to console me, but I paid it dust.

I couldn't believe it. All my efforts to organize an act of charity had failed. To top it off, there was more trash lying around now than when the storm hit. And . . . I seemed to have lost track of Mateo. He didn't need a babysitter, but I wanted him to meet with the rest of the crew before he went ghost. It was just as well. My attitude was on ten right now, which meant no one was safe from getting told off. No need to harm the innocent when my real target was—

"Alyssa? Alyssa!"

The scream had me spinning around. I recognized that voice. It was Ryon.

"Alyssa!" he was shouting. "Come on, wake up! Alyssa!"

So many questions popped in my head. Where was everyone going? Why was Ryon yelling? The urgency in his tone propelled me forward, while the demand for reason slowed my pace.

"She's not waking up!" one kid yelled. "Someone call an ambulance."

"An ambulance? What's wrong with her?" asked someone behind me.

Nothing about what was going on made sense. Every forward motion was met with resistance, every inch of room challenged by a nosy bystander. As I got closer, I saw Ryon kneeling on the ground, bent over someone lying at his knees. His wide back blocked the face, but his cries and the reddish-blond hair strewn across the grass made it clear who it was.

"What's wrong with her?" I asked everyone and no one.

And everyone and no one replied:

"She said that she wasn't feeling well—"

". . . She looked dizzy, she kept swaying a lot, right?"

"Yeah, she said something about being tired—"

". . . She just collapsed, man. She was staring off into space for a second and then boom! It was lights out."

"Stand back. Give her some air!" one of the first-aid workers bellowed, parting the crowd with his arms. More EMTs ripped through the growing mob, medical bags in hand.

Ryon kept yelling her name, even as the medic knelt by Alyssa's side.

"It's all right, son. We need to look at her," the man said.

They checked her pulse and listened to her chest for signs of life. Another teacher pulled Ryon back to make room for the stretcher.

I called Ryon's name, but he couldn't hear me. His stare remained glued to the medics working on Alyssa. More kids huddled around her, obstructing my view even more. I craned my neck and hopped over shoulders to gain a decent view while listening to Ryon's desperate pleas for her to wake up.

From what I could see, the medical team had deposited Alyssa onto the stretcher. The crowd watched on and whispered nonsense.

"We need to get her to the hospital now! She's in cardiac arrest." At the announcement, the kids backed away as if whatever caused her condition was now airborne. Panic locked me in place, yet the world began a rapid spin, smudging everything in my periphery. It was a clear indication that I was about to cry, go ape, or both, but I needed some answers first.

Ryon beat me to the punch and yelled, "What's going on? Someone tell me what's wrong with her!"

If hearing Ryon was this painful, then I was glad I couldn't see his face. The rapid motion around me blurred my vision, but Alyssa's limp body lying on the stretcher had my full attention. Her pale coloring, the oxygen mask on her face, the way her head lolled back and forth—it all proved that a crisis was happening in front of me. It was real.

My brain ran at high speed, and my thoughts veered off in eight different directions, an incoherent blob of images and emotions. I couldn't click away from the scene. It had no PAUSE button, no X in the top right-hand corner of the screen. There was no ESC or CTRL + ALT + DELETE keys to close the program. This clip, this corrupted file, kept playing, and I couldn't make it stop. All I could do was watch.

Ryon wiped the tears from his sleeve and yelled after them. "Which hospital? Just tell me which hospital!"

"Mount Sinai!" one of the medics called back. "It's closer."

And with that, Ryon took off. I watched his shoulders tear through the crowd as he headed toward the end of the park, no doubt to his car to meet them in the emergency room.

"Someone needs to call her mom. Does anyone know how to find her mom?" a kid asked in the crowd.

The question gave me purpose. I pulled out my phone and dialed Alyssa's house phone. I'd deleted the number ages ago, a redundant act of defiance since I knew it by heart.

The call went to voice mail. "Hello. You have reached the Weaver residence. At the tone, please leave a message."

"Mrs. Weaver? This is Janelle Pruitt. You need to get to Mount Sinai Hospital. Alyssa collapsed in Aberdeen Park. She's on her way to the hospital. Please hurry." I hung up and fought the urge to chuck the device toward a nearby tree. Someone needed to tell Mrs. Weaver what was going on. Was she at work? If so, which job?

"Think. Think. Think." I beat my temple with the phone. Maybe I could go to her house.

My legs felt weightless and heavy at the same time as I dashed through the park. Craning necks and bobbing heads kept me from seeing the grass. My body twisted and contorted, and I willed myself smaller to squeeze through the gaps between trees and people.

I tore across the street and ran three blocks to my car, where a battle of keys took place. They fumbled in my shaky hands and kept missing the lock and scraping the door's paint. When I finally got inside the car, they refused to slip into the ignition. In a final act of rebellion, the keys fell to the floor under my seat. There was no time for this! While one hand patted for my wayward keys, the other scrolled through my phone for something, *anything* that could help.

"Janelle!" A boy called my name. "It's me, Mateo. Janelle, open the door. I'll drive you home." The voice grew louder, followed by soft tapping on the glass.

I ignored him. "I need to call Alyssa's mom. She's not at home and I don't have her cell number."

"It's okay. The teachers will contact her."

"They can't help her! I need to call her mom!" I hadn't meant to yell, but he wasn't helping. "Her insulin is at home. She can bring it to the hospital. She'll know what to do. She always knows what to do." I kept scrolling, though I couldn't see the numbers anymore.

"Okay. Just calm down. Did you call her?" The soothing voice he was using was bugging the crap out of me.

"What's it look like I'm doing?" I yelled. "I can't find her number!"

My lungs couldn't capture air fast enough, and the lack of oxygen made spots appear before my eyes. A wave of terror hit me so strong that I couldn't move.

Then I heard Mateo again, but his voice sounded garbled, as if he were in another room. "Hello, Mrs. Trina? It's Mateo. Do you know a girl named Alyssa Weaver? Yeah. Do you know how to reach her mom?"

I looked up and saw him pacing outside the car with his phone to his ear. "Do you have her cell phone number? Her daughter had an accident and is on her way to the hospital. Yeah, it's bad. They mentioned some sort of shock. Okay. Thanks." He snuck a glance at me, then said, "Not so good. I will. No problem." Ending the call, he stooped down to look me in the eye. "Your *abuela* is calling her now. Can you open the door? Please?"

It took a lot of coaxing on his part to get me moving again, but I managed to unlock the door and slide into the passenger seat. I expected him to climb in and start the car. Instead, he reached between us and pulled me into his arms.

I understood the action, but I couldn't register the sensations that went with touch and condolence. A black cloud framed my vision, growing larger until all that was left was a pinpoint where I saw his hands hold mine.

"See? Problem solved. Mrs. Trina knows everyone's mom,

right? You said so yourself, remember? It's gonna be okay," he whispered. "You want to go home or to the hospital?"

"I don't know." I could've sworn I'd spoken the answer out loud. Maybe I'd heard the question wrong, because he kept calling my name over and over.

"Janelle? Can you hear me? Janelle? Janelle?"

CHAPTER 5

My blackout only lasted for a few minutes, and that was enough to spook out Mateo during the drive home. Luckily, I'd had other panic attacks like that in my life. The first one happened when I was eight while on a shaky flight to the Philippines in monsoon season. Another had occurred after Pop-Pop's funeral.

When I arrived home, my grandma already knew the drill and told me to sleep it off; this was the Pruitt go-to remedy for fried brain.

That's how I spent the rest of the weekend—phone off, curtains drawn, cocooned inside a blanket until my eyes opened Monday afternoon.

By then, my phone had lit up with so many notifications, it drained my newly charged battery. Grandma Trina had spared me the usual lecture about missing school, but she'd kept insisting I eat something. Even through a closed bedroom door, she could somehow tell I *looked* hungry. I did finally emerge from my room to have the dinner Mateo had prepared. We didn't speak, other than grunts from my end whenever he asked if I was okay. He knew what despair looked like and how it didn't allow for deep conversation. It didn't allow for personal hygiene, either, but I rallied enough strength to shower and then crawl back into bed with my phone.

Word of Alyssa's collapse had gone viral in a matter of hours and had the whole school shook. Kids who'd attended the cleanup party posted clips online. Total strangers were encouraged to view a girl's violent descent into toxic shock and to click the LIKE button. Friends crammed her Instagram and Facebook with inspirational memes, while others hyped up the incident like the latest blockbuster. The extras in the background had embellished their roles and tried to win the award for Best Supporting Actor.

Dude, I'm telling you, I was right there when it happened. Watch the video again. The black jeans and the Converse—that's me! It was so trippy, bro. I thought she was dead.

My dad knows a guy who works at the hospital. He said that she's got like maybe a month or so to live.

I never knew she was sick. I thought she was on that gluten-free diet. I stopped eating carbs and everything.

I heard she has stomach cancer and has to get a bunch of chemo. That sucks. She has really nice hair.

There was always someone who had a friend who dated a guy related to someone who had dirt on Alyssa, when in truth they didn't know her at all. And what wasn't known was invented on the spot to stay relevant. Compassion? Loyalty? Privacy? What dat do?

On Tuesday morning, Mateo drove us to school. The thought of interacting with people had me ready to transfer, but I needed to make an appearance at the student council meeting today.

Mateo parked the car and cut off the engine. "I can take you home if you want."

My eyes rolled from the parking lot to his face. "You say that *after* we get to school?"

"There's still time. You're not gonna faint again, are you? Kinda freaked me out last time." When I shook my head, he said, "Last chance to call in a sick day."

"I would need a sick month. But thanks, though," I told him, and reached for my backpack. "You can be really nice when you wanna be."

"No point in both of us being uptight. Need to find some balance in the universe." He graced me with a quick smile, then climbed out of the car.

Was he sympathy flirting with me? I didn't have the energy to decipher hidden signals today, so I followed him to the school's rear entrance.

The senior class officers sat in the history classroom, awaiting news and encouraging words from our leader. I'd heard Ryon was absent yesterday and I'd expected him to be a no-show again, but duty called to us all. I could respect that, though why Joel Metcalf was filming the meeting remained a mystery. He stood two rows behind me and adjusted the camera's position on the tripod.

"Hey, Spielberg! Could you put that away and join the meeting?" I called over my shoulder.

Joel poked his head from behind the camera. Oily black hair flopped around his eyes. "Can't. It's for the vlog."

"What?" I turned completely in my seat to rail at him. "We're in the middle of a crisis and you're talking about a stupid vlog? Are you mental?"

"Ryon told me it was okay. Said he didn't want to repeat himself," Joel explained, then kept filming.

I turned to the front of the class, where Ryon held a white-knuckled grip on the podium's edge. Gone was the put-together overachiever we were used to and in his place stood a burnt-out star who'd hit rock bottom. His eyes, dark and red-rimmed from crying, stared at his notes. Watching him fight for composure held all the nerve-racking suspense of a Jenga game. Pull one block from the stack, say one wrong word, and the entire tower fell apart. Would he or wouldn't he burst into tears? Would I?

"Um, you are all probably aware of what happened at Aberdeen Park on Saturday," Ryon began. "I'm sure you all have a lot of questions. I was able to speak with Alyssa's mother at the hospital. She sends her thanks to all who offer their prayers and condolences."

When the murmurs died down, he continued.

"Alyssa had been battling with health issues for a few years now. They were able to keep it under control, but . . ." He cleared his throat and tried again. "An infection caused her kidneys to shut down, which led to toxic shock and cardiac arrest. Alyssa's been in a coma for three days, but the doctors are confident she'll come out of it soon. The main concern is to get her kidneys back online before the damage is permanent."

The silence that followed was misleading. There was no peace in it—just a prelude to a boatload of grief. It felt similar to when I'd stub my toe on the bedpost in my room. There was that quiet, that split-second delay before the pain hit. I'd clench my teeth, shut my eyes, and brace for impact, because it was gonna hurt! Nerve endings I never knew existed were put on notice. It would seem that Alyssa was the pinkie toe of my life right now, and all I could do was sit still until the sting died down.

I wasn't the only one trapped in temporary paralysis. The whole council, heck, the whole county knew the situation. Now, hearing the specifics from a reputable source brought it home for us. And I was already in a bad mood.

"Does she have a kidney disorder?" Sera asked, breaking the silence. The group gawked at Sera and her oddly precise diagnosis. "What? I watch *Grey's Anatomy.*"

Ryon nodded. "They said it's common for people with diabetes. It's one of the leading causes of kidney failure."

"Wait, she's diabetic?" Sera's stare volleyed from me to her brother, realization flashing in her eyes with each pass. "Janelle, you knew about this? Is that why you freaked out at the park? Why didn't you say anything?"

I really, really hated being put on the spot, and as much as I loved Sera, she picked the wrong time to come at me sideways. "First, I didn't know her health had gotten that bad. Second, why would I tell you? Are you a doctor? Do you specialize in checking glucose, electrolyte, and potassium levels? Yes, I also watch *Grey's Anatomy*. Third, it's no one's business but her family's, and I don't know why you felt the need to have this bootleg press conference explaining all of this, Ryon." My attention shifted to our president. "Not one of these kids are paying her doctor bills or sitting at her bedside. All they're gonna do is pile up her inbox and make it all about them."

"Thank you for that constructive feedback, Janelle," Ryon replied tightly. "You raise a good point about finances. I've opened a crowdfunding account for anyone who wants to contribute to Alyssa's medical bills and show support. Also, T-shirts that Alyssa designed for *Active Beauty* will be sold in the cafeteria. The proceeds will go to her and her family."

"Those shirts were made for the disaster relief project!" Clearly still in her feelings, Sera waved her arms in a fit and raved, "Does everything have to be about her?"

"Sera, I don't know if you left it at home or in your locker, but you need to find your chill or borrow one from the group." Devon Shapiro spoke up. "Alyssa is unconscious, poisoned by her own body. Her kidneys stopped working. Chemicals that are supposed to come out through your pee are polluting her bloodstream. Think about that next time you get up to take a leak."

The room fell quiet, and Sera slumped in the chair next to me, properly chastised. Looking annoyed by the curious eyes on him, Devon explained, "My grandma had diabetes. Same thing happened to her. She stayed on dialysis for years until she died."

That didn't help with the silence in the room, nor did it help with the mental horror show that had been playing in my head all weekend. But at least now we had a bit more perspective. This wasn't about some web series or a cleanup effort. This was a life, one that was currently in danger.

"So where do we go as far as the cleanup campaign?" Tabatha asked.

"We keep going," Ryon said with conviction that had been missing all through the meeting. "There are still people who need help. The park still needs repairs, more benches and fences to repaint. We need to focus more on what we can fix than what we can't."

When the meeting adjourned, I walked a tightrope of frayed nerves. Everyone was scared to do anything without the class vice president at the helm. Needless to say, nothing productive got accomplished.

"Janelle, hang back for a sec," Ryon called after me.

I gathered my books and strolled toward the podium. "What's up?"

He kept his stare trained on the door. "I wanted to tell you away from the others since you know more about the situation. I've been at the hospital the past three days. The doctors said she has twelve percent kidney function and the damage is permanent. It's only a matter of time before they stop working completely. They've put her on dialysis to flush out the toxins."

There went that banged-up toe again, along with a pain so raw that I couldn't move. Only this pain lodged in my chest.

"People live on dialysis all the time," I said, trying to think rationally. "They can live for years." I knew Alyssa didn't keep the strictest diet, but she'd been fine before. She was always fine. She'd get through this, too.

He scoffed. "Barely. Dialysis does maybe a fourth of what a real kidney does. It's meant to keep you alive until you can get a transplant. Thousands of people die waiting for one. Look what happened to Devon's grandma." A head shake and a shudder followed his response. "That's not gonna happen to her."

Was he saying what I thought he was saying? I had to ease back a step or else tip over from shock. "You're gonna donate a kidney?"

"Can't. I won't be eighteen until February. But I'd be lying if I said that it hasn't crossed my mind this week."

"Why can't her parents do it? I'm sure her mom would go for it."

He rubbed his eyes. "I'm just thinking ahead, that's all. Been thinking a lot these past few days."

"I can tell. When was the last time you slept?"

His brows puckered as he strained to recall. "Three days ago."

I thought so. "You should go home and get some sleep."

"And you should visit her," he replied.

I bristled. "What?"

"You should visit her. I'm gonna head back there at lunch. Feel free to tag along."

And do what exactly? Even if she was awake and in a talkative mood, what would I say to her? Keeping my distance seemed the better option. "Nah, that's okay."

He dipped his head until our eyes met. "Have you even gone to see her?"

"No." I couldn't get out of bed all weekend, much less operate a vehicle. Quiet as it's kept; I wasn't ready to see her yet.

He searched my face with narrowed eyes. "Trust me, it's gonna eat at you until you go and see her for yourself. You guys used to be friends—"

"Yeah, used to be, but that was a long time ago," I was quick to let him know.

"Not according to Alyssa," he countered. "I've been in her room, Janelle. That's all I'm gonna say on that. Anyway, I can tell that you're just as upset as I am. Whatever feud you two have, you might wanna set it aside and focus on the bigger picture. Life is too short to be bitter and too long to have regret."

He scooped up his wilderness backpack and quit the room, leaving me to swallow a big ol' slice of humble pie. It would take a gallon of water to wash that down, but all I had available was one salty tear.

74

CHAPTER 6

Mateo had to take a make-up quiz, so I wasn't in a rush to get home after school. More important things weighed on my mind and had me driving on autopilot. Impulse turned the steering wheel, fluency pressed and released the gas pedal, and habit brought me to the driveway of what I once claimed as a second home. Mrs. Weaver's traffic-cone-orange Camaro was parked in the driveway, so I'd come at a good time.

Feeling every bit the prodigal child, I dragged my feet to the door, then rang the bell. While waiting, I considered the house that held so many memories. It was a brick one-level rancher with flower beds wrapping the property. I remembered Alyssa's room sat at the rear and boasted a scenic view of the cracked patio floor where grass, bikes, and old toys went to die.

"Janelle Lynn, is that you?" a soft voice with a Dixie twang called from the door.

I turned and met the same hazel eyes as Alyssa, but edged with crow's feet and thick black eyeliner. "Mrs. Weaver?"

The small woman stepped around the door in a cloud of fried blond hair and copious perfume. She was once a true redhead (unlike Alyssa, who had just a tint) with bony arms covered in freckles. Though she was still pretty, her age had begun to show, likely due to worry and her fondness for tanning beds. Her long, hot-pink nails tapped the door frame by her head.

"C'mere. It's good to see ya, hon." She pulled me in for a hug, her bracelets jingling as she patted my back. Then she stepped back and appraised the merchandise. "Take a look at ya. You've gotten so big. Sproutin' up like a beanpole. Fillin' out in all the right places."

I was too dark to blush, but my cheeks burned. Alyssa's mom was a trip. Aside from being an undercover pack rat, she was what kids in our neighborhood classified as the cool mom. No topic was off-limits, and going by the stories she'd tell about her wild rocker days, she'd seen it all.

"What brings you here, Janelle? I figured you'd go to the hospital." She motioned me inside.

"I just came by to . . ." The words died in my mouth on sight of the living room. The place was spotless, and I could actually see the floor. The trash had been sorted and lined in rows by the patio door. Either Mrs. Weaver had overcome her bag lady habit or they were about to move.

I hid my shock with a grin. "The place looks great."

"Yeah, things got tight and I did a huge overhaul before the storm. Had to sell a few things, too. My weddin' ring and her daddy's old albums went for a pretty penny on eBay—God rest him." She made a quick sign of the cross with her hands.

The answer had me choking on air and spit. "Omigod! Alyssa's dad died?"

"Oh, no, hon. He's alive and well. He's at the hospital now watchin' over Lyssa while I grab a shower and make a few phone calls. But a girl can dream, right?" She winked. "You want somethin' to drink?"

"Uh . . . Sure." I wasn't gonna touch that hornet's nest of a topic, so I followed her into the kitchen and listened to that familiar click-clack of high heels on linoleum tile. Tapping nails, jingling bracelets, clicking teeth, popping gum—the woman was a living, breathing sound effect.

I let my gaze wander around the living and dining room. Bills—medical bills, given the cross-and-snake emblem on the letterhead—were piled in several stacks on the table and organized by priority. The clean house, the pawned valuables, the surplus of pill bottles, and the blood pressure cuff sitting on the kitchen counter—all of it pointed to dire circumstances.

The whole scene was one big question mark, and Ryon's words this morning had me looking for meaning in every square inch of space. That was my real purpose for being here. He mentioned Alyssa's room as if it held evidence of a crime I didn't commit or told a secret that I should already know.

"So, how you been, Miss Janelle? Been givin' your grandma a hard time?" Mrs. Weaver asked, then poured me a glass of apple juice.

I guffawed. "It's more the other way around."

"Oh, I believe it. That woman used to catch me kissin' boys behind First Baptist and whooped my tail worse than my own mama did." She chuckled and handed me the glass.

Her story had me doing long division in my head to figure out Grandma Trina's real age. If Mrs. Weaver was young enough to catch a grandma beatdown, and she was in her forties now, then carry the one . . .

"Alyssa don't mention you much." Her voice brought me back on track. "I was wonderin' why you didn't come 'round no more. Figured you two had a fallin' out."

"Something like that. But we're in student government and we see each other all the time." *More than we want to*, I thought as I sipped my juice.

"Figured that's what it was. Don't let it get to you. I'd had girl-friends on and off for years. One minute, you can't stand 'em; the next minute, you're inseparable. Happens all the time."

It was a bit more complicated than that, but I let the woman enjoy her fantasy.

"You've always been a good friend to my Lyssa, unlike them other gals she brings 'round now. I swear, them gals plain ol' high sidity. If their noses was any higher, they'd be sniffin' cloud water."

So she'd met the Borg? Fascinating.

"So how's Alyssa? I, um, heard she's on dialysis," I asked, waiting for her to debunk the rumors and erase the past week with a playful laugh that echoed around the walls.

Instead, she said, "She's still in a coma, but she's stable now. They did surgery to implant the tube in her to better fit the machine." Eyes closed, Mrs. Weaver rubbed her forehead in small circles. "My baby'll probably be on that thing for the rest of her life. I hear each treatment wipes you out for days, then you gotta go back and do it again. She'll have to work around school or learn from home."

I couldn't imagine being strapped to a machine every week and walking around with tubes sticking out of my stomach. But having to leave school, too? "Is it that bad?" I asked.

The woman's expression told me it was. I knew that look: the glassy eyes, the far-off stare as the mind drifted to somewhere dark and hollow. If my own grief was a stubbed toe, then Mrs. Weaver's was a full leg amputation, and I felt like complete trash for pointing out her limp.

I set down my empty glass, then motioned toward the hallway behind me. "Um, I let Alyssa borrow a book for class. Is it okay if I get it from her room?"

Shaking off her daze, Mrs. Weaver cleared her throat and stood up straight.

"Yeah, go ahead back there. I doubt she'd mind. You remember the way, don't ya?" she teased.

"I'm sure it'll come back to me." I smiled, then left the room.

Drenched in beige, lilac, and a party store's worth of glitter, Alyssa's command center looked like someplace a child pageant winner would live. Frilly pillows galore, cushy footstools and chairs, clothes and beauty products strewn everywhere. A humongous dressing room vanity with light bulbs framed the mirror. For a girly girl, Alyssa had always hated pink. Abhorred pink. Reviled pink. She said it reminded her of uncooked flesh, which had turned me off the color since.

While snooping for some elusive smoking gun, my attention moved to the items cluttering her dresser. Beyond the costume jewelry and nail polish sat rows of orange prescription bottles. A thin pamphlet wedged between the pill bottles caught my eye. It was a brochure for a place called the Atlantic Wellness Center, over in Arlington. The cover showed a photo collage of smiling people and a doctor in a white coat holding a red, love-shaped heart in his hand.

ORGAN DONATION
THE GIFT THAT KEEPS ON TICKING

Was Alyssa already looking into organ transplants? How long had she known she'd need one? The creases in the brochure implied that it had been folded and refolded, considered then reconsidered a number of times.

I backed away from the dresser and took a wide, all-inclusive pan around the room. Then I saw it, the big clue Ryon had hinted about. Only it wasn't one thing.

Every item in the room told a story. The band poster on the wall was from our first concert without our parents. That hubcap on her bookshelf came off my car when I first learned how to drive. Alyssa had rescued it from a ditch and painted it with gold glitter. Not even bleach could remove that orange stain on the carpet in front of her TV (where I threw up after eating three bags of Flamin' Hot Cheetos on a dare). I'd outgrown the cable-knit sweater balled up at the top of her closet that she borrowed and never gave back. The same went for the board games peeking from under her bed.

No wonder Ryon was spooked by Alyssa's room. The place was a historic landmark; a tourist attraction made famous by its own destruction. This was the *Titanic*, the mummified ruins of Pompeii—locked in time and too fragile to disturb. Ghosts haunted these grounds as well, sucking me back in time to where Alyssa and I talked alike, dressed alike, and shared everything. The enchantment lasted a few seconds before I remembered who we were now and what we weren't anymore. And with that, it was time to go.

Mrs. Weaver sat on the living room couch, staring into space with the phone to her ear. One of the medical papers I'd spotted in the kitchen dangled between her fingers. Her veiny legs crossed at the knee and bounced in the nervous staccato of someone who'd been placed on hold for too long.

She saw me headed for the door and asked, "You leaving already, hon?"

"Yeah, I've got tons of homework. I'll catch you later."

"Okay. Make sure you come back and see us now, stranger." She shot a finger gun at me.

Instead of telling an outright lie, I fired off a finger gun of my own and then stepped out of the house.

In the quiet of my car, in the void of open road ahead of me, Mrs. Weaver's words floated between my ears. *You've always been a good friend to my Lyssa.*

The jury was still out on that one. But the question remained: Was I a good one now? Good friends visited each other in the hospital. Friends cheered each other up when one was sick or upset. Friends set hurt feelings aside and showed support.

That was the problem. My feelings for Alyssa were a tray of paper clips—you could never just pull one out. Other emotions latched on and dangled from the loops: love, confusion, sympathy, resentment. Much like her room, that tangled mess was locked in time and too fragile to disturb. I thought it best to leave the paper clips chained just as they were—or else risk upending the tray completely.

CHAPTER 7

I was about seven when I first heard the word *dialysis*. My family and I were in the airport and I saw an old guy sitting at the food court. His protruding gut sat on his lap. Sticking out from the potbelly was a clear tube like the kind you'd see attached to a flotation device.

I remembered the man constantly patting the bandage around the tube to make sure it stayed in place. The black box by his foot looked like no suitcase I'd ever seen.

I'd tugged my mom's sleeve and asked her if he was a terrorist with a bomb.

"No, baby," she'd replied. "That's just his dialysis machine. He keeps it in the box so he can get his treatment while he travels."

"His what?" I'd asked.

"His artificial kidney," Sheree had explained. "Some people's organs don't work the way they should, so a machine does the job for them."

That sounded like sci-fi to me. "You mean like a robot?"

My sister's eyes darted to Mom, and then to me, and she gave a lopsided smile. "Uh, yeah. Sure. A robo-kidney."

I hadn't thought of that man in years, but he'd been on my mind all this week. Was he still alive? How bad was his condition anyway?

Ever since I'd visited Alyssa's house, I'd spent my evenings researching information about kidney damage. The average dialysis patient had to have 15 percent kidney function when introduced to the kidney robot. Alyssa was at 12 percent and dropping. Not a good sign.

That Friday afternoon, I gathered the courage to see Alyssa at the hospital. I signed in at the front desk, slapped on my printed name tag, and moseyed on down to room 5471 with no idea what to say, do, or expect. Sources claimed that she'd returned to the conscious world and been moved to a cushy recovery room on the fifth floor. And by sources, I meant Ryon. He mentioned that the specialist had done something to her arm to help with her dialysis.

"Whatever you do, don't, I repeat, do not stare at her fistula," Ryon had told me at lunch. "She just had it put in and she's a little self-conscious about it."

I was lost on two counts: I had no idea what a fistula was or why he'd given the warning with such dread. It nearly distracted me from the red blotch on his left cheek. At first, I thought it was a reaction to the drop in temperature outside, but under closer inspection, it was the remnants of a hearty slap.

Best I could do was a nod. "Okay, sure. Just one thing though. What the heck is a fistula?"

As soon as I entered the hospital room, I had my answer.

"Oh my God!" was my initial reaction. I leapt back and clutched my chest.

"If you're going to stare then get out!" Alyssa glared grisly murder at me from the bed.

"I'm not here to harass you. I come in peace. Look. I even brought balloons." I showed her the bright-yellow bunch in my hands.

Alyssa scoffed, unimpressed. "Yeah, because Lord knows I need more flowers, balloons, and cards."

She was right. Child birthday parties weren't this lit, even with a hired clown. Foil balloons crowded the ceiling. Teddy bears and fancy bouquets hogged all the free counter space. Looking at my meager offering, I said, "But . . . but they're all pink."

"You know I hate pink."

"I *do* know that. That's why I bought these." My smile widened.

Her eyes narrowed into two razor slits.

Inviting myself in, I scoped out the new digs. The room looked like a hotel suite, with cream-colored walls and dark wood accents. A flat-screen television was mounted on the wall across from the bed, and a chaise longue sat under the window. That was where Mrs. Weaver no doubt spent most of her nights. Then my gaze moved to the dreaded dialysis machine next to Alyssa's bed.

Its omnipotent bulk would not go ignored. The robo-kidney demanded acknowledgment and a steady diet of unfiltered blood.

"What did I tell you about staring?" she asked.

"Sorry." My eyes lifted to the ceiling. "Does it hurt?"

"Yep. But once the swelling goes down, it should be fine."

As hard as I tried to avert my gaze, it somehow kept landing on that thing on her arm. It looked like a sausage link embedded into her skin just over the left bicep. Right now it was covered in bandages, but when I first walked in, she'd been picking at the stitches. I'd seen more parasites, lesions, keloid scars, and boils in my life than anyone should and still maintained a healthy appetite. But that? That was just nasty.

Finally, I asked, "What is that thing?"

"It's an artery and a vein surgically fused together with two outlets poking out of my skin that connect to the tubing that connects to the dialysis machine. A fistula." She said this as though reading from a script, completely monotone and full of apathy. I probably wasn't the first person she'd explained it to.

"I thought it goes through your stomach," I told her.

"Same game. Different field. Only this way the filtering action happens outside the body." She nudged her head toward the machine. "Fewer risks of infections this way."

"All righty then." I tied the balloons to her meal tray stand and planted my butt in the chair next to her. Crossing my legs, I asked, "So, how was your week?"

She fought hard not to smile but failed. "Worst week ever."

"How long are you gonna be stuck here?"

"Until the infection clears. Then I gotta go to a center across town for treatment three times a week. Mama's trying to get one of those home filtration kits, but there's a lot to it. You gotta take a class just to plug the machine in. She works too much to be home with me and she can barely operate the microwave. Best let the pros do it."

"Good call." I nodded. "I can go with you if you want?"

She hesitated for a moment. "Not sure if visitors are allowed during treatments. But I'll check."

"Okay." I searched the room for a new topic. "So, about what I said in class the other day—"

"Don't apologize. You're not sorry. Don't pretend that you are just because I'm sitting in a hospital bed. I'm still me. You're still you, and we can't stand each other. Let's not break tradition, okay?"

I could tell she was lying—sort of. She was all shifty-eyed and looking around. Dead giveaway. If she really wanted me out, she'd just press the CALL button for the nurse. But the comment was a good lead-in to another question I had waiting backstage.

"Why are you so set on pushing me away? Who ran over your cat in the street?"

She grabbed the remote and began channel surfing. "Ain't got a cat."

"Which further proves how baseless your stank attitude is." I paused as Ryon's face flashed in my head. "It also explains the handprint on *Sugar Booger's* cheek. Are we having a domestic dispute, ma'am?" I asked in a tone full of syrupy sweetness.

"I told him not to touch my incision. It's still tender." She pointed to her bandaged arm. "But did he listen? *Nooo.*"

"So beautiful, man. Gets me right here." I patted the spot over my heart.

She wiped the damp strands of hair from her face. "Look, if you're gonna stay, don't mention anything that has to do with me or any of this machinery attached to me, okay?"

"All right. Don't come at me slick, and I won't start pulling tubes and pushing buttons. Got it?"

"Fine!" She turned up the volume on the TV.

"Fine!" I shifted in my seat and crossed my arms, my attitude dropping to an 8.5. Then I caught what played on the screen. "Oh! *The Golden Girls!* We used to watch that show with your mom all the time." I grinned.

The Golden Girls had been our introduction to the world of throwing shade, and those cranky broads were our mentors (along with my grandma).

"Used to?" Alyssa asked. "I *still* do. They're the coolest old ladies ever. I'm so Blanche, it's not even funny."

"No. Your mom is Blanche. I'm Dorothy and you're the dumb one."

She sniggered. "Just shut up and watch the show."

And that's how we spent the next two hours of my visit. The back-to-back episodes turned out to be a full weekend marathon.

It was nice not having to say anything, or to come up with something witty or positive. There was nothing positive or healthy about Alyssa's situation. The same could be said for our relationship, and neither required further discussion. We just sat together watching four old women act a fool in their Miami home.

"I want to be like them when I get old. These chicks are awesome," Alyssa said after the fourth episode.

By then, I'd scooted my chair closer to the bed, my head resting on top of my folded arms over the blanket. But at her words, the air shifted in the room and something dark crept under the door, a phantom presence that had no business in the peaceful space we'd created. It loomed behind me and leaned close to my ear. Its icy breath tickled the hairs on my neck as it whispered, *She'll never live to see old age.*

I jumped to my feet. The chair teetered backward; its legs scraped the floor. "Wow! Look at the time. I was only supposed to be here for an hour. I should get back home."

"Already?" she asked, the way a child pleads to stay up past her bedtime.

"I've got a lot to do at home." I collected my bag and jacket from the back of the armchair. "I'll come back soon though."

"Okay." She spoke in a small voice. "I mean, you don't have to."

"I know. But I will." I closed the door behind me.

Outside her room, I spotted Mrs. Weaver in the hall. I would've told her goodbye, but she appeared to be in a heated conversation with the doctor. Her hands sliced into the air, and words were spoken in harsh tones that sounded too loud to be real whispers. It was best to stay out of grown folks' business, but I needed to move closer to get to the elevators in the next corridor.

I tiptoed across the floor, creeping down the hallway. Mrs. Weaver faced away from me and the doctor was too concerned with calming her down to notice me. I'd just made it around the corner when I heard Mrs. Weaver say, "Why can't she have mine?"

"I'm afraid your HLA levels make you incompatible."

I froze mid-step.

"How can that be if we're the same blood type? I'm O and she's O. We're the same blood type," she argued.

"There's more to it than that, Mrs. Weaver. The number of antibodies in your system is too dangerous for your daughter's body. It's a high probability that she will reject the kidney."

My back pressed against the wall. I inched closer, not daring to peek around the corner. Thanks to the hallway traffic mirrors mounted in the top corner, I didn't need to.

"So you're tellin' me that my daughter's gonna die? Is that what you're tellin' me?" Mrs. Weaver demanded.

"If she doesn't get a kidney soon, then her body will shut down," the doctor rephrased. "But there is still time to locate a suitable donor. Have you discussed this with her father?"

"He can't help her," she groused. "The way he parties and drinks, he'll be on that waitin' list right along with her."

"There is the donor exchange program I spoke to you about," the doctor said.

"The what?"

"The donor exchange program. Since you're already in the database, we can line you up with a patient you're compatible with, and their donor will match with Alyssa."

Mrs. Weaver reared back as if slapped. "I'm not givin' my kidney to some stranger! I'm doin' this for my daughter! *My child!* And you wanna pass me off to someone else?"

"It will be an even exchange," he assured her.

"I thought you said you couldn't find a match. You sayin' you found a donor in this program to trade with?"

He nodded. "As a matter of fact, we've found several patients that you are compatible with—"

"*For her!*" Mrs. Weaver pointed toward Alyssa's room. "Did you find a match in your database *for her?*" When he didn't reply right away, she sucked her teeth. "Yeah, that's what I thought. Back to square one."

"Mrs. Weaver, I understand this is a difficult time for you—"

"No!" She cut him off again. "*Difficult* is holdin' down three jobs to pay for these medical bills. Difficult is pinnin' a five-year-old still while givin' her insulin, or forcin' juice down her throat when she has an attack. *Difficult* is havin' your child depend on a machine to keep her alive. *Difficult* is doin' this all by yourself because your husband can't handle a sick kid. But goin' in that room and tellin' my baby that she only has a few weeks to live? That ain't *difficult*, Doctor. That is *impossible*. Now, I want you to go to your office, make some calls, write some emails, send up a Bat-Signal, whatever you gotta do, and get my daughter a donor!"

"I'll see what I can do," the doctor said, then moved quickly down the hall, hopefully to his office to do what she'd asked. I wasn't sure because all my focus was set on Mrs. Weaver.

I studied the fragile woman leaning against the wall. One arm was wrapped around her waist, the other hand clasped around her mouth. Her sobs fell quiet under tremors that ran all the way to her knees. I couldn't see her tears, but I could hear them in every sharp gasp of air. It was like a swimmer punching through the water's surface and drawing breath before plunging back down into the soundless deep. Or maybe she was drowning.

I turned around, ran to the elevator, and pushed the DOWN button. The numbers above the door hadn't changed. I pushed it again. Again. Again, again, and again, until finally, the numbers climbed to my floor and the doors slid open.

My body slumped against the elevator wall and I balanced my weight on the metal railing.

"Can you hit lobby, please?" I asked the elderly woman in the elevator with me. I didn't recognize my voice. It sounded croaky and wet with phlegm. The blockage spread to the back of my throat, allowing only shallow hiccups of air to pass through in quick sequence. My vision was blurred; my eyes prickled with unshed tears.

The woman in the elevator asked me if I was all right and I remember thinking the words *yes* and *fine*, but they couldn't be heard. Not underwater. Not while drowning.

The doors opened again and I almost collided with the lady to get to the exit. I ran through the emergency room doors and into the hospital parking lot. I found my car, got in, locked the door, and stared at the row of vehicles ahead.

There, in the privacy of my car, that drowning thing swam toward the light and broke through the black surface of the water. My first breath ended with a scream that should've shattered the windows. My head throbbed, my jaw cracked, I was certain I popped a capillary, and yet I kept screaming. I punched and kicked and pushed back against my seat with all my weight, and not even my best attempts had an effect. I didn't care if I broke the steering wheel or busted the airbag or if the car exploded—this pain had to go somewhere. The horn went off. People in the parking lot were staring, and if they knew what was good for them, they would back off.

At some point, I stopped screaming. Sometime after that, I started the car and peeled out of the lot. It could've been the change of the season or sitting in an air-conditioned hospital for hours, but the chill I'd felt in Alyssa's room clung to me like body odor. At every stoplight, my eyes strayed to the rearview mirror, paranoid that the phantom had followed me home.

• • •

I scooted past the dogs, then trudged upstairs on legs that felt like half-cooked noodles. I heard Mateo moving around in his room and fought the temptation to knock. That would lead to him answering the door, which would lead to talking, which would lead to feelings becoming vocal and poorly translated. Best to skip all that and just sleep it off. I zombie-shuffled to my room, landed facedown on the mattress, and then had what I felt was a fully deserved cry. I'd kept it in for too long, something I had promised myself I'd never do. After all, tears were signs of something wrong.

Tears came from cuts that others can't see. That's why they run clear, Alyssa told me once.

If I had to pinpoint the cut, that one dominant emotion, it would be helplessness. This issue, this crisis, couldn't be fed, clothed, or given fresh drinking water. I couldn't collect money, signatures, or imperishable goods. I couldn't rally, boycott, march the streets, hold up a sign and scream out to the world, "MY FRIEND IS DYING!" Lord knows I wanted to, though. But this was an internal battle, an area completely out of my depth. How do you gain freedom when your body is the oppressor? It's not like you could get a new one . . .

My head shot up as I remembered something I found in Alyssa's room. The medical brochure for organ donations on her dresser. Was that the program Mrs. Weaver was talking to the doctor about? I'd forgotten the name, but I remembered that the hospital was in Arlington.

As I stood up from my bed, helplessness fell away and made

room for something else. Curiosity. Hope. It's what dropped me into my desk chair. It's what opened my laptop and it's what typed keywords into the search engine. And that was how I ended up on the Atlantic Wellness Center's home page.

The hospital's national score ranked in the top ten. The patient testimonials, however, left me paranoid, heartbroken, and reassessing my life choices. I clicked on the link for the donor questionnaire, just to see what it was about. A quick skim, nothing too serious. What could it hurt?

One hour later, I crashed on my bed, mentally drained from the twenty-five-page donor application I'd just completed. Peekaboo nestled by my side, contently chewing on my left sock while I stared at the glowing stars on my ceiling. Those stars, too, were straight out of the dusty archives that were me and Alyssa. I was a gawky tween again, gazing at this sticker galaxy, discussing crucial topics that wouldn't matter in a week with Alyssa at my side. The memory felt like a comfy pair of slippers, that beloved T-shirt with the faded letters, the song you hadn't heard in years yet still knew the lyrics to. If I closed my eyes, I could almost hear the tune in my head, a faint harmony of two girls whispering in the dark.

POLICY 7.2: SUPPORT SYSTEM

FOUR YEARS AGO

"Janelle! Janelle, wake up!"

My eyes flew open. I couldn't recognize the setting at first because everything looked black. I was sitting upright on something soft, and after piecing together the where and what, the new locale had to be my room. I wasn't at the cemetery or the hospital or downstairs in the kitchen where the nightmare began. But it felt as if I was still there.

"Janelle, shh. It's okay. You're awake. Stop screaming," Alyssa's voice called in the darkness. "It's the middle of the night. You'll wake up the whole house."

I sensed her close by, which made me finally look to my left. The light from my window outlined her wavy hair and silver-blue, moonlit face. My breath pushed past my lips in little hiccups, much slower than when I ripped away from the dream.

"It's okay. Just breathe. In . . . and out," Alyssa coached while inhaling and exhaling in time with me. She sat facing me, her hands squeezing both of mine. Her fingers felt so warm, or were mine just that cold? It was a chill I couldn't shake. It had been that way since the funeral. Strange, because I remembered the church being hot inside and packed with people.

I saw singers in robes and the minister aiming his prayers to the shiny box on the altar. Too much black cloth flapped and twirled around me, but I remembered Daddy's hand on my back, pushing me toward the casket. My movements had felt like skating, a smooth glide toward the sleeping giant.

Pop-Pop had always slept on his back. In the den in his favorite chair, on the porch bench after dinner, and snoring so loud he'd wake himself up and then look around for the culprit. But he was way too quiet to be asleep.

When I touched his cheek, I flinched. The texture felt closer to stone than skin. That hard, cold feeling ran up my arm and sank bone-deep, marrow-deep, all the way to the blood. That wasn't a good way to be, so I asked Daddy if Pop-Pop was chilly in the coffin.

"Cold is the natural state of the universe, baby," my dad said behind me, his big hands squeezing my shoulders. "The gaps between the stars are freezin'. Only livin' things understand hot and cold and your granddaddy can no longer tell the difference."

Alyssa's voice came out in a firm whisper. "Stay with me, Janelle. Come on. Breathe, okay?"

I blinked a few times and found her staring at me in the

dark. The moment was gone, but the paralysis stayed the same.

No one had to tell me that these panic attacks I kept having were side effects of grief. I'd watched enough talk shows to know that much. That didn't stop my waking thoughts from going rogue. Sleep came in short bursts these days and I hadn't left my room since the funeral.

Neither had Alyssa. I barely looked at her during the service, but I'd felt her soft hand and quiet spirit sitting next to me in the first pew. In fact, she hadn't said much since I told her the news over the phone. A true mercy, because speaking hurt. Listening was worse. My thoughts would scatter from place to place, little stops and starts with no pattern.

In and out. Inhale . . . and exhale.

After three more rounds of breathing, Alyssa asked, "You feeling better?"

That question sounded like math, and I sucked at word problems. "A little. I just need to lie down."

Sharing a pillow, we lay head to head, temple to temple, and studied the stuck-on stars on my ceiling. My indifferent universe. My parents could be heard through the walls, even at two in the morning. Muffled sobs, nose-blowing, and whispered phone calls to relatives in other time zones drowned out the cicadas outside.

They tried to keep quiet, but I could still hear them. Grown folks talking to other grown folks, but not really. Stay strong.

Hold it together and act like you hadn't been gutted like a fish. Pain was selfish and rude and interrupted every conversation. Yet we Southern folk were raised to be polite—say "please" and "thank you kindly" to everybody we met. Nothing got under my skin or boiled my blood faster than someone acting fake.

I'd rather hear a hair-raising scream than a whimper trapped behind a hand. At least I'd know I wasn't alone. I'd sooner ram a fist through the wall before I'd dab a single tear from my eye. Why should I? They'd earned the right to be there.

If being a grown-up meant hugging strangers and eating Aunt So-and-So's disgusting casserole while bleeding inside, then let me stay fourteen forever. Let me sit on Pop-Pop's lap and hear about his travels. Let me play chess at his table and lose one more time.

In the darkness of the room, I felt Alyssa's hand touching my face.

I brushed her hand away. "Stop."

"I'm just trying to help." She crumpled the wad of tissue between her fingers.

"I know, but don't touch them. They're doing what they're supposed to do," I said. "Pop-Pop said that tears are signs of pain, and you only feel pain when something's wrong. Like when you step on a nail. It hurts because the nail's not supposed to be in your foot. It's wrong, and the liquid that leaks out is the proof." I turned my head and looked to her, tears spilling over my cheek onto the pillow. "Something's wrong, Lyssa."

"I know. My mom says that tears are like blood but in your head. They come from cuts that others can't see. That's why they run clear." She brushed the hair away from my face with her hand. "I don't know how to help you, but I get it."

That was all I really needed right now—for someone to accept the ugly and not cover it with makeup. Hearing another condolence or prayer would drive me to violence. It was all vapor, wind passing around the body and never seeping through.

"You don't have to stay. You've been here all weekend," I told Alyssa.

"What's the point? If I was home, I'd be more here than there. Might as well keep everything in one place." She tapped her temple. "That's the twinsie connection right there. Just a thought and we're in two places at once. So no matter what, even if I wanted to, I'm not going anywhere without you. Got it?"

"Got it." Smiling, I closed my eyes and allowed sleep to take me again. This time around, I'd drifted to somewhere warm where things never moved away, grew sick, or died. It was a nice place to visit. Too bad I didn't live there.

CHAPTER 8

Curled in the back seat with my knees tucked under my chin, I gazed through the fogging windshield at the rear end of my school. The cars parked in the row ahead were formless colors behind a thick sheen of rain and glass. Hiding out in my car wasn't the best way to spend my lunch period, but it was quiet and removed from all the crocodile tears and pretense that polluted the campus. A bad case of the Mondays? No. More like a case of the stay-out-of-my-face-if-you-don't-want-to-end-up-on-the-news Mondays.

When jaws weren't flapping about Alyssa, the other topic my classmates wanted to dish about was Mateo and our imaginary dating status. Seeing two attractive seniors carpool to school every day was bound to launch a few shipping wars. But wow, I didn't know there was a fandom for broody, mysterious guys who liked to bake. Kids that didn't even know me or Mateo wished us well in the hallways. Last week, a girl in my physics class asked to see my engagement ring. And the Borg? Well, I'd rather not go there.

The tapping on my window startled me back to the present. Ryon, with his giant backpack, stood by my door. The car keys in his hand suggested that he'd either arrived late to school or was leaving early.

"Want some company?" he asked.

"Sure." I clicked the locks.

Ryon climbed in the back seat with me, shook the rain off his jacket, and removed his hood. I immediately noticed the bags under his eyes.

"Why are you hiding out?" he asked.

"I couldn't stay in that building another minute. They're more focused on themselves than her," I said, eyeing the back doors of the school with disdain.

"I hear ya. If I see another phone or camera, I'm gonna break somebody's face. They're not gonna turn me into the next viral video."

I shifted in my seat to look at him fully. "Well, the vlog was your girl's idea in the first place, and it's too popular to quit now. That's a good thing, right?"

"It would be if she'd get some peace." Ryon frowned at the murky view out the front window. "The vlog was supposed to help with the disaster relief, not become a trashy reality show. Now they want to—and I quote—'capture the vulnerability of a future widower.' That's what everyone's calling me now, like she's already dead." His head rolled along the backrest to look at me, his face hard and full of determination. "She's not gonna die."

Unsure if that was a question or a statement, I nodded anyway. No sound entered the car except for the warm air blasting through the heating vents. The impulse to tell Ryon about my decision was strong, but I held back. Giving people false hope was cruel.

He angled his chin toward the parking lot. "We were all standing over there, helping out with the food drive. You and Sera had a booth set up right there, right? Wow. Feels like a decade ago."

I looked to where he was staring and felt the eerie time-jump as well.

"Yeah, it does," I said as the bell rang. The lunch period was over and so was my respite from the world. "We should get goin—"

I paused at the sound of soft snoring to my right.

Ryon's head was back against the seat, his mouth open, totally knocked out. You'd think he and Sera would get along on account of how similar they were in features, voice, and the ability to fall asleep anywhere.

Waking Ryon would've been inhumane. This whole situation with Alyssa had proven that we were all at the mercy of our bodies, and Ryon's demanded sleep—class or no class.

I shut off the car, grabbed my bag and umbrella, climbed out, and left him in peace.

I joined the herd of students corralled in the main corridor. Kids leaving lunch, kids doing a mad dash to the bathroom or their lockers before the tardy bell. It was both disorder and routine, busy bodies mingling until the last minute. I walked past

Alyssa's locker. Notes, cards, and flowers were heaped on the floor in front of it. Not that she'd seen any of them.

The usual frenzy over the homecoming dance was merely an afterthought. There'd been some talk of making Alyssa an honorary queen, extending her rule for a third year. Someone had the bright idea to have the dance at the hospital, but that went nowhere fast.

Joel Metcalf and other media students filmed Liz Aronson and Destiny Howell by the soda machine. The other members of the Borg manned the T-shirt stand by the cafeteria. Naturally, they'd pump the "Alyssa Illness" well until it was bone dry. Posters for the *Active Beauty* vlog hung every ten feet.

"We're starting a new campaign in time for Halloween. We're calling it the Hallow-Clean." Destiny smiled at the camera. "If you want to participate, just hashtag #Alyssa4Life and #Halloclean and you can win a free T-shirt. Details in the description box below. Be sure to Like and comment. Every click counts, guys." She blew a kiss at the camera, slinging spittle into the lens.

"Uh, yeah, we can edit that out." Joel grimaced, then wiped the front of the camera with his shirtsleeve.

Destiny looked at me and smiled with fangs on full display, her amber eyes following my every move. "So, Janelle, what's your take on the Alyssa Weaver tragedy?" she asked. Before I could answer that question, she went right into another. "Rumor has it that you two have known each other since the sixth grade. Is it true that you weren't smart enough to enter kindergarten on time, so you got held back a year? Is that why you're so old?"

"Actually, I was in Ethiopia, Chad, Yemen, and parts of East Asia," I replied matter-of-factly. "I was homeschooled while my folks brought food and supplies to impoverished villages. Public school didn't really come into play until middle school." I gave her a curious look. "Alyssa didn't tell you that part? What a convenient thing to not mention. I guess you're not as tight with her as you thought, huh?"

Destiny appeared flustered, and then she remembered the camera aimed at her face. Assuming we were done here, I turned my back to leave, but Destiny was dead set on trying me today.

"I also heard you and Mateo Alvarez are shacking up together," she said in that innocent baby voice she used to get out of trouble. "Would that be you sniffing around for my leftovers?"

Not only had the rest of the conversation in the hall stopped, but so had time and my ability to move. Nope. This chick did not just blurt that out in front of half the school. Nah, Joel Metcalf was not filming the whole thing on his HD camera.

Did I forget to mention that Destiny was Mateo's ex-girlfriend?

Destiny was Mateo's ex-girlfriend.

They dated sophomore year and it lasted two months before Mateo dumped her, but their relationship was still a sore spot for me. I'd be lying if I said that that wasn't part of the reason why I kept my distance from Mateo. I couldn't be bothered with past events—I was too busy denying this current situation.

It didn't take a genius to figure out what was really going on within the Borg. Now that the baddest chick in the game was out of commission, the rest of her crew was vying for the top spot.

But I was not gonna become the Angry Black Woman by going after Destiny in the middle of the hallway. Curbing my need for retribution, I walked away on robotic legs and chanted the Pruitt Family Commandments in my head. *Thou Shalt Not Be Ratchet. Thou Shalt Not Show Out in Public.*

As I approached my locker, Sera sidled up next to me, phone in hand. "So according to this," she said, "Mateo Alvarez is hiding from the mob and y'all had a secret wedding this summer so he could stay in the country. You two plan to adopt a bunch of kids from overseas like Brad and Angelina and have your first names legally changed to 'Janteo.'" Sera flashed me her phone and revealed a lengthy entry on the *Active Beauty* message board. "Where do they come up with this stuff? You barely know the guy."

"When has that ever mattered in the world of gossip?" I dumped my bag and keys into my locker.

"Anyway, have you seen my brother?" Sera asked.

I slapped my locker shut and kept walking. "He's asleep in my car."

"What? Why?" She fell into step beside me. "Never mind.

I need to get my car keys back from him. My house key is on the link."

"Third row, center aisle." I pointed to the exit. "Hey, did he, um . . . mention anything to you about organ donation?"

"No. Why?" Her face lit with indignation when it dawned on her. "No! No way! There is no way he's doing that for her! Dad would flip out!"

"Relax. He can't do it anyway until he's eighteen. But . . . my birthday was in September." Not my smoothest segue, but I just wanted to see what her reaction would be.

I didn't have long to wait, although it took a moment for Sera to collect her jaw from the floor.

"You can't be serious!" she cried. "Why would you want to help that demon spawn? She wouldn't do it for you, that's for sure."

That's why the act is called *giving*, not *earning*. Or maybe I was just as blind and optimistic as my sister. "Don't you care at all that she could die?" I ask, careful to whisper.

"Yeah, but not enough to lose sleep like Ryon does. Look, I feel bad for her family and all, but this chick has brought me nothing but torment. She's not as perfect as everyone thought and that reality check is freaking people out. It's not like she's really gonna die or anything."

On second thought, maybe Sera and Ryon weren't so similar after all. I'd suffered far worse treatment from Alyssa, and I wasn't about to send her to the guillotine.

Maybe Sera didn't know the full extent of Alyssa's condition. Maybe she was just sick of the hype. Maybe this was actually Sera's stunt double talking to me and not the friend I did activist work with over the years. I'd believe any explanation other than what I just heard.

The bell rang, and she rushed off to class before I could respond. Confusion and annoyance followed me to physics class and kept me distracted. We had a substitute teacher today and I didn't notice until the end, because Sera's attitude threw off my whole routine.

People don't volunteer or give money out of the goodness of their hearts. They do it out of guilt, for bragging rights, to follow a trend, to get into heaven—whatever. In the real world, everything *is business and* everybody *has an end game.*

Alyssa's words came back to me, and though it pained me to admit it, she might have a point. Everyone I knew networked and settled debts on the I'll-scratch-your-back-if-you-scratch-mine payment plan. I knew that wasn't how true friendships worked, but that was how things ran at White Chapel High School. Finding a die-hard friend was rare. No wonder I had so few.

If I had to sit down with a shrink and explain my relationship with Alyssa Weaver, I'd probably get diagnosed with something incurable and hard to spell. We were those grouchy old neighbors who showed affection by trashing each other's lawn displays at

Christmas. I'd driven around town, pitting the reason why I should visit against reasons why I shouldn't. It was a tie.

Alyssa took her time answering the door. Word on the street was she'd just gotten out of the hospital today, so she was probably stiff and groggy. She emerged through the opened door and— Yeesh! It was worse than I thought. No makeup, hair giving me Medusa teas, with sunken eyes glaring at me like this train wreck was my fault.

Giving up that warm, Southern welcome, she asked, "What do you want?"

"An apology for you coming to the door looking like Cynthia from *Rugrats*," I replied. "Also, I wanted to . . . I don't know, hang out and stuff."

Squinting, Alyssa stretched her neck closer until her nose was an inch from mine. "You've been crying. What happened?"

Another reason for driving around town was the crying jag that occurred out of nowhere. All my fears, memories, and emotions were beyond suppression. Alyssa didn't need to know all that, so I said, "People getting on my nerves."

She rolled her eyes. "What else is new? You'll have to use the chair or the floor." She lumbered back into the house and down the hallway.

I closed the door behind me, still blown away by the transformation. The interior walls were white. The carpet was tan. Their furniture was . . . There was furniture! Two couches—one against the wall, the other under the front window with a glass coffee table between them. Two giant bookshelves flanked a TV stand and the fifty-inch flat-screen dominated the center.

When I reached Alyssa's room, she'd crawled back into bed, her lilac covers tucked under her chin. A humidifier pumped steam into the room. It was seventy degrees outside. She had on flannel pajamas and she was still cold?

The bed and the butterfly chair were the only viable seating options in the room. The chair now operated as a hamper, so I'd have to make do with the floor. I checked the closet for a blanket to sit on. I was shocked to find the old purple sleeping bag crammed against her shoe rack. That thing had seen some wild nights of makeovers and pizza parties. There was still a pepperoni stain on the zipper that wouldn't come out.

"You sure you okay with me crashing here for a bit?" I asked Alyssa.

Channel surfing at rapid speed, she said, "I would've slammed the door in your face if I wasn't."

Seeing her point, I fluffed the bag a few times until it draped evenly on the floor.

After kicking off my shoes, I sat with my legs crossed and stared up at her. "I can't believe you still have this thing. I'm surprised you haven't burned it."

"Yeah, I have an issue with letting stuff go."

My stare dropped to my lap and stayed there for several of the most awkward minutes of my life. What could I say to that? I wasn't reading into things, but neither of us had the strength to unpack the baggage between us. Alyssa sure didn't.

What in the world was she gonna do about school? She was due back next week, but she clearly wasn't ready. Her mom had mentioned pulling her out of school altogether, but it was still up in the air. Her whole life had been up in the air since she was a kid. Her family, her coin, her diet, her treatments, her energy— everything was managed but never resolved. An unending cycle of modified schedules, the additional steps needed to start the day.

Glancing around the room, I realized this was hoarding of another kind—the hoarding of procedures. Medical stuff was piled to the ceiling, and every inch of wiggle room had to be squeezed through just to get out the door. Day in and day out: sanitized incisions, fresh bandages, new needles. Beeping machines, daily records in journal pages. Nutritional fact labels with each bite of food tasting like a percentage. I looked at Alyssa's thinning hair, the translucent white skin that hadn't felt the sun in days.

It was her childhood battle with insulin all over again, times a thousand. The sick little white girl up the road with the junky house. The business partner who sold cookies and lemonade each year and refused to sample any of it. When would it end? One way or another, it had to.

I cleared my throat, let the air dry my eyes, then asked, "So, you wanna—"

"Okay, the first rule of this hangout is that you do not talk about my condition or anything sappy. I've just got through dialysis. I'm totally drained, my head is killing me, and I'm ready to blow chunks."

"I was gonna ask you if you wanna Netflix and chill," I clarified.

"You are not a hot Korean guy with a sexy raspy voice, so no. I politely decline your offer. Plus, I don't have Netflix anymore. Mama considers it a luxury expense. Cutbacks." She said this last part with a crook of her upper lip.

What? Miss Shop Till You Drop finally got that credit card cut up? Say it ain't so. I couldn't kick the poor dear while she was down—not from my angle on the floor anyway. This was her being civil, and what better way to call off a two-and-a-half-year feud than by presenting a peace offering?

Her eyes, droopy and dead to the world, sparked like flickering embers when I said, "You can use my password."

CHAPTER 9

"Janelle Pruitt?" the nurse called from the receptionist window.

I approached the front desk on legs that had fallen asleep.

"Here's your ID and insurance card back." The nurse slid a clipboard through the slot in the window. "Go ahead and fill out this form and bring it back to the desk when you're done."

"Thanks." I returned to my seat, leafed through the papers, then zipped through the usual questions. Single. Not pregnant or nursing. Nonsmoker. Hepatitis, malaria, and HIV negative. No known allergies. Haven't traveled abroad in six years.

Each new form I filled out had the same questions, as if they were trying to catch me in a lie. It was all part of the process, according to the Living Donor Program Companion Guide. That hella thick, spiral-bound booklet was currently sitting on my lap and provided a hard surface to fill out paperwork on. It gave a full rundown of policies and issues addressed during the procedure, you know, in case there was an open-book quiz later.

POLICY 2.1: MEDICAL HISTORY
POLICY 6.2: RISK ASSESSMENT
POLICY 8.5: ARE YOU SURE YOU WANT TO DO THIS???

Okay, the last one was fake, but it's pretty obvious the powers that be were trying to weed out the poseurs by assigning homework. Not only did I have to bring the workbook with me to every appointment, I also had to write journal entries inside for each step of the procedure. Fun times.

Once done, I handed my form to the nurse, then spent the next five minutes people-watching. Patients in varying degrees of illness occupied every seat. On the left sat an elderly couple. The husband appeared to be the sick one, judging from the oxygen tank by his chair and the missing leg. My attention moved to the girl sitting in the center cluster of seats with her mother. Her bald scalp hid underneath a pink baseball cap, and I tried not to stare. Poor kid. I often complained about my high-maintenance hair, but now I counted my blessings and gripped my shoulder-length braids in a protective clutch.

It appeared that everyone in the room had a sad story, each with a sense of mortality I could never appreciate. When I did volunteer work overseas with my parents, death had to literally stare me in the face for me to see it. I'd never known famine until I spoke to a skeleton with brown skin and dust-covered hair. Five little fingers and a thumb told me her age when she was too weak to speak and too foreign for me to understand.

Oh man, why did bad things happen to good people?

I was sure those sitting in the waiting room had asked that question at least once, and it might actually apply in their case. Alyssa Weaver, however, was not good people. She wasn't even nice people half the time, and I wouldn't put it past her to let our town burn to the ground if it upped the viewership on her vlog.

So why was I here? Why had I taken time out of my day, ditching school to get tested for something that might not happen? The answer came by way of a phone call I'd gotten three days ago.

I'd been in the middle of another after-school-special crying fit, the one where you hugged the steering wheel because you were triggered by a stupid song on the radio. Taylor Swift was singing about how she and some chick got bad blood, which might as well be the theme song for Alyssa and me. The fast beat didn't fit the typical bawl-your-eyes-out power ballad, but my tear ducts had their own agenda.

Apparently, so did the person blowing up my phone.

Around the eighth ring, I put me and the caller out of our misery. "Hello?"

"Hello? May I speak to Janelle Pruitt, please?" a man asked on the line.

"This is she." The confusion was understandable. I didn't sound like myself, but more like Sera with a head cold.

"Oh! Okay, then. Hello, Janelle. This is Dr. Ian Brighton from the Atlantic Wellness Center. We received your online application and we wanted to follow up with a few questions. Is this a bad time?" he asked.

My head lifted from the car steering wheel. "No! No, not at all. I've been waiting for your call."

"Great. It's my understanding that you wish to partake in our Living Donor Program."

I pushed up into a sitting position and wiped the tears and snot from my face. "That's right. I know the person I'm donating to."

"Yes, an, uh . . ." Papers rustled in the background. "Alyssa Ellen Weaver. She's in our database. May I ask your relationship with the patient?"

There was no need to lie, so I went for the short and sweet approach. "Old friends."

"Well, as the transplant coordinator, I'm here to walk you through the procedure. I also serve as an elective advocate, in cases of personal preference and convenience, though one will be assigned to you. Our facility is fully staffed, so all the testing you'll need can be done in only a few appointments, should you decide to have them done here."

"That's fine. You're about an hour drive from me," I said.

The phone interview ran nearly an hour and I hadn't entered the building yet. At first, I thought it would be an in-and-out process until Dr. Brighton ran down the dream team of doctors I'd have to meet: a general physician, the surgeon, the kidney specialist, the psychiatrist, the health insurance worker, and a partridge in a pear tree. All I could say was "Wow."

And now here I was, ready to begin the process in real time.

The door to the back room opened and a nurse in blue scrubs stepped out with a medical chart in her hand. "Janelle Pruitt? This way, please."

I followed her down a white hallway with doors on either side.

Her head was buried in the folder in her hand. "So you've already had a physical and blood work by your GP. Is that correct?"

"Yes. My doctor faxed them here yesterday."

Sounding real hype about the whole appointment, the nurse said, "You've documented all of your medical history. Just to be sure, no one in your family has high blood pressure? Diabetes, heart, kidney, or liver disease?"

I strained to recall. "No."

She frowned at an entry marked in the file. "You indicated a stroke. Is this correct?"

"Yes. My pop—" I cleared my throat, then tried again. "My grandfather died of one when I was fourteen."

"I'm sorry to hear that. Did he have a preexisting condition?"

"Not that I know of. It happened out of nowhere." Alyssa's

collapse happened out of nowhere as well and both people were at the mercy of their own bodies. Yeah, best not to dwell on that right now.

The nurse snapped the folder shut and led me into an examination room, where we began the initiation rite that all must partake in before setting eyes on a real doctor. This had been Alyssa's life since she was five and I didn't envy her for a second.

Now, seated on what looked like a kid's high chair with padded arms, I was getting a sneak preview of the Alyssa Weaver experience. A rubber tourniquet wrapped around my bicep. The strap was pulled tight and tied in a knot, pinching my skin. Goose bumps sprouted on contact with the rubbing alcohol on my inner arm. Gloved fingers traced the crook of my elbow, seeking a vein, and the tap, tap, tapping against my skin made my molars grind together.

The sharp prick felt years longer than the few seconds the nurse promised me, yet her cheery manner made me calm. The nurse looked to be in her forties, with large, sympathetic eyes. Seeing blood must've been old news for her, plus it wasn't *her* life force piping into the vial in her hand.

"There. That wasn't so bad, was it?" The nurse taped the needle in place.

"I guess." I opened one eye to look at her but avoided glancing down at my arm. My gaze moved to her baby-blue scrubs, then settled on the name tag fastened to the pocket.

BAMBI GOLDBLUM, RN

Hold up. I was having blood drawn by a grown woman named Bambi? Who on earth were her parents? Did they not love her? It had to have been a nickname because I could see the endless teasing in school as clearly as if it were happening live.

"You're doing great, Janelle. This is a really noble thing you're doing," Nurse Bambi said with a warm, maternal smile.

My free shoulder twitched in a half shrug. "It might not lead to anything."

"Maybe so, but just the act of volunteering speaks volumes about your character," she argued. "Not many people would be quick to do this."

Yeah, and I was one of them. Nurse Bambi had no idea how much convincing it took for me to book this four-hour appointment. You had to have a few screws loose to agree to get cut up for parts. Sure, I had ORGAN DONOR marked on my driver's license, but I figured I'd be very much dead before someone took me up on the offer.

I remembered what Dr. Brighton had said to me over the phone:

"I know it sounds overwhelming, but you need to be aware that this is a long process and we're only in the evaluation stage. Once we have your test results, we can determine if you're a possible candidate. We need to be careful with these types of procedures, especially for someone so young. So tell me, what made you decide to donate?"

My answer could've gone several ways. I could've waxed

philosophical about what constituted a friend and an enemy and how they were sometimes the same thing. I could've gone the humanitarian route, run down statistics I'd researched online, and ranted about the plight of mankind. But the truth, the *real reason* was more complicated and far too personal for casual conversation. So I gave him the quickest and most generic answer I could:

"It's for a good cause."

PART 2

EFFECT

CHAPTER 10

"Is this what you really want to do?"

Sheree's face dominated my computer screen with an expression that seemed foreign. Her smile, her pep, her rainbow-kitten-pixie-dust were unavailable for our Saturday video chat. And it all had to do with my big reveal.

I couldn't keep a secret this juicy to myself. Those who really needed to know would likely cuss me out, so it was best to do a practice run with big sis. But the convo wasn't going so hot, judging by the severe side-eye she threw my way.

"I'm just getting evaluated. It's not that serious." My reply did nothing to remove that stubborn crease in her brow.

"But what if it's more than that?" she asked. "What if you get approved? What happens then? If you, hypothetically, are a match and then you back out, do you think that's fair to Alyssa?"

Only if Alyssa finds out that I applied as a donor. Which is not going to happen.

"Come on," I said. "What are the odds of us being a match?"

"Then what's the point if you're so sure? Are you doing it just to say you tried to donate? Is it for a personal pat on the back?" Sheree's tone reeked of accusation, and the vibe was stinking up my room.

"If that was the case, then I'd post it all over the internet," I argued.

Sheree possessed the marked ability to read a chick for filth with an iceberg stare, a curled upper lip, and a click of the tongue. No words required. It was enough to shut me up.

"Okay then. If it's not for credit then it might be for revenge. Are you making a power play? You're gonna hold this over Alyssa's head to get her to act right?" she asked.

Before I could answer, a disturbing image came to mind. I was dangling an organ over Alyssa's head and she was hopping around like Peekaboo to catch it from my fingers.

Here you go. You want a kidney? Who's a good girl?

Oh yeah. Totally messed up.

"What's with the hostility, Sheree? I'd think you—of all people—would be happy for me." If she was this upset, there was no telling what our folks would say. This call was supposed to be the dress rehearsal for that, but my sister done flipped the script.

"I am happy for you, really," Sheree replied. "But I'd be happier if you were doing this for the right reasons. A few weeks back you were telling me how much it bugged you when Alyssa brought those clothes to the fund-raiser. Why were you mad?"

"Because she was just doing it to show off. She was going to throw that stuff out anyway," I explained, getting irritated all over again.

"Exactly! And you just saying you're donating, but without the passion of going through with it, it's no better than her handing castoffs to homeless people. Where's the sacrifice? Where are the man hours and elbow grease? Anyone can be generous when the gift costs them nothing. But this gift's gonna cost you. Big-time. And I'm not even talking about the physical part. There's controversy and emotional strain. Brace yourself, sis. 'Cause it's coming."

Nope, that didn't sound ominous at all. "Can you elaborate on that?" I asked.

"Facts: Black people don't donate organs, especially while we're still alive," Sheree explained. "Think about it. How many black folks do you know would give away body parts? We won't even go to therapy if we need it. If Jesus don't fix it, then it's gonna stay broke. And because of that, people are gonna feel some type of way about you saving a white girl and not some sistah on a ten-year waiting list. The struggle is real on these streets, Janelle. Some are willing to pay top dollar for minority organs and will resort to abduction and human trafficking . . ." She let the subject hang, as if saying more would invoke a curse.

That reply wasn't terrifying in the slightest and would by no means give me nightmares tonight. The chill tickling my spine was just a side effect of the weather, I swear. "Okay. Let's keep it one hundred. Do you want me to do this or not?" I asked.

It took some time for her to answer, but she said, "If Alyssa doesn't get a transplant, then she's gonna die. So, yes, I want you to do this. Listen, I know you wanna help out in the world like the rest of us, but you need stamina and stiff principles to get you through the rough parts. There's a lot of wrong in this world, but does this particular wrong heat your seat?"

The saying brought a smile to my face and a flood of memories. A thousand little words of wisdom told to me and my sister over dinner, a game of chess, or from an old man's favorite armchair.

Not every battle is yours to fight, baby girl. But when conviction burns so hot it heats your seat and you hop out the chair swingin', then you've found your callin'.

"Pop-Pop would say that all the time," I told Sheree.

"And he was right." She leaned closer to the screen. "You know I've got your back in whatever decision you make, just as long as you have a clear reason for it. If it doesn't work out—fine. But see it through 'till the end." Finally, like the sun peeking through clouds after a storm, her twinkling smile appeared. "So, keep me posted, okay?"

I smiled back. "Sure. Love you."

Once the screen went black, I closed my laptop, then checked my phone for any new messages. Saturdays meant disaster relief business, and the cleanup team was supposed to meet at the park entrance in an hour. Theoretically. At least one student council member would flake—I could bet money on it. Today's dropout was none other than Joel Metcalf. According to his text, he was stuck editing Alyssa's tribute video, which included the Borg remake of Beyoncé's "Run the World." A small clip was already posted on the *Active Beauty* fan page. The atrocities captured on film were numerous and unspeakable.

After throwing on some jeans, sneaks, and my volunteer T-shirt, I went downstairs for some semblance of food. I'd planned on grabbing an off-brand McMuffin at one of the cafés in Aberdeen Square, but the scent wafting from the first floor canceled that order.

The dogs nipped at my heels and stalked me into the kitchen.

Mateo stood at the stove and scooped flat donut holes from a baking pan. He glanced up at me, and his smile revealed deep-seated dimples.

"I'm glad you're here. I need you to try this." He handed me a piece cooling from the plate.

I eyed the pastry wearily. "What is it?"

"*Polvorones de Canela.*"

"Provolone Cornella." I nodded thoughtfully. "Meaning what exactly?"

"*Polvorones de Canela.*" The words rolled off his tongue in a low purr that made me consider adopting a cat. "A cinnamon cookie. It's my secret recipe. Go on. Try it."

Watching him watching my response, I took a timid bite. Flavors exploded on my tongue in a celebration of spice, sugar, and all things decadent and fattening. The treat ended too quickly and my tongue swiped my lips for more.

"These are bangin'! You should sell these at our next bake sale." I dove for another one.

"Maybe. I still need to tweak a few ingredients." He scooped raw dough onto the cookie sheet.

"So I'm guessing you're skipping out on the cleanup party today. Did you get proper clearance from the warden?" I asked, sneaking cookie number three.

"Mrs. Trina's at some church meeting, so I've finally got a few hours of peace. Now I'm in the zone." He hooked his thumbs into the neck strap of his apron. The front of the apron had a cartoon of a talking hot pepper with the words EL CALIENTE! floating inside its little speech bubble. "Speaking of skipping," Mateo added, "I noticed you weren't in class yesterday."

The comment forced my food to go down the wrong pipe. "How would you know that? We don't have any classes together," I said between coughs. I grabbed a bottled water from the fridge.

"I didn't see your car out in the parking lot and when I asked your friend Sera, she said you hadn't showed up." He stared pointedly at me. "Does Mrs. Trina know you played hooky?"

Could a girl get some warning before having to lie on the spot? I'd timed my appointments perfectly so I'd make it home around three in the afternoon. Since Mateo no longer needed to bum a ride, I figured no one would suspect that I ditched school.

I should've known Chef Boyar-Hotness would be trouble when I saw his pride and joy hogging the driveway. It was a rusty green *Sanford and Son* pickup, held together by duct tape and prayer. It had gotten trapped in mud during the storm, and he was more thrilled over saving that hunk of bolts than his mom's recovery. I assumed it was another memento from his dad, though I couldn't be sure.

Mateo stirred a bowl of batter contentedly. I could tell he was waiting for my response. "Well?"

"'Well' what?" I gulped my water and stalled for time.

"Fine. Don't tell me. I know where you went anyway."

I swallowed hard. "You do?"

"You went to get tested, right? You're thinking about donating a kidney to Alyssa Weaver."

The bottle slipped from my fingers, and catching it in time was a juggling act of pure fail. The plastic bounced from hand to hand, to countertop, to bar stool, to the floor, and then to the mercy of my German shepherd. The dog left the room with a new chew toy between his teeth. Meanwhile, I leaned against the kitchen island and acted like none of that just happened.

Playing it cool, I asked Mateo, "Wh-what makes you think that?"

"Several things. Your reaction when Alyssa passed out in the park. Your knowledge of her condition. The internet search history auto-directing me to bookmarked sites when I borrowed your laptop. The medical binder you left in the back seat of your car that says, 'Living Donor Program Companion Guide.' The dates marked inside the planner lining up with the days you've missed. And the Band-Aid inside the crook of your arm shows that you've had blood drawn recently." He glanced down at said arm, then dismissed the point with a shrug. "Then again, I could be wrong."

Wow. Did he moonlight as a private eye or was I just that clumsy? Either way, the need to explain myself was dire. "I just wanted to see if I'm a good candidate. It might not even work. I just had to see, you know?"

"What if it does work?"

Oh great. First Sheree and now him? "I guess I'll cross that bridge when I get there. I still have a few more appointments until they can tell me if I'm approved or not."

"I take it I'm the only person who knows about this."

"Just you and my sister. So please don't tell anyone." With hands clasped together, I was calling in a favor *and* praying in tandem. I would need both prayers and favors if Grandma Trina found out.

"Sure." Mateo plucked a cookie from the plate and took a bite. He made a face. "Needs more butter."

I blinked, completely thrown off guard. He had to be playing with me. "What do you mean, 'sure'? You mean you won't tell?"

"Yeah. I think it's cool what you're doing. I had to give my mom blood when she was first taken to the hospital. It's not the same, though. Not many Hispanics donate organs. It's shady business, especially in Mexico."

My head moved closer to his and I had no idea why I was

whispering. "You're talking black market stuff? People don't go to doctors down there?"

"Who do you think is running the scam?" he said, then continued working. "Why waste time treating a poor, sick person when you can harvest their organs after they die? It's a huge racket that makes people scared of hospitals. Not all, but you learn quickly which ones to avoid."

What was I supposed to say to that? He was sounding more like Sheree by the second.

Mateo bumped my arm. "Relax. I'm sure you'll be fine. And your secret is safe with me."

"Thanks." I drummed my fingers on the table when the conversation lagged. Not that it would change my mind or anything, but I just wanted to know—"You don't think I'm crazy for attempting this, do you?"

Brows knit in concentration, he arranged the balls of dough so they were evenly spaced on the baking pan. Sculptors weren't this meticulous.

"Nope. I don't really know Alyssa that well. But I can tell she means something to you. Near-death experiences can put things into perspective and show you who your true friends are." Mateo handed me a cookie. "Stop thinking so hard. The brain and the heart will trip you up every time and have you going in circles and nothing gets done. Just follow your gut. That's what I do." He rubbed his belly.

I leaned back and stared him up and down. Had Mateo always been this deep? "Check you out, Chef Yoda, Jedi Master of the kitchen," I finally said with a smile. "I didn't know fortunes came with these cookies."

"Mmm," Mateo replied. "Mind what you have learned. Save you, it can."

Somehow, he'd sounded exactly like that little green dude from *Star Wars*, and I. Was. Rolling. My eyes watered, my stomach muscles tied into triple knots, and my legs gave out as I laughed and leaned against the counter for support.

I was learning something new about Mateo every day. Today, I'd learned that he was a low-key fanboy and he could say something that would cause choking or a deadly case of the giggles. I'd have to remember that in the future.

It had been a while since I'd had a good, face-splitting belly laugh. The weirdest part was that in the past, nearly all of those occasions had somehow involved Alyssa.

POLICY 10.2: DONOR-RECIPIENT RELATIONSHIP

FOUR YEARS AGO

"Don't. Say. A thing." I pushed the command out through a locked jaw and clenched teeth. It required every muscle in my face to keep from turning toward Alyssa's direct line of vision. One glance, one nudge, one *psst* from that fool would open the floodgates of hysterical laughter. I knew what had caught her attention, but I possessed enough home training to not stare outright.

The scruffy man in the tan trench coat and safari hat slid down the buffet line. Eight chicken legs and four tiny milk cartons sat on his dinner tray. As volunteers, we didn't pass judgment or ask questions about the people we served, but that *thing* cradled in the man's arms raised a grocery list of them. The bundle squirmed inside a blue blanket and clutched a baby bottle between its two black claws.

Not even trying to be subtle, Alyssa's bugged-out stare followed the man to a table across the room. Her strawberry-blond head, crowned with the same reindeer-antler headband as mine, turned as far as it could go without getting whiplash.

"Not one word, Lyssa," I warned again.

She lifted her hands in surrender. "I wasn't gonna say anything."

Holding my breath, I started the countdown in my head. *Five, four, three, two . . .*

"But let it go on record that that's gotta be the ugliest baby I've ever seen," she whispered.

"That's because it's not a baby. It's a raccoon, not even full grown." I slapped creamed corn onto the dinner tray and passed it to the next person in the chow line.

"Are you telling me that guy brought a raccoon to a soup kitchen?" Alyssa raved. "Dude's got that thing swaddled in a blanket like Jesus in the manger."

"Shut up, Lyssa," I hissed.

We couldn't make a peep without Grandma Trina catching wind of it. She stood across the room, chatting with the charity organizer. But my grandmother was the rare creature with eyes on the front, back, side, and top of her head. I averted my gaze and could still feel the looming threat of danger if I so much as cracked a smile.

We were in the multipurpose room in our town hall. The room transformed into whatever was needed: an auditorium for town meetings and pageant plays, a conference room for a guest speaker, or a ballroom for every prom in every school district. But it was mostly a playroom for Thursday night bingo. Today, it had a more humble purpose: serving food to the unfortunate.

Rainbow lights flickered on the eight-foot Christmas tree in the corner. Tinsel and garland hung from the ceiling, and all us volunteers wore reindeer-antler headbands and red rubber noses. Some lady in a squeaky voice sang "Santa Baby" on the radio. Her cutesy-wootsy voice crooned through two monster speakers at the front door and jabbed ice picks in my brain. It helped distract me from the laughing fit that was bound to pop off at any minute.

"Girl, I'm telling you right now—don't look at me." I slapped mushy meat product onto a tray. "You're not gonna get me in trouble today. Nope. No way."

Alyssa had the nerve to sound appalled. "How would I get you in trouble?"

The question was too dumb to warrant a response. I'd gotten grounded for a week for selling candy with her for our class field trip. Everyone in school was peddling goodies, but their efforts didn't result in two minors getting charged with trespassing. Neither Grandma Trina nor the sheriff who drove us home could grasp the marketing genius of running shop inside every nurse's station, daycare center, and Lamaze class in town. That's why I was minding my p's and q's today. Grandma Trina was famous for making gifts disappear from the tree if we acted up. The speed with which she approached our table told me that more presents were about to go missing.

"What are you two doing? Didn't I tell y'all to split up?" Grandma Trina demanded.

Alyssa wrapped her arms around my shoulder and clung to me tightly. "I know, but we'll be good. I promise." She batted her lashes at Grandma Trina, but the woman wasn't having it.

"Promise nothin'. Y'all ain't gonna be embarrassin' me up in here with all that gigglin'. Show some respect. Now, you go back to the canned food station and y'all can play after the dinner." Grandma Trina pointed across the room in the way she'd order our dogs to sit in the corner.

Alyssa made a production of the separation. Her arms stretched out as she pulled away and whimpered, "Stay strong, Janelle. We will be together again someday."

"Noooo! Come back!" I cried, my hands reaching out for her.

"Oh, for the love of . . ." Grandma walked away in a huff, completely done with the whole scene. But we weren't. Alyssa was halfway across the room and we were still going at it.

"I'll never forget you!" I wailed. "The memories we shared will stay close to my bosom!"

Carrying a box of Styrofoam plates, Sheree stepped

between our outstretched hands and shook her head at us. "Really, guys? You two need serious help," she muttered, then walked away.

Not even thirty minutes after her banishment, Alyssa somehow made it over to my side again. While on my break and en route to one of the long banquet tables, I felt her nudge my arm.

"*Aaand* I'm back by popular demand." Keeping a lookout for Grandma Trina, Alyssa added in a hushed tone, "So can I stay over tonight? My dad's in town and I'm really not feeling that holiday reunion."

Did she not know what day it was? "Yeah, but aren't you gonna open gifts tomorrow?"

"No gifts, just gift cards. All gift cards. No need to open them until I get to the store. Besides, they're just gonna fight and blame each other for their failings in life."

Okay, my parents had fights. Alyssa's parents had WWE matches. Whenever I'd stay over, she'd turn up the TV in her room to drown out whatever cookware hit the walls. Her folks' marriage was over long before her dad moved out, but that didn't mean they didn't love her. Heck, most of their arguments were about caring for her. Was that what she meant by "their failings"?

I turned to ask her, but she grew distracted by someone entering through the double doors.

Ryon Kimura stepped into the dining hall, wearing a frumpy blue sweater with a giant snowflake on the front. If I had to bet money on it, that getup was from a mandatory photo op where everyone in the family dressed the same.

He approached our table and smiled. "Hey, Janelle. You guys got any more of those to-go boxes?"

I ran the inventory in my head. "Um, yeah, we—"

Alyssa hopped from her seat and stepped in front of me. "We have plenty. How many do you need?"

"As many as you can spare." His glance roamed across the two dozen dining tables that were full to capacity. "It's pretty packed in here. Some are getting turned away at the door. We've got food to spare, but not enough room."

Alyssa slapped her hands over her mouth and gasped. "Oh no! Not on Christmas Eve!"

"I know. It's heartbreaking. My dad and his crew have something set up at the community center. So we're directing everyone over there and sending to-go plates with them," Ryon explained.

Alyssa sighed deeply and carried on with quivering lips and misty eyes. "There's nothing more gratifying than the act of giving. Can you imagine all these hungry people with nowhere to go for the holidays?"

So now that was a point of concern for her? If I rolled my eyes any harder, I'd go blind. "Go ask my grandma over there. She'll get you what you need." I pointed to the buffet line.

"Thanks. I'll catch you later. Merry Christmas." Ryon winked, then walked away to the sound of Mariah Carey singing "All I Want for Christmas Is You." Alyssa's hand reached for his retreating back as she lip-synched the lyrics in his honor.

I watched her antics, then said through a mouthful of pie, "They've got bottled water at the buffet table if you're feeling thirsty."

"Oh, shut up." She dropped into the seat next to me. "Let's not go into secret crushes around here. Unlike you, I plan on going after what I want."

I stopped chewing and asked out of the corner of my mouth, "What's that supposed to mean?"

With elbows resting on the table, she tucked her hands under her chin and stared longingly at the pie on my plate that she couldn't eat. "Nothing. No tea, no shade."

Before I could call her out, I felt a tap on my shoulder. I turned to the chair to my right and saw an adorably tiny woman wrapped in a matted fur hat and coat.

"Sweetie, are you drinking that?" She pointed to the clear plastic cup of water between us.

"No, ma'am. You can have it." I slid the cup closer to her.

"Oh, thank you, dear," the woman said, then stuck her thumb in her mouth, popped out the top row of teeth, dropped it into the water, then continued eating.

Alyssa and I sat locked in place. My eyes turned straight

ahead, looking at nothing, not my food on my plate, not the dentures floating in the cup, and *especially* not Alyssa's face. The moment I did, the second we made eye contact, I would be done for.

"Not one word," I grunted out, my body shaking with suppressed laughter.

"I can't hold it together," Alyssa croaked.

This was an act of human torture—having to swallow down humor while across the room your grandma stared you down with promises of bodily harm dancing in her eyes. And then Alyssa and I both caved and gave in to our laughter. We cracked up at the same time, but within moments, Grandma Trina was cutting through the tables like a raging bull to reach our side.

Horrified, Alyssa and I voiced our approaching doom at the same time, "Uh-oh!"

There was no question that my portion of gifts under the tree would be MIA. I'd be lucky if I was left with a gift card. I guess Alyssa and I really were twinsies—we both had a lame Christmas morning to look forward to.

CHAPTER 11

There was no doubt about it—Dr. Brighton looked like a Ken doll. His floppy blond hair, golden tan, and straight white teeth were too flawless to be natural. He was probably a vegan who juiced everything and did triathlons twice a year.

I sat in the chair on the opposite side of his desk, trying to figure out what products he used to get his hair so bouncy. The front part fanned downward, then swooped over his forehead like an ocean wave, and I imagined rocking that style when I finally took my braids out. My face was rounder than his, but I'd still look cute. My hair would need a straight press and maybe a trim, but—

"Janelle?" he said after what sounded like numerous tries for my attention. "Do you have any questions on what I've explained so far?"

"Huh? Oh! No—I don't understand anything about white blood cells, antibodies, HLAs, HPAs, or HBO. I wouldn't know a genetic crossmatch from a city crosswalk. I just need to know if I'm compatible."

"You're very compatible. In fact, you're a near perfect candidate."

English was my first language, yet I was gonna need a translator for that response. "How? We're not related." Then again, Mrs. Weaver hadn't made the cut, and she'd given birth to Alyssa.

"You have type O blood, which is universal, and you have four of the six required antigen markers—"

I had to stop him right there. "Please. Two syllables or less."

"Your blood types are the same. Her immune system won't try and off your cells for invading their turf. Your organ tissues have similar enough DNA to attempt to pass as her own."

I kept to my original question. "*How?*"

"You're from White Chapel. That's a small farming community, am I correct?" he asked, and I nodded. "People have been there for generations. It's like a large tribe, and ancestors of the original founders are still living there."

So Dr. Ken Doll had jokes. "Okay, it's not even like that, sir. This is Virginia, not West Virginia, and we're not that small of a town."

"I'm only implying that this country is a melting pot. People marry into different ethnicities. Genes are passed down, and it's often harder to find a match for some people because they're so blended, but sometimes that can work to our advantage. We happened to luck out in your case."

Yeah, real lucky. Now I was questioning my family tree. I knew that slavery and illegal race-mixing did happen in the South, so it might be possible, somehow, somewhere, in a galaxy far, far away, that Alyssa and I had a relative in common. I knew DNA was weird, but this suspended all boundaries of belief. Or maybe I didn't want to believe it. That thought was more alarming than the test results.

After another ten minutes of watered-down med school vocab, Dr. Brighton flipped to a new section in his file. "Now that we've tackled the medical side, it's time to delve into the mental and emotional side."

I rubbed my clammy palms on my legs. The friction burned my thighs. "Meaning what?"

"Meaning you need to assess the risks involved in going forward," he replied. "What if the kidney fails?"

Baffled, I pointed to both the open file and the computer on his desk. "You just spent twenty minutes telling me I was a perfect match."

"No one is a perfect match, Janelle. Not even identical twins are a sure thing. There's always a possibility that the transplant will fail. It could be right away, a month, or three years from now. There is no guarantee when it comes to the human body." With hands clasped together, Dr. Brighton leaned in, ready to drop some hidden knowledge. "Nearly a quarter of the transplants we perform here every year are re-transplants. Some organs fail sooner than others. But organs from living donors are far more successful and have a longer shelf life. The recipient will have roughly fifteen years."

My hand gripped the chair to keep from falling over. "Fifteen years? That's it? What happens after that?"

"The recipient may need a new transplant."

I jumped out of my chair. "What? She'll need a new one when she's thirty?"

"Or sooner. We'll have to see." His chair rolled toward the computer and he wiggled the mouse to wake the screen. "So this is why I want you to think long and hard about this procedure. How will this affect your relationship? It's one thing to donate to a complete stranger, but could you live with seeing Alyssa every day knowing what you've lost and that she still could die? Will she blame you? Will you blame her?"

We do that anyway, I wanted to say, but a growing knot caught in my throat. Blinking away the prickling tears, I looked over at the file cabinet, the plaques, the family photos on the wall, the view of the parking lot through the window, anywhere but the pity on Dr. Brighton's face. Spotting the water cooler in the corner, I went over for a drink. I still felt his steely blue eyes track my every move. I refused to show weakness, not today.

"I'm not trying to scare you but to give you realistic expectations," he continued. "Organ donation is not a once-and-for-all fix but an extension of a life span and better quality of the time given. Patients spend up to four hours on a dialysis machine three days a week. That's twelve hours a week, two days a month, and nearly a month out of an entire year. Imagine what your friend could be doing with her life with that time—because that's what we're campaigning for. It's why your case has jumped to the head of the line among thousands, and why in a few weeks we're at the mid-point of a process that takes close to a year to complete. Time. It is what we're racing against and chasing after." His fingers tap-danced on the keyboard as he typed notes into the spreadsheet.

I nodded, drinking in his message and washing it down with my cup of water.

"So, should you agree to proceed with the evaluation, we'll arrange a session with Dr. Langhorne. She's our chief socio-psychologist and very good at what she does."

I stared out of the window and mulled over the concept. "I've never gone to therapy before. Is she nice?"

His hesitation made me turn around. He seemed lost for words, or rather in a struggle to choose the right ones. "She's . . . efficient. You'll meet her soon enough."

Dr. Brighton's words rode shotgun with me on the long drive home. Decisions like these took time, which apparently was a dying resource.

Mateo's Fred Sanford truck hogged the driveway, so I parked at the curb. While gathering my stuff from the passenger seat, I got a text from a person I'd thought I deleted from my address book.

ALYSSA: Come to my house after school. Thanx.

Stop the presses! I'd been summoned by the queen herself, and who would dare decline a royal engagement? By God, I must tend to her council at once. Yeah, right. If it were a real emergency, she would've called directly, or sought professional help via 911. I could count on zero fingers the times I'd jumped at her command, so why quit that habit?

I went inside, took a shower, ate some of Mateo's bomb quesadillas, walked the dogs, then found my way onto Alyssa's front yard around 4:15.

Before my foot hit the stoop, the door opened and Alyssa appeared, wearing pajamas and a ticked-off expression.

Since that was her resting face, I needed context. "How you feeling? What's your flavor?"

Alyssa flashed me a smarmy grin, then scrolled her phone with her thumb. "Sour. I texted you two hours ago."

Smiling wide, I showed her my own phone. "Yes, and I dropped *everything* and ran right over."

She scoffed and shook her head slowly. "I swear, Persian rugs lie better than you. Anyway, can you take me to my dialysis appointment? I'm too weak to drive."

My gaze swung to the white Rabbit convertible in the driveway and then to the orange Camaro that wasn't there. "Where's your mom?"

"At work. And Ryon's got SAT prep today."

"I thought the hospital didn't allow visitors. And where's the

Borg?" They were her friends, after all. Or had I imagined the last two years?

"I told you I'd check about visitors. They approved it," she said, completely dodging the last part of my question. "So can we go?"

"Depends. You got that gas money?"

She lifted her head to the sky and groaned. "Omigod, Janelle! Could you do me this one favor?"

That sounded like something friends would do. You know, the people she *didn't* call. But whatever. "I'm just messing with you, you big baby. What time's your appointment?"

"Four thirty."

I checked the time on my phone. "See, look at that. I came just in time."

Her puckered lips and sidelong glance spoke volumes. "I knew you'd take your sweet time coming over. That's why I texted you so early." Bag in hand and a pillow tucked under her arm, she stepped out of the house and closed the door behind her. "Let's roll."

The Peninsula Dialysis Center was a small clinic on the outskirts of the county. The place looked more like a nail salon than a hospital, with wall-to-wall windows, bright lights, and a chemical stench in the air. The lobby had that white, high-tech sleekness featured in every sci-fi movie. The tall blond behind the counter could easily play the hot alien that the star captain would hook up with.

Thinking of nerdy stuff reminded me that I needed to text Sera. We were supposed to hang out at her place this afternoon. It had completely slipped my mind because—life. I checked my phone and Sera had already texted me.

SERA: R U coming later?
ME: IDK how late I'll be. Rain check?
SERA: Sure. ☹

"Texting my replacement?" Alyssa cut her eyes at my phone as she pulled her ID from her wallet. "Does your new bestie know you're with me or are you keeping it on the low?"

"I know how testy you get when people put your medical issues on blast, so no. She doesn't know. How does it feel being the side chick?" I gave her a sorry-not-sorry smirk.

She returned the look. "Oh, Janelle Lynn. We both know I'm never the side chick."

There went that jealousy thing I'd picked up on before. I'd caught it during the school food drive and it hadn't made sense then, either. She had four loyal disciples on her squad and half the school on her friend list, yet she was checking for me?

Maybe besties were like spouses: You can only have one at a time. Any more than that and you'd run the risk of starting a cult.

After Alyssa and I signed in at the front desk, we chilled in the sitting area and read magazines until she was called to the back room. I expected to wait in the lobby until she was done, and maybe catch a nap. To my surprise, she waved me to come along.

"Normally, visitors aren't allowed in during the 'put-on' and 'take-off' parts of the treatment, but I put in a special request for certain people to come, namely you and Mom," she explained, but left out one critical part.

"Why me?" I asked.

"Because . . . reasons." She hedged. When I stopped in the middle of the hall, she went on to say, "I trust you, okay? You're better at handling weird than most people, and the registration form asked for two contacts in case something happens. My dad lives too far away, Ryon would only cry the whole time, and the others . . . You're just the first contact that came to mind, is all."

That made me smile a bit. "You telling me I'm *your person*?"

"Ugh! You're still hooked on *Grey's Anatomy*, I see. I gave up on that show after McDreamy died," she muttered, then kept walking.

The dialysis room was a large, open space divided into ten stations with leather recliners set in a semicircle. After she got a quick physical exam, Alyssa hopped into her assigned lounger and fluffed the pillow she'd brought from home.

The nurse handed me a face mask, safety goggles, and a long-sleeved smock to avoid contamination. Then I was asked to sit at a safe distance from Alyssa's seat during the "put-on" process. For the next ten minutes, I sat amazed, watching the nurse hot-wire the robo-kidney with blurring speed. Alyssa wasn't kidding when she said that people needed to take a class to operate the machine. No way would I try that at home. A cartridge slid here. A pouch of fluid hooked there. Tubes connected to knobs that wrapped around wheels that clipped onto more tubes that inserted into Alyssa's arm. And the poor girl had to do this three times a week? *Twelve hours a week, two days a month, and nearly a month out of an entire year.* My mind couldn't wrap around a problem that big.

An hour into the process, Alyssa and I entered a strange area of physics where we occupied the same space, but in different dimensions. I was on my phone. She was on hers. Both of us avoided the things that were really on our minds.

Loud snores caught my attention. An old woman two stations away lay sound asleep in her recliner. The paperback novel she'd been reading rested on her stomach. Her head lolled to one shoulder while her short salt-and-pepper wig twisted in the opposite direction. At first glance, I mistook the hairpiece for a gray poodle sleeping on her head. It even swelled and contracted as if it were breathing on its own.

And no, I was not, *absolutely not*, going to look at Alyssa. The moment we locked eyes, the second she cracked a smile, I would burst out laughing, and we were too old to cut up in public.

"You know you saw that. Don't act like you didn't," Alyssa mumbled, her thumbs clicking away on her phone.

"What is wrong with you?" I whispered. "That's a little old lady. Be nice."

She shrugged and kept texting. "What do you mean? I love old people. I want to be old people. But if I see something funny then I'm gonna laugh—simple as that. You did see that thing move, though, right? It wasn't just me?" When I didn't answer, she said, "Because the sign at the front door clearly says NO SMOKING and NO PETS, but old girl gets to waltz in here with a dead squirrel on her head."

"Shut up, Lyssa," I gritted out. "You are so wrong for that. I swear, I can't take you anywhere."

Setting her phone on her lap, she lifted her chin high and proud. "Unfounded and untrue. I may be a diva, but I'm also a lady."

I had to lean all the way back in my chair on that one. "Need I remind you of all the times you ran your mouth? You almost got kicked out of school because you're forever talking back to people that you're not supposed to."

Her hazel eyes swept up and down my frame like I was the short one in our duo. "I'm gonna need receipts."

"I've got plenty." I ran down the front-runners on my fingers. "That time you made Sera cry in the middle of a pep rally."

She waved off exhibit A. "It was self-defense. She kept harassing me for calling Ryan 'oppa,' like I don't know what that means in Korean. He's two months older than me *and* he's my boyfriend. He fits the profile."

It was true, but the point was winning the argument no matter what. I kept going. "Or when you cussed out that pregnant cashier at the fro-yo shop."

Hand resting on her chest, Alyssa looked dismayed. "That chick had the nerve to call me fat. The. Nerve!"

I moved on to my third and most incriminating piece of evidence. "Or when you made the guidance counselor quit her job."

After a long pause, she said, "Hey, you don't sit behind a desk, talk crap about my mom being trailer trash, and not have your life flash before your eyes. It's just not how things are done in my world, especially while in the middle of a custody battle. Mrs. Cline found that out the hard way."

Case: dismissed. The smile I didn't know I was wearing melted from my face. I fell against my chair and watched her in silence. That part of the story had been conveniently left out of the hallway tabloids, and not once had I thought to ask Alyssa for the real scoop. What other details had I missed?

Sighing, Alyssa stared dead-eyed at the ceiling for so long, I looked up, too. It had that speckled Styrofoam tiling you'd see in every office building.

"Remember that time I went to Finnegan's for my birthday and I ordered that nasty shrimp platter?" she asked out of the blue.

I recalled the event vividly. "I think half the waitstaff remembers that night."

She shuddered at the memory. "It looked nothing like the picture on the menu. It was like five shrimps, dry as could be, shivering on the plate. I made the waitress take it back to the kitchen and ended up ordering the best salad I ever had. Why can't life be that easy, you know? You just flag over your server and tell them to fix it."

I'd give anything to know that answer for myself. My hand swiped the air, indicating an invisible tagline. *"Excuse Me, Life? This Is Not What I Ordered.* That would make a cool T-shirt."

She considered the concept for a moment. "That's a great idea."

"I've been known to have a few in my day."

Her gaze drifted across the room in recollection. "Yeah, you have."

The minutes ticked away before either of us said another word. Finally, I asked, "Lyssa, can we just say what we really wanna say to each other?"

Her head tipped toward me. "You wanna go first?"

As a matter of fact—no. The question felt hopeless, and simply asking it caused exhaustion. But I had to get the ball rolling. "How did we get here? We used to be best friends and finish each other's sentences. This is not what I ordered."

She gave me a chin-quivering smile, the kind that fought off tears. "It's not what I ordered, either. But what else is on the menu?"

I extended my arm and slipped my hand in hers. "Hopefully, something fresh."

Alyssa squeezed my hand and smiled in earnest.

POLICY 11.2: COERCION AND UNDUE PRESSURE

FOUR YEARS AGO

"Come on, Janelle. No one will know it's you." Alyssa slapped her hall pass against her thigh in an impatient beat as she checked her phone. "The bell's about to ring in three minutes."

We stood outside of Mr. Russo's art class, casing the row of lockers across the hallway. The corridor had to be free of witnesses, so we'd gotten out of social studies at the same time to make the drop. It had to go down during last period to avoid risking Mateo losing the note between classes. Alyssa had planned our operation down to the second. All that was missing was the *Mission: Impossible* theme song piping through the intercom. And my courage.

My head shake came off like a tremor as I literally held my heart in my hand. Crushed between my fingers was pent-up emotion inside heart-shaped pink construction paper. Every wish, fear, and daydream I'd hidden since last semester was carefully spelled out in colored marker and scratch-and-sniff stickers. None of Alyssa's matchmaking efforts had worked, and we'd only seen Mateo a few times during summer break anyway. So she'd decided on the anonymous approach in a controlled area, which meant waiting until the first week of school.

"I can't. Here, you do it." I handed the note to her.

She held her hands in the air and backed away. "No, no, no. And by the way, no."

"Why not?"

"Because it's not my letter, not my feelings, and not my crush," she replied. "If you're not brave enough to be a secret admirer, then you don't deserve having a public boyfriend."

Whoa! Jumping the gun a bit, weren't we? I'd settle for a simple wave in the hallway. "I'm not asking for one!"

"Yes you are, but you're too chicken to go after what you want. It's the perfect way to tell him how you feel without all that goofy stuttering you do. It's therapeutic." She scooted behind me and gave me a shove. "You got two minutes before our entire mission goes bust. Now hurry up. I'll keep a lookout." Staying close to the wall, she skirted to the end of the hallway and peeked around the corner.

Alyssa made everything a special ops mission: dress shopping for the school dance, raising money for class field trips, getting dirt on some girl she didn't like. It was all done with high stakes and action movie flair.

I drew in a deep breath and placed one foot in front of the other. I'd memorized his locker number, which stood exactly eighty-two feet and forty-six lockers away from mine. We were practically roommates.

"Ninety seconds," she whispered.

"I'm going! Gosh!" My hand reached up and aimed the card into the locker's vent. Then it got stuck. The note was too wide and the ends began to tear when I tried to force it in. Pulling it out would rip it even more. "It won't go in," I told her.

"Oh my God! Must I do everything around here?" She stomped to my side and yanked loose the card, causing a sticker to fall by my feet. I folded the ends, then eased the paper through the vent hole, but this time it was too thick. Together, we shoved as much of the note as we could into the slot.

Alyssa checked the time on her phone. "We've got ten seconds to clear out."

I tried to push in the last half inch, but my fingers couldn't catch a grip. "There's still some poking out."

"No time! Let's go!" She grabbed my arm and dragged me down the hall.

Alyssa's powers of persuasion never worked on me save this one occasion, and I'd be lying by saying I didn't resent her for making me write the letter in the first place. She saw it as nothing more than a transaction, a means to an end, but inside my weak prose lay real heart, delicate as the paper it had been printed on. That extracted organ would never grow back, and once given away, its fate was out of my control.

CHAPTER 12

"I got it." I passed my bank card to the cashier, but Mateo ripped it from my fingers.

"No, you don't. *I* got this." He retrieved his wallet from his back pocket.

"No, I do. It's fine." I snatched back my property only to have it taken by the wrong person.

Cutting his eyes at me, Mateo grumbled, "I've got money, you know."

"Never said you were broke." I tried the exchange again with the same result.

This clash of wills was brought to you by the aptly named Brew-Ha-Ha Café, located across the street from Aberdeen Park, where you could get shoddy service and the most childish banter this side of recess.

We'd entered with the other cleanup teams for a late morning pick-me-up when the argument kicked off at the register. I blamed the coffee guy. He mistook our close-standing position for a joint venture.

The cashier watched my bank card triangulate around the counter while our unpurchased items grew cold.

Tired of the roundabout, Mateo blurted, "I'm not letting you pay for my coffee! I'm not that big a mooch."

"What's this 'my' stuff? I'm getting coffee, too."

"Wow! Is this a macho male ego thing?" Tabatha Morehouse stood behind us with her arms crossed. "Because she's a woman, she can't pay for her own coffee? Does seeing a female in charge emasculate you somehow, Mateo?"

"You should probably ask your boyfriend that question after you buy his coffee." Mateo slapped his forehead at his deliberate error. "Oh! That's right. You don't have one."

Everyone in line, which ran seven deep and climbing, joined in with a loud, *"Ooh."*

With a duck-lip pout, a rolling neck, and blue hair swinging, Tabatha said, "I'll have you know that I'm single by choice and I don't need a man to get me through life."

"No one does! That's what coffee's for!" Devon Shapiro's head jutted from the back of the line to glare at us. "So could y'all hurry up and pay already? You're holding up progress!"

"Okay! We're going!" I ripped my card from Mateo's clutches and passed it to the clerk, while growling through clenched teeth, "Dude, just let me get the drinks."

Transaction completed, Mateo and I waited outside for the rest of the team. Rocking on the edge of the curb, I watched Mateo sip his latte and lick his wounds. "I know the rumors say we're an old married couple, but we don't have to fight like one," I told him.

He hung his head, shoulders drooping. "Sorry. I'm just not used to handouts, okay?"

"Learn when to pick your battles, man. It's just coffee. And it's not even good coffee." I tipped my chin toward the café doors. "This place is just close to the park and Al CapPacino's got shut down for repairs."

"Yeah, well, when you've been on your own as long as I have, you tend to see any type of kindness with caution."

"You're saying people can't be nice for the sake of being nice?" I asked.

He shook his head. "It's good in theory, but every good deed has a motive."

I was beginning to understand that. "And you've been trying to figure out mine?"

"Not just yours. Everyone's." He moved closer and asked, "You ever talk to some of the kids here? They have no idea what's going on and they couldn't even spell altruism. When you ask, you'll hear something like, *It looks good on my transcripts. There's a girl here I really like. The Lord told me to do it. The establishment is dragging the people down, man. Stay woke.*"

I almost spat out my coffee. Once again, I'd been caught off guard by Mateo's humor. Recovering from laughter, I asked,

"What kind of talks do *you* have? Most kids I come across are just doing it for the 'gram."

"True. And I doubt anyone else in school would have the guts to do what you're doing for Alyssa. I wish it was for someone else, but it's good of you to look past all that and see the bigger picture. I respect that."

Was that a compliment? "Wow, if I didn't know any better I'd think you're starting to like me."

"Do you want me to?" Eyes trained on me, he sipped his coffee and waited.

No way was I touching that one. This conversation was heading into flirty territory, and I had to stay on task. "It's not a requirement, but a nice bonus."

He grinned. "I'll take that as a yes."

Oh my goodness! We'd officially entered the city limits of flirty territory. Heat spread across my cheeks and my stomach began to quiver. Thankfully, the rest of the team poured out of the shop before I ruined the moment by saying something dumb.

"All right! It's go time!" Devon rolled his neck and shoulders, ready to jump into the ring of a heavyweight fight. The others cheered and pumped fists in the air.

I was pretty hyped myself, and I quickened my pace across the street toward the park.

The turnout wasn't as big as the first cleanup party, but two dozen volunteers had made an appearance. After the first week's fiasco, the school board and the principal had laid down the law and stripped down the shenanigans. There was no band, no stage, no skaters, no car show, no mosh pit, just a group of devoted citizens who weren't scared to get their hands dirty.

We signed up at the activity table, grabbed our gear, and joined the lighting team at the tree-lined path. The debris had been cleared away, but only the lights on the left side of the trail had been restored. Since we kids weren't authorized to do major wiring, lighting detail was idiot-proof for anyone who knew how to decorate a Christmas tree. The only two setbacks were that we had to use a heavy ladder and work in pairs. And guess who my partner was for the day?

On our way to the work site, Mateo asked, "So what's it like going to all those appointments?"

I took a moment to think of the right word and came up with three. "Tedious. Awkward. Intrusive." I told him about my first appointment with the nephrologist.

Mateo hefted a tall, metal stepladder under his arm and moved to our approved spot. "What's a nephrologist?" he asked.

"Just a fancy word for kidney specialist," I explained, and slipped on thick utility gloves. "See, kidneys aren't identical twins. One usually works harder than the other. So the nephrologist runs all these tests to point out the bigger, better, faster, stronger twin, so Alyssa can adopt the weaker one."

Mateo propped the ladder against our tree of choice, then tested its stability. "Did they do X-rays and stuff?"

My laugh came out as a bitter whimper. "Oh, Mateo, my sweet, innocent *hombre*. You don't know the half of it."

In four hours, I'd had my blood taken three times, was forced to pee in a cup twice, had weird fluid pumped through my veins. Then I was made to lie on a floating bed that fed me feet first into the world's most tricked-out donut. With each pass through the CT scanner, a computerized voice inside the machine would tell me to hold my breath. Add an empty stomach to the mix and a girl was trippin'.

Mateo's only response to that was, "What kind of fluid did they put in you?"

Really, dude? That's what you took from my story? Opening the waiting box of Christmas lights, I grumbled, "A few."

My doctor had explained that the first injection had been saline solution. It'd felt like ice chips were tunneling through my veins, moving up my arm toward my heart. The second fluid they injected into my arm had apparently given my veins and organs a mutant glow that the CT scanner could detect. The warm sensation had played a childish prank on my bladder, like a hand dipped into water while sleeping.

"*¡Híjole! ¡Eso suena loco!*" Mateo cried after I'd filled him in. "And that's just *one* of the doctors you have to see?" When I nodded, Mateo shook his head. He began spooling an extension cord around his arm from elbow to thumb.

He seemed right at home with this type of work or anything that meant using his hands. From cleaning out the spare room at home to changing the oil in his truck, he was a regular Mr. Fix It. I couldn't see him in a suit and tie, pushing papers in some boring office job. Mateo Alvarez was a rugged, roughin'-it-in-the-wilderness type. I imagined him rocking a flannel shirt, wielding an ax, and chopping firewood for our log cabin home in the mountains—

"Hold on. Aren't you a flight risk or something?" Mateo's question brought me back on track. "You and your family traveled to all those places and you're still allowed to donate a kidney?"

"Yeah, you get tested for everything. But I'm squeaky clean. It just depends on what part of each country you visit. And when you come back, you gotta wait about a year to—"

"You're donating?" A familiar and distinctly hoarse voice busted through our conversation.

Ryon set down his paint buckets and approached slowly. Awe and trepidation propelled each step, and his hands shielded his eyes from the bright glimmer of hope. Or maybe the sun was in his face. "Is it true? You're donating a kidney to Alyssa?"

"Bruh! *Shh.*" I took his arm and dragged him away from the nearby group members. "These trees have ears."

Not caring one bit, he asked again, "Is it true?"

"I'm trying. I've gotta get evaluated, then get approved by the league of extraordinary doctors. I think they gather around a campfire and vote people off the island."

Mateo eyed me askance. "I'm not a medical professional, but I don't think that's how it works."

"This is so awesome!" Ryon hugged me, kissed my cheek, and squeezed me even tighter. "Thank you."

"Hey, hey! What's with all the touchy-feely, Kimura? Go ahead and reel that back in," I said.

Ryon backed away with his hands in the air. "My bad. I wasn't trying to move in on your girl," he told Mateo.

I'm not his girl. That sad truth was set to fly from my mouth, but Ryon's next question kept it grounded. "Does Alyssa know?"

"No! And don't you tell her, either." I pointed a finger in his face. "I need to make sure it's a done deal."

"Okay, I won't." His nod didn't look convincing at all.

"I mean it, Ryon." I pinched his arm hard. "One word and I'm calling off the whole thing."

"Ow! Okay! I promise I won't tell!" he whimpered before I let him go. When I did, he scrubbed his face and pushed the hair out of his eyes. "Wow. I just . . . wow. Thank you so much."

"Don't thank me yet."

We were getting ahead of ourselves. There was one more appointment to make, and I still needed a unanimous vote by the transplant team. Nothing was certain, except the likelihood of Ryon getting a full night's sleep tonight. Seeing the relief on his face was worth the blowback to follow. Best believe it was coming, and I could almost smell the rain in the air from the impending storm.

This same thing had happened before, in the fall of our freshman year. That, too, had involved Ryon and my inability to stay in my lane and keep my mouth shut.

POLICY 12.2: ETHICAL ISSUES

THREE YEARS AGO

Relax. Breathe. Just breathe. Oh God, this is bad. So, so bad. Sheree, please hurry up.

My sister had run to the car to get Alyssa's swim bag and should've been back by now. The emergency kit and blood sugar meter were packed in that carrier, so why didn't Alyssa just bring it inside and store it in a locker? That's what locker rooms were for.

Wrapped in a beach towel, Alyssa slumped against the tiled wall, shaking like a leaf. "No built-in . . . locks . . ." she answered between breaths. "Don't want stolen . . . Kate Spade . . . tote."

"Are you serious? You can afford a designer bag, but not a five-dollar padlock? Priorities, Lyssa. Have some. They're free." I shouldn't have been snapping at her, but I wasn't good with medical emergencies. The last one involved my pop-pop lying stretched out on the kitchen floor. Needless to say, I was triggered, and it took all my willpower to keep it together.

"Are you *absolutely sure* you don't want me to call your

mom?" I asked for the fifth time. My phone was fired up and ready to go. She only needed to say the word.

Alyssa shook her head. Wet strands clung to her face and pool water dripped down her neck as she stared at the ceiling. "Not yet. Use kit first."

Lord, give me strength! This girl was stubborn. Even in the middle of diabetic shock, she wanted to save face. But this wasn't her first rodeo and attacks like these didn't require a trip to the ER if treated quickly. With that said—where the heck was Sheree?

I pulled back the privacy curtain and peered into the empty locker room. We were at the community pool with a few other kids from school, a final bash before the pool closed its gates for the fall, but things weren't going the way we'd hoped.

I knew something was up when I caught Alyssa sitting at the lip of the pool, rubbing her head as if she were dizzy. Her legs trembled in the water; her body listed to the side. Red flag. I swam to her side, then tapped her knee. She was breathing too heavy to respond and clutched her chest, indicating a racing heart. Double red flag.

I'd searched the pool area for my sister, our unofficial guardian and chauffeur. Sheree wasn't going to let a drop of chlorine anywhere near her freshly relaxed hair, so she occupied the lounge chairs with her senior friends. I'd waved her over and with our combined strength, we'd helped Alyssa to the changing room without causing a scene.

It came with the job of being Alyssa's friend: doing damage control while keeping her alive. I couldn't 100 percent blame Alyssa. Nobody wanted this kind of attention, especially her.

If anyone asked—and they did—we played it off as "female trouble" and kept it moving. Ryon Kimura wasn't so easy to shake off, though. He followed us through the slippery hallway, offering assistance until the GIRLS ONLY sign outside the locker room held him at bay.

Now, hiding in the private stall, I waited for backup to arrive. The emergency tutorials Mrs. Weaver always gave us upon every outing played in my head. Alyssa was in a relaxed sitting position on the wooden bench. Check. She remained calm and responsive to voices. Check.

"It's okay. You're gonna be fine." I cupped her face in my hands and touched my forehead to hers.

Outside, the locker room door opened, followed by the quick flapping of sandaled feet racing across the floor. The curtain flew back and Sheree appeared with Alyssa's bag on her arm.

"Okay, I got it. The vending machine outside only has soda, and the juice in her bag got hot in the car." Sheree knelt next to me in front of Alyssa.

Sighing in relief, I rummaged through the bag and pulled out her emergency stash of sweets. "That's fine. Get her to open her mouth."

Alyssa liked the cherry Squeeze Pops because she didn't have to chew or risk choking. Sheree held Alyssa's jaw open while I poured the candy into her mouth, pushing the red goo from the tube like toothpaste. Then Sheree chased it down with hot apple juice.

According to the clock on my phone, the whole ordeal lasted fifteen minutes, but I collapsed on the floor like I'd just given birth. With our backs pressed to the opposite wall, Sheree and I watched for any change in Alyssa's symptoms. We cradled our phones in both of our hands—Mrs. Weaver's number preset on my dial screen, 911 set on Sheree's. Our thumbs hovered over the CALL button as we waited. And waited.

Slowly, color returned to Alyssa's cheeks and her breath released in long, even puffs. Sheree used the kit in Alyssa's bag to check her blood sugar. Luckily, Alyssa was coherent enough to walk us through the rest.

Once my heart returned to its original position in my chest, I stepped out into the hall. I was on a mission to get carbs for Alyssa and much-needed air for myself. My brain hurt trying to process what just happened and could've happened. A montage of worst-case scenarios flashed before my eyes, and there was a high chance that I would throw up before it was all over.

And how long had Ryon been standing there?

Wearing only wet swim trunks, he watched me from the

end of the hall. He wasn't my type, but I could see why Alyssa liked him. He had six-pack abs and his smoky, deep voice was better suited for a jazz club than the debate team. Right now, that voice sounded almost menacing when he asked, "What's wrong with her?"

I didn't need to ask whom he was referring to, and I tried to make light of the situation. "That answer could take all day."

"I know she's lying about her girl issues," he said. "I have a sister. She's never turned pale or gotten the shakes at that time of the month." He drew closer, his flip-flops slapping on the wet cement floor. "Look, you've known her longer than all of us. You know what's going on with her—that's why you covered for her just now. What am I missing? Can you tell me? Please?"

Good gracious! His face was a moving portrait of pure heartache. But then this *was* Alyssa Weaver we were talking about: writer, producer, director, and star of her own drama. "It's not for me to tell—"

"*What* isn't?" he pressed. He wasn't going to let this drop, which made me even angrier for being put on the spot. How do you keep a lifelong medical condition a secret from a guy you've been dating for two months? Riddle me that, Batman.

"Fine!" I took a deep breath. "Alyssa hates needles, okay? She's hated them ever since she was a kid. She'd take insulin and get her blood sugar tested every day."

I liked Ryon, but that was all he was getting: clear-cut facts, condensed and downplayed for Alyssa's benefit. No one needed to know the out-and-out terror she faced growing up. The whole thing traumatized her in ways that exceeded vocabulary, so those details would remain closed to the public.

"Alyssa has diabetes?" Ryon asked, though he didn't seem fazed by the news. He just blinked a few times and raked his hands through his wet hair. "Okay, so what? What's the big deal? Why didn't she just tell me?"

"She hasn't told anyone. Whatever her reasons are, you're not supposed to know, so you can't talk about it, all right?"

Frowning, he brushed past me and headed back to the pool. Not the response I was looking for.

I caught up with him and tugged on his arm. "Ryon, you can't tell her I told you."

"I won't, but I can't pretend that everything's okay. I have to help where I can. Besides, I'm not good at secrets." He kept walking.

I couldn't shake the feeling that I'd betrayed Alyssa somehow. She went out of her way to not tell people about her condition, and unlike our classmates, I knew the meaning of discretion without having to google it. There was no way I would've told Ryon unless there was a good cause for it. It seemed like one at the time.

CHAPTER 13

Dr. Langhorne consulted her notes and flipped back a few pages in the file on her lap. "From what I understand, you come from a philanthropic family and have a long history of advocacy work. Do your parents know about your decision to donate?" she asked.

I sat in the armchair opposite to hers, chewed my thumbnail, and racked my brain for a brilliant reply. "Not exactly."

"Is there a reason for that?" A fancy pen twiddled between her manicured fingers as she awaited my answer.

I had every right to be nervous. The woman's dark, probing stare made me second-guess every word out of my mouth, be it true or false. A lot was riding on acing my psych evaluation, but glossing over info just to look good might put me on her bad side. And her bad side was a rough part of town that no one in the building wanted to visit.

Before I walked through the door, it had been made clear that Dr. Edith Langhorne, sociopsychologist of the Atlantic Wellness Center, was not one to mess with. The way the staff never looked the woman in the eye, the speed with which her assistant delivered a file and scurried off, and how she'd kicked Dr. Brighton out of the office for talking over her had driven the point home. The first thing to catch the eye inside her office was the engraved stone tablet above the credenza that read:

MY HEARING IS ASTUTE, MY PATIENCE IS MINUTE,

MY WRATH IS ABSOLUTE,

SO KEEP IT CUTE OR KEEP IT MUTE.

Yeah, sistah girl was fierce, and no exam had ever worked my sweat glands as much as her question. Maybe it's because the answer wasn't so simple. Either way, I gathered enough nerve to say, "My parents and my sister are thousands of miles away, and I don't want to pull them from whatever they're doing for something that might not even happen. I'm not looking for a pat on the back or a merit badge, and I wouldn't be doing this if there wasn't a dire need for it."

"Fair enough." She jotted down more notes. "But at some point, they will need to be notified and interviewed, if possible."

I recoiled. "Why? I'm eighteen."

"Just barely, and that makes the situation even more precarious," she explained. "You're still technically a teenager—a high school student, and susceptible to peer pressure and rebellion. This might not be a way to impress your family, but perhaps it's an act of defiance against them. Some applicants expect money, which is not only unethical but illegal. I've had people come in here suicidal, hoping to die during the procedure. We have to be absolutely certain that you're making a well-informed decision and are mature enough to handle the consequences of that decision."

I shook my head. "I'm not depressed or suicidal. Trust me; I've grown attached to living."

"Donating a kidney is not like donating blood," the doctor went on. "This is a major, life-altering surgery that involves a number of risks, including death. And there's always that small chance that you may experience complications during or after surgery," she added. "You need to be aware of all the risks and the long- and short-term effects before going forward. That is the whole purpose of this evaluation. However, you are under no obligation to continue and you are free to opt out at any time."

I nodded, though to be honest, she wasn't doing a great job at convincing me that any of this was a good idea.

"Now, we won't contact your family at the moment, but once we move further into the process they will need to be notified," she said, getting back to business. "Someone needs to know where you are and to be able to care for you after the surgery. And it's essential that you have a solid support system established beforehand."

I hadn't thought about the hospital stay or the recovery time. It would take weeks to recuperate, and I considered the odds of Grandma Trina signing that absence note.

Sorry, I can't go to school for a while. I just had a kidney removed and I need to rest up.

I shuddered at the thought.

For days, the idea of the *big reveal* dangled over my head like an overdue assignment. I'd have to tell Grandma Trina at some point, and it was better that the truth came from me. The medical team required a next-of-kin contact for emergencies. And honestly, I didn't want to go through the process by myself.

As soon as I entered the house, whatever delicious concoction Mateo had fixed dragged me into the kitchen by the nose. There were no pleasantries. No "hi," no "how was your day," just me heading straight to the pot on the stove.

"What on earth is that?" I closed my eyes and inhaled the spicy aroma.

He stirred his masterpiece with a wooden spoon. "Birthday gumbo."

I had to facepalm at that one; I'd been so caught up with my appointments. "I completely forgot your birthday."

"That's cool. You've got time. It's tomorrow."

"Oh, good." I sighed in relief. "What do you want?"

"That's a loaded question. I just want something fun to do," he said.

My lips twisted left and right. "I can think of something."

"That's a loaded answer." He winced at the slap on his arm. "Ow!"

"That's what you get. I'm two months older than you. Learn to respect your elders."

"You're not an elder. Elders are accomplished leaders in their community who pass wisdom and resources to the next generation. You're just old. You get no respect."

His reasoning made sense, but I had an argument to win. "I—I have wisdom."

"Debatable. What else you got?"

I sensed a challenge, and the need to always be right brought out my snarky side. Twirling a braid around my finger, I gave him my best Alyssa Weaver answer. "I'm pretty."

That made him smile, but he didn't deny the point, which was progress. "You think that's enough?"

I batted my lashes. "It's a start."

He plucked the braid from my finger and coiled it around his own. "It's distracting."

"From what?"

His eyes fixed on my mouth, appraising each line and curve before he whispered, "I don't remember. That's the point."

"Janelle? Janelle Lynn, where you at?"

Grandma Trina's booming voice shattered the moment. The ruckus had me searching for a weapon, ready to fend off home invaders. Were we under attack?

She stormed into the kitchen with the phone in hand. "You mind telling me why I'm getting calls from school saying you've been out twice this week? You've missed four days of school last month. What have you been up to, young lady?"

My eyes strayed to Mateo, who offered a shrug and an "I'm sorry. I didn't know," under his breath.

It wasn't his fault. He was doing me a favor by delaying a bomb that was going to explode eventually. It was best he stayed out of the way and ducked for cover.

"I went to the doctor," I told Grandma Trina.

For a moment, she looked concerned, but I knew that wouldn't last long. "Why? What's wrong with you?"

"I was getting tested." I inched toward the opposite side of the counter.

She stepped closer. "For what?"

"I'm getting tested for organ donation. I agreed to give a kidney to Alyssa Weaver."

"*Who?*" She paused, struggling to recall the name. It finally clicked for her. "Oh! Leslie's little girl with the junky house." I nodded. "Have you lost your mind?" Grandma erupted, startling the dogs by her feet.

"According to my psych evaluation—no."

"You might wanna get rechecked, 'cause there ain't no way you doin' this, so you go ahead and tell them people that you can't do it."

I'd known my decision wouldn't go over well with the fam. I'd

176

expected it. But there was no way I was backing out now. I'd been through too much and couldn't allow my fear of my grandmother's authority to get in the way of what was right. "I can't do that."

"Oh yes, you can and you will." With a speed that defied her age, Grandma Trina marched deeper into the kitchen. Even the dogs knew something was up and they stayed close to the pantry.

Looking both confused and terrified, Mateo lingered by the stove, wooden spoon in hand. Grandma Trina, still holding the phone, opened the drawer and retrieved an address book as thick and beat-up as her Bible. The pages were the color of parchment, covered with the names of every living and dead soul in the county.

I cleared a path as she stomped over to the kitchen table. Mateo and I drifted toward each other, our gazes trained on the woman flipping through the raggedy pages with angry swipes and mumbling to herself the whole time. That was never a good sign.

"This child done lost her mind. Gonna come up in my house and tell me what she gonna do. Don't even know where the kidney is and talkin' 'bout givin' one away . . ."

Mateo leaned in and whispered, "She knows we can hear her, right?"

"Dude, just lay low," I hissed out. "You gonna get us both killed."

Mateo was a slow learner. "What are you doing?" he asked my grandmother.

Grandma Trina put the phone to her ear. "What it look like? I'm callin' the Weavers."

Oh no! This was going down the wrong road fast. Alyssa's mom had no idea about my decision. It wasn't fair for her to get chewed out over help she hadn't even asked for. Thank God the call went to voice mail. My whole body sighed over the brief reprieve.

"Hello, Leslie? This is Katrina Pruitt. I've come across a situation that requires your immediate attention, so I'ma need you to call me as soon as you get this message. No matter the time. Talk to you soon." Grandma ended the call and aimed her missiles at me.

"Janelle, you're entirely too young to be considerin' that type of surgery. There are risks," she said. "You know minorities are at the bottom of the list to get a donated organ? People don't donate like that."

"See? There you go. Donors are in short supply, so that's why I need to step in," I argued.

With not one lick of feeling or hesitation, she said, "The answer is no. I'm sorry about your friend, but I can't let you do that."

That answer had me doing a double and triple take. Had she really said that? Her?

"But Alyssa needs a new kidney. She'll die if she doesn't get one," I pleaded.

"I understand that, baby, but why you gotta be the one to do it?" she asked. "There are thousands of people who can come forward. Why don't you do a fund-raiser and get people to volunteer? You're good at that sorta thing."

That was an option I'd already thought about. "All of the kids in school are underage—I'm the only one who's eighteen. Alyssa's mom tried to donate, but she isn't a match. Plus, we're a bit on a time crunch here. Grandma, I can't sit by and let someone die. I'm eighteen years old. Legally, I'm able to have the procedure without parental permission."

Her head and shoulders sloped back in feigned astonishment. "Oh, so you're grown, right? You're grown enough to get your own place and pay your own way?" When I didn't reply, she said, "That's what I thought. As long as you live under my roof, you will not be gettin' this surgery. So no more talk about givin' away organs. Now take your grown tail up them stairs and go to your room."

I looked at Mateo, who stirred his pot slowly, waiting for my response. I rolled my eyes and ran to my room. There was nothing he could do anyway. He was just as powerless as I was under this roof.

Once upstairs, I slammed the bedroom door. My screams left my mouth in a grunt, too soft for Grandma Trina to hear. It was all I could do not to punch a hole through the wall, remodel the entire house with my fist. Hypocrites! All of them! But fine, if she didn't want me here, then I'd go someplace else. I called Sera and asked if I could spend the night.

I packed a couple days' worth of clothes, my laptop and charger, then carried the load downstairs. On the way out, I found Grandma Trina on the phone in the living room, no doubt snitching to my parents.

"Elijah? Hey, it's Mama. Call me when you get this. Your youngest child has gone wild up in here, talkin' 'bout giving a kidney to a girl from school. I'ma let you handle that. I'm too old for this mess. Love you—bye." She ended the call, dropped her cell phone on the coffee table, and turned to me in a clear sign of a challenge. To the death. "And where do you think you're going? I told you to stay in your room."

"I'm going to Sera's. You said if I was grown enough to donate a kidney, I was grown enough to get out of the house. So that's what I'm doing." I opened the door and stepped out into the crisp fall air.

"Little girl, who you think you're talkin' to? Janelle Lynn, you get back in this house!"

I broke into a full run to my car parked on the curb. If this were a movie, there would've been an ax murderer or a possessed doll in the house trying to kill me for all the fuss I was making. The barking dogs and Grandma Trina screaming at the door didn't help the situation.

I threw my bag in the passenger seat, started the engine, and tore down the street. Once I turned the corner and settled onto the main road, my world fell blissfully quiet again. I finally had the freedom to think in peace. Too bad thinking was the last thing on my mind.

Some friends were so extra that you enjoyed their company just to drown out your own issues. That was Sera, full stop. She did everything to the extreme, and being within the hemisphere of her weirdness mellowed me out in ways sleep medicine couldn't. For the past two years, her house had become my vacation home when I wanted to get away from it all.

Sitting on Sera's bed with a warm plate of pizza bites between us now, we tuned out the rest of the world. Our textbooks and binders lay open on our laps so it appeared as though we were doing homework in case her parents checked in on us. In actuality, we were binge-watching the latest season of an anime show on Sera's computer.

"Hold on. Is this a beach episode?" I asked with my mouth full. "Why is there *always* a beach episode in these things? It goes nowhere. This guy has six girls *literally* tripping over themselves for him. Just pick one, *senpai*!" I yelled at the computer screen.

Sera lifted her hand to me, demanding silence. "Patience, *hoobae*. The true payoff is in the shipping wars beforehand."

She'd called me *junior* in Korean; *junior*, as in inexperienced, which was true in terms of my knowledge of foreign cartoon protocol.

Sera and I turned to the door at the sudden noise from the bottom floor. Angry footsteps pounded the stairs, growing louder as they moved up the hallway. There was some heavy breathing followed by a slamming door across the hall that shook the figurines on Sera's bookshelf. Going by the layout of their house, it had to have been Ryon entering his room. What was his deal?

"*Ooh*. Somebody got their report card in the mail," Sera sang, and did a little snake dance with her neck and shoulders.

I turned to her, my mouth gaping open in shock and then realization. Midterm report cards had been sent out this week. The envelopes were always addressed to parents or guardians, and if I remembered correctly, the report revealed class attendance. Codes and mathematic formulas danced in my head as I considered the various outcomes of this afternoon's drama. No matter how it came about, the blowup with Grandma Trina would've happened anyway. Oh man, I could never become a criminal mastermind; I'd leave too much of a paper trail.

I looked at Sera. "Is Ryon failing?" I asked.

Wearing a menacing grin, she nodded. "Failed two tests and skipped three classes."

"But you skip class all the time," I argued, not seeing the point.

She shook her head. "My folks don't really care what I do. They only care what the golden boy is up to." She shrugged. "Ryon is stuck with a whole other set of standards. He might just meet them if he wasn't so obsessed with a certain redhead who shall not be named."

I rolled my eyes. Could she be any more obvious? "How would you feel if someone you cared about might die before graduation?" I challenged her.

Sera gave me a look. "She's not gonna die, Janelle. She just wants people to feel sorry for her."

Were we talking about the same person? "Actually, that's the last thing she wants."

"How do you know?" she asked.

"Because I know her!" I hadn't meant to yell, but it was crystal clear that Sera didn't know the real deal or the real Alyssa. Part of that was my fault for shutting Sera out of my decision. And if I told her now, she'd get mad over my secrecy and overanalyze our friendship needlessly. Was it cowardly to want to keep one small part of my life safe and normal? Couldn't I just stay in this little oasis with Sera? Or was that selfish?

"Yeah, I know. You guys have this long, epic backstory." Sera's tone had that irritated drone you'd have after hearing a song one too many times on the radio. "I've seen married couples like that. After the breakup, they'd start dating people that remind them of their exes."

I had to think about that for a minute. Did she mean Alyssa's friends resembled me, or that she, Sera, resembled Alyssa? Either scenario had me cutting my eyes at her for the rest of the beach episode. Where had that come from?

A soft knock came at the door. Ryon appeared from the other side with a phone gripped in his hand. "Hey, Janelle. It's for you."

Slowly, I climbed off the bed and moved toward the door, my stare volleying between the phone and Ryon's red, swollen eyes. He'd definitely been crying but bringing that up might embarrass him, so I asked instead, "Who would be calling me on *your* cell phone?"

"Your boyfriend." Ryon pushed the phone closer, indicating that I should take it.

I stopped moving. There was only one person who fit that description. The idea of him calling me on *Ryon's phone* at ten at night seemed more fictitious than our dating status.

But when I put the phone to my ear, his voice came through the line loud and clear.

"Janelle. It's me, Mateo. Why is your phone off?" His question sounded like a reprimand, which spiked my attitude to a 9.8.

"I didn't want to talk to anyone," I answered. "How did you find me?"

"Hate to break it to you, but you don't have that many friends. Didn't need a search team or the K-9 unit on this one," he replied with more humor in his voice than I had patience for. "Anyway, you need to come home. Now."

My heart caught the hiccups. The jolt made my chest hurt. Mateo wouldn't have called if it wasn't an emergency. Questions flew out of my mouth before I could make sense of them. "Is it my grandma? Is she okay? Did something happen?"

"No, nothing like that," Mateo said quickly. "She's fine, everyone's fine. You just need to get over here as soon as you can."

I needed a minute to get my blood pressure under control. "Don't scare me like that, yo! If it's not a life-or-death situation, I'm staying put right here with Sera."

"Alyssa and her mom are here."

That was the last thing I'd expected him to say. Whatever fun

I'd been having tonight shriveled up and died. Silence spread between us for so long that Mateo asked, "You still there?"

"Yeah." I snuck a glance at Ryon and Sera, then spoke softly into the phone. "I'll be there in twenty."

When I finished the call, I handed Ryon his phone, then gathered my books and my backpack from the floor.

Sera uncrossed her legs and rose from the bed, concern etched on her face. "You're really leaving?"

I slid my book bag over my shoulder, then searched the floor for my overnight bag. "Yeah. Family emergency."

"What kind of emergency? Does it have to do with why you came over?" she asked, following me out the bedroom door. "You sounded really upset on the phone."

I still was upset, but now wasn't the time to get into the gruesome details. It would only lead to a fight, and I already had one of those waiting for me when I got home.

"It's just family stuff driving me crazy again. It's no big deal," I told her on my way downstairs.

She didn't make a fuss—a blessing in itself—but I could almost see the tiny question marks floating overhead like the anime characters we'd spent hours watching. I gave her a reassuring hug along with a promise to call. Dragging my feet, I stepped out into the cold night.

So much for my mini vacation. Time to face the firing squad.

CHAPTER 14

Exactly eighteen minutes later, I sat on the love seat in the living room beside Mateo. Mrs. Weaver and Alyssa sat across from us on our living room sofa, with a throw rug of dogs curled at their feet. We all watched Grandma Trina pace the floor in front of the TV.

"All right then. We're gonna do this like we did in the old union days and bring this to a vote," she announced, and rubbed her palms together.

Mateo raised his hand. "Union? Like versus the Confederates in the Civil War? How old are you anyway, Mrs. Trina?"

"Watch your mouth, boy." Grandma pointed a lethal finger at his face. "I'm thirty-five; that's all y'all need to know."

Palms up, shoulders hunched, Alyssa appealed to the lady of the house. "I just wanna know why we're here."

"For you, baby," Grandma replied, then realized Mrs. Weaver hadn't explained the nature of the late-night meeting. "We brought you here to discuss a solution to your medical condition. Janelle volunteered to be an organ donor. *Your* organ donor."

The room fell quiet as the Weaver women sipped slow on that new information.

I kept my eyes trained on the floor, braced myself for Alyssa's response.

A soft voice came from across the room. "I can't accept."

I jerked my head up. "What? Why?"

"Because *I don't want* your kidney," Alyssa replied as if the very idea disgusted her.

She picked this time to try and act brand-new? It's not like I had cooties or anything. "Why not?"

"We're not talking about having a wisdom tooth pulled. That is a huge operation that might not even work, and I still might need dialysis afterward. It's not worth it."

Mrs. Weaver touched her daughter's back. "But honey—"

Alyssa shrugged the hand away. "No. I'm not doing it."

"Well, that settles it." Grandma Trina's firm clap served as a gavel. "Janelle, you can call the doctors tomorrow and cancel the testin'."

Alyssa was clearly stunned by that little detail. Her irate stare swung from Grandma Trina to me. "You've gotten tested?"

"Yeah. I've completed all of my appointments," I said, feeling proud of myself. This wasn't all big talk; it was the real deal. "The lab results say that I'm a good candidate. Our blood types are the same and the crossmatches are negative, so it's a go. And I just finished my psych evaluation. The coordinator might request another phone conference before my case is reviewed, but for now, we just have to wait."

Alyssa slowly rose from the sofa, her expression puzzled and suspicious. "You're a match?"

"Yeah."

"That must've been steep. How did you get it done so fast? How'd you even know who to contact?" Mrs. Weaver asked.

"I found the brochure on Alyssa's dresser when I came over," I answered while ignoring the mass homicide flashing in Alyssa's eyes. "They knew your case and passed me through quickly. And since I'm the one donating, I don't pay a dime. Just the checkups afterward."

Alyssa nudged her head toward the hall. "Janelle? Can I talk to you for a minute? Alone?"

"Sure." I stood and led her to the kitchen.

We barely made it into the room before she went in on me. "How long have you had this great plan of yours?"

"I applied a few days after your collapse. And I had my first appointment after I visited you at home."

Crossing her arms, she asked, "When were you going to tell me about it?"

To be honest, I didn't want to tell her at all, and I should've opted for an anonymous donation. Wincing, I answered, "Right before the surgery?"

Her mouth fell open. "Are you serious? You just automatically assumed that I'd be okay with getting hacked and scarred and tampered with just to have it fail and get it done all over again?"

Who said it was gonna fail? We were a match. That was half

the battle right there. "What choice do you have, Lyssa? You can't live on that machine forever. Your condition is terminal, and we all know it."

"What *I do know* is that you had no right to do this without asking me first," she snapped. "You went behind my back, *again*, making decisions for me that aren't yours to make, *again*, and treating me like a child, *AGAIN*!"

I raged at the ceiling. "Omigod, you are so petty! Don't you see that I'm trying to save your life?"

"Don't you see that I don't want you to?" She strolled back and forth in front of the kitchen table. "I'm not one of your starving orphans in the Congo, Janelle. I don't need twenty-nine cents a day, I don't need to be adopted, and I don't need to be spayed or neutered. I'm not one of your causes!"

Her hands were buried in her hair, gripping the roots. "I just wanted a friend who I could hang out with and be normal with. I wanted to talk about shopping, boys, movies, why the Earth spins at a tilt and why Pluto isn't a planet anymore, and if there's such a thing as female angels or if that's just a gimmick to sell underwear. Just random stuff where I don't have to think about what's going on in my body.

"That's why I hooked up with another crowd who had no idea I was even sick. People who saw me as fierce competition, not a charity case. *That's* why we stopped being friends, Janelle. That's why we fight and slam each other all the time—'cause that's the only way I can *actually talk* to you. That is why I did what I did, knowing full well it would crush you, because I'd rather have you hate me than pity me."

Silence dominated the kitchen. The adults stopped talking in the living room, no doubt having overheard Alyssa's rant. Everything went completely still. No response came to mind, no excuse was adequate, and no words made it past the pinch in my throat. This would be the part where I'd say, *Why didn't you tell me you felt that way?*

The answer was she had. Countless times, and I didn't listen. I was listening now.

Alyssa held her face in her hands, fingers pressing into her eyes to keep from crying, but tears leaked down her wrists all the same. She straightened up, tilted her head back, and blinked wildly.

"This is my decision. *My life.*" She sniffed and wiped her face. "My body controls me enough. I don't need any more help from you. Cancel your application to the organ donor program or get reassigned if you really want to sacrifice a body part. But it won't be to me." She left the kitchen. Not a stomp. Not a run, but a quiet departure of a ghost.

A part of me had seen this coming. It was why I made Ryon keep quiet. It was why I tried so hard to cover my tracks. And it's what I'd tried but failed to explain to Dr. Langhorne in our session the other day . . .

• • •

"You have the right to remain anonymous; however, we encourage all living donors to attempt communication with the recipient," Dr. Langhorne had said. "What do you think her response will be?"

"She won't be throwing a parade in my honor, if that's what you're getting at," I answered, glancing at my feet. "I'd probably get chewed out, like usual. She hates pity or being treated differently. That's why she didn't tell me . . ."

"Tell you what?" the counselor prodded.

I kept my stare grounded and my voice low. "That she was getting worse. All this time I thought she was handling it, that it wasn't so bad. There were so many signs, so many clues I missed."

"Do you blame yourself?" the doctor had asked. "Like if you were a better friend, you would've prevented this somehow?"

I saw where she was going with this line of questioning. I wanted to shut that assumption down, but I hesitated. If I'd tried to get through to Alyssa, if I'd done more research on her condition, if I'd gotten out of my feelings long enough to see the symptoms, and on and on it went. "What ifs" and "if onlys" always showed up late to the party, offering insight that would've been useful weeks ago, months ago, years ago.

Dr. Langhorne sat straight in her chair and leveled me with a stern gaze. "Janelle, I'm not at liberty to discuss the recipient's case with you, but you need to understand that none of this is your fault. And going through this procedure is not a proper form of atonement."

"I know. That's not my reason," I told her, though I wasn't entirely sure that was true.

"It might not be the main reason, but it's something to consider. You need to go into this situation with clear and realistic expectations. If the surgery is successful, this experience could bring you closer together or tear you further apart. If it's unsuccessful, it may deepen the wound already there. I believe it would be best if you spoke with her, sooner rather than later. Get whatever unresolved issues out in the open before you make any major decisions . . ."

Braced by my arms, I slumped against the kitchen counter and controlled my breathing. *In . . . and out. Repeat.* Again and again, until the function came automatically and no longer needed coaching.

I heard soft murmurs from the living room, Alyssa insisting on leaving and her mother's protests to stay. Eventually, the front door opened, then closed. Locks turned and chains slid into place. After that there was silence. Utter silence. If you heard it long enough, it almost sounded like screaming.

Brilliant idea, Dr. Langhorne. What could possibly go wrong? Aside from absolutely everything?

POLICY 14.2: MEDICAL HISTORY

THREE YEARS AGO

Angry footsteps advanced and broke my writing flow. Before looking up, I felt the negative energy, the slight shift in the air of a fast-approaching person. The sentence I'd written lay incomplete on the page and was swallowed up by the shadow that now darkened my notes. The chatter at my lunch table stopped as classmates watched the fiery cannonball that was Alyssa Weaver.

She loomed over me with balled fists and a hostile stance. "We need to talk."

Where was all of this attitude coming from? I dropped my pen and closed my textbook. "Um, okay. What's going—"

"Who told you to broadcast my medical history to the entire school?" she demanded in a low voice. "Seriously, who? I want names. Point them out, because it sure wasn't me."

"You better add Janelle Pruitt to that list, 'cause it wasn't her, either," I replied.

"Then how come kids in school are talking about it? Why is Ryon Kimura following me around, handing me juice and crackers and asking about my blood sugar? Oh, and why is there a booth set up in the commons for diabetes aware-ness?" She pointed to the double doors behind her.

My eyes scanned the cafeteria for witnesses. Kids became super focused on their food or buried their noses in their books, which meant they were ears-deep in our business.

Collecting my tray, I whispered, "We should take this out in the hall."

"Oh! So *now* you wanna keep things hush-hush." She fol-lowed me as I dumped my food and left the cafeteria.

In the hallway, I squared off with her and explained, "Look, I may have mentioned something to Ryon, but only after he saw you almost faint when we went to the pool last week. I didn't expect him to host a telethon about it."

She recoiled, her face etched with resentment and betrayal. "You had no right to tell him."

"He was worried about you, that's all," I said in my defense, but the reasoning sounded worse out loud than it did in my head. Being open with Ryon was coming back to haunt me, but I never thought she would take the news this hard. "I'm sorry, Lyssa. I was honestly trying to help you. Why are you getting so upset?"

She threw up her hands like I was the unreasonable one. "Look around, Janelle. We're in high school now, the worst place to be different. I don't feel like explaining to a bunch of morons what diabetes is. What kind of social life am I sup-posed to have with people thinking I'm made of glass?" Her fist pounded her chest. "I am self-sufficient. I'm able-bodied. I'm competent and I can do anything everyone else can do, beat them at it, and send them home crying."

"Nobody said you weren't." Furthermore, if anyone looked ready to go home crying, it was her. Her eyes were runny and unfocused, her feet couldn't keep still, and her fingers fidgeted with the ends of her hair. Why was she acting like this? Was she on some new medication?

"But they will, as soon as this gets around school." She wiped her runny nose on her shirtsleeve. "If my dad couldn't deal with my issues, how do you expect a guy like Ryon Kimura to handle it?"

Better question: How could she possibly compare the two? I hated seeing her like this, so down on herself when she'd done nothing wrong. Her parents' divorce wasn't her fault. Her illness wasn't her fault, but no one could convince her otherwise. "That's not fair. Ryon really likes you. Why do you think he came to the pool to begin with? To be with you."

For a second, I thought I was getting through, but she rejected the idea with a shake of the head. "No. He pities me. But hey, I should be thanking you. If he dumped me now, he'd come off like a shallow jerk and his do-gooder reputation would be ruined. Well played, Janelle. Never thought you'd take a page from my playbook."

Okay, I got that she was upset, but that was not how I rolled and she knew it. I needed to keep calm and not add more fuel to the crazy. "Lyssa, come on now, don't say that. Maybe you can talk to Ryon and he can call off–"

She held both hands in front of my face. "Stop. Just stop talking. It's easy to talk about problems that aren't yours when you're never the one in need. It's always someone else's misery being exploited. But it's all for the greater good, right?"

"What's that supposed to mean?" I reached for her arm, but she flinched away.

Baring her clenched teeth, she growled, "Just leave me alone, all right? Don't follow me." She marched off, not looking back. The hall echoed with her angry strides, a receding storm.

Halfway down the hall, Alyssa stopped next to Destiny Howell at the drinking fountain. Destiny stood straight, flipped back her twisty braids, and the two started chatting and smiling like buds from way back. They'd been getting awfully chummy these days.

I couldn't stand Destiny. It wasn't because she was the most popular freshman in our class. The girl was a straight-up klepto, stealing everything from chewing gum to class project ideas to hairstyles. Two days ago, she stole my chemistry homework and passed it off as hers.

Before I could save Alyssa from herself, someone bumped my arm. A box fell open and a rainbow of colored paper fanned across the floor. Falling right after it was a petite Asian girl with black hair cut in a diagonal bob.

"Oops! Sorry. I didn't see you. This big box is in the way." The girl swiped the papers into a pile. She was barely five feet and wore black skinny jeans, worker boots, and a red flannel shirt wrapped around her waist. But that wasn't what caught my attention. That voice sounded like an old dude with asthma. Though one of a kind, it was very familiar.

"What's all this?" I squatted next to her to help clean, all the while straining to place her face. I didn't recall seeing her in any of my classes.

"Fliers for the Diabetic Awareness Rally this afternoon. We're getting things set up in the commons. Did you know that one in four people can get the disease in their lifetime?" She touted the stat as though forced to memorize it.

Bereft and needing to be the smartest person in the room for a minute, I threw some medical trivia her way. "Which type? One or two?"

Her body went into a flash freeze. "Um, either? I mean, what's the difference?"

Maybe I'd been hanging with Alyssa for too long or I'd binge-watched too many episodes of a certain doctor show, but the answer had me eyeing the girl like she was slow. "The pancreas, for one thing. You know, the organ that makes insulin? With type two, the body repels insulin so the pancreas is forced to make more. Type one is less common, and the body attacks itself because insulin isn't made at all. There's other stuff, too, but that's the gist."

The world's greatest magic trick danced in her eyes. "Whoa! I really didn't know that. To tell the truth, I'm just helping my brother in one of his bleeding-heart crusades. I wonder why he picked this topic, though. So random."

Not really, but I wasn't gonna spill that kind of tea. Heck, after what went down in the cafeteria, I wouldn't even go near the cup. In any case, recognition struck me hard at the word *brother*. "You're Ryon's sister. Sera, right? Aren't you guys twins?"

Her smile fell away as she was quick to inform me, "No, absolutely no, and in every language of the word 'no.' He's older by ten months and we're nothing alike. He's all rainbows, butterflies, and unicorn farts, and I live in a cold, noisy place called reality. It's actually a good thing we're not twins since I would've probably eaten him in the womb. Survival of the fittest and all that."

Cynical and slightly morbid. I liked her already. "You've pretty much described my sister to the letter. Siblings aren't so bad, though, and yours is a sweetheart. In fact, my friend's dating him." I pointed over my shoulder.

"What? This is news to me. Where is she? What friend?" Sera looked around the empty hallway.

I looked back to the water fountain and found Alyssa and Destiny gone. Searching the hall from corner to corner, I was left asking the same question. *What friend?*

CHAPTER 15

Okay, I was confused. When you told someone not to blab about something, that meant *not* having an open forum discussion during our student council meeting. I'd assumed that was a given.

My warning must have gotten lost in translation, because Ryon stood behind the podium, set down his notes, and blurted out, "Janelle is donating a kidney to Alyssa." No transition, no lead-up, no *oh, by the way*.

My hands shot into the air. "I'm sorry. What does that have to do with the cleanup project or the Thanksgiving parade or midterm exams?"

Joel Metcalf, who sat at my left, swiveled in his seat to gawk at me. "You're going to give Alyssa a kidney? But you're black."

The dumbness was on and poppin' today, and so was my sarcasm. "I'll take your word for it, being that I was taught to not see color."

Joel must've taken the statement literally. "Really? But you can see tints, though, right? Even from a black-and-white photo, it's obvious you're several shades darker than Alyssa."

The meeting had just started and fondue boy was getting on my nerves. "Your point being?"

"Is that even scientifically possible? I mean, genetics and all that?" he asked.

I turned to Tabatha. "You hear that?" I pointed to Joel. "That right there was racist. Sic 'em!"

"I'm not racist! White blood cells are racist!" Joel cried in his defense. "It's science. The blood groups have to be similar. That's why the best matches are from relatives."

Feigning a yawn, I inspected my nails. "My lab results say I fit the profile. I have a universal blood type—"

"But it's not just blood, though," Joel disputed. "Seriously, how do you give a black kidney to a white person?"

Tabatha jumped into the ring, gloves on. "Why is this such a big deal for you?" she demanded of Joel. "It's not the skin color that matters. Kidneys are pink. It's DNA and tissue. Some match and some don't. Move. On."

"Joel's got a point." Devon Shapiro spoke up. "Blood groups have a unique code that's passed on by the parents. But this is America. Everybody's mixed with something around here. I've got Cherokee in my family."

"So Janelle and Alyssa are related?" Joel's eyes widened in surprise. "That makes so much more sense now."

The others groaned, not bothering to correct him, likely for fear of losing brain cells.

Devon covered his face with his hands and mumbled, "Joel, you are a prime example of why the gene pool needs a lifeguard."

"I'm just stuck on one thing." I scratched my scalp with my pencil. "What part of medical board review do you not understand, Ryon?"

"You said you passed your medical exam, so you're good. Besides, Alyssa said she knows," he replied.

"Did she tell you that she refused to have the operation?" I asked. "So this whole announcement was a waste of time."

Ryon leaned over the podium, his hands gripping its edges. "She *what?*" he yelled.

"Yeah, she doesn't want me interfering in her life, so I'll respect her wishes."

"I'll talk to her," he said with confidence.

He was gonna need all the confidence in the world to get her to change her mind. So far no one could, not her mother, not Dr. Brighton. Even Grandma Trina grew concerned about her decision.

"You think the child just wanna die in peace?" she'd asked at the breakfast table this morning.

"*No lo sé*. But when you've suffered for as long as she has, sometimes death is a relief," Mateo replied thoughtfully, and buttered his toast.

I wasn't trying to hear that defeatist mess. Alyssa wasn't the type to just give up on life, although she never really had a choice on the kind of life she wanted. But she had a choice now, and she was throwing it away over stupid pride.

It was fair to say that nothing got achieved during our Tuesday meeting. All conversation gathered around me and Alyssa. The girl bathed in the spotlight three times a day, but I preferred to soak in private. Sera had her own private immersion going on throughout the meeting. She sat next to Devon at the end of the row and looked away from me the entire time.

After the bell, I ambled to her desk as she shoved books into her messenger bag. Devon skirted behind her, whispered something that made her smile, and then sauntered away as cool as he pleased. Had I missed something?

"Wow. I see y'all are getting along," I said. "Is it official?"

Her smile fell with a slam I could almost hear. "Not yet. We're just talking."

She got up and I followed her to the door. "What's with the silent treatment?"

She spun around; her straight ponytail almost slapped me in the face. "What's with you not telling me that you were going to donate a kidney to Alyssa Weaver?"

Oh, that. "I did sorta tell you. You weren't really feeling that idea then, and by the looks of it, not much has changed."

"But *why*?" Sera demanded.

"Why you got it in for Alyssa? I don't know. My guess would

be a thin skin and unresolved emotional trauma." I'd learned that from Dr. Langhorne.

Clearly, Sera was not impressed with my new interest in psychology. "I mean, why go through all that trouble? You could die, you know? You won't have a kidney. What if you start having problems with the other one later on in life?"

"Well, I won't because I'm not doing it. Alyssa said no. Plus, the remaining kidney would grow bigger and pick up the slack."

"What if the kidney stops working altogether?"

Was this a pop quiz? "Then I'd be first in line for a kidney donation. That's one of the perks of being an organ donor. You automatically shoot to the front of the line if things go south. No waiting list for me. But that's all speculation because *she doesn't want to do it*." I spoke really slowly so she could catch that last part.

Sera's whole body language screamed *challenge*: crossed arms, pinched lips, one leg kicked out. "What if she changes her mind? Do you really think it's worth it?"

Do you really think it's not? "That would imply some sort of profit. There's no money to be made. There is no fame to be had, and I'd have months of pain and rehabilitation to look forward to. I'm taking Ls all around. I'd be doing this because a friend deserves a better life. If I'm her one chance at having it, then I'd give it to her. No charge. No start-up fee."

Sera reared back as if I'd spat on her. "I thought you guys weren't friends?"

So did I. Sort of. "It's complicated."

"Doesn't sound complicated to me. Sounds like you made up your mind already."

I nodded. "I had, but it doesn't matter now. I just wish you could've at least been happy for me. Or at the very, very least been supportive of my decision."

You would've thought I asked for *her* kidney. "Sorry," Sera said softly. "I don't think I can do that. Not with her. This is a good thing, though. You would've thrown your life away over someone who isn't worth it."

"Who are you to say who is worth saving and who isn't? She's not a serial killer or a terrorist, Sera. She's just like you and me."

She sucked her teeth and hurried to the door again. "Whatever."

I blocked her exit. "Just so you know, that is the worst read ever invented. That's right up there with 'yo momma.'" I took a breath. "I really could've used you in my corner. But now I see that you're no better than the Borg that you hate so much. You think they're fake and stupid and conceited. Yet you're standing here, telling me to let someone die because they hurt your feelings. Who's the fake around here?" I turned to go, then doubled back. "Oh! And *that's* a read. Take notes."

After school, Mateo and I each headed home at the same time. Claiming the prized parking spot in the driveway turned into a scene out of *The Fast and the Furious*. There was a lot of engine revving and glaring behind the wheel while waiting for the street light to change. Tires screeched and smoke clouded the asphalt as we tore through the residential area at a breakneck speed of thirty miles per hour. Grandma Trina's van was already in the driveway, and her lopsided parking only allowed room for smaller cars to squeeze through it. Mateo and his monster truck were left sitting curbside while I claimed the victory.

"You didn't win," he explained, then followed me to the front door. "As a gentleman, it seemed the proper thing to do to let you have the driveway."

"Whatever helps you sleep at night, buddy." I stole a quick glance at him from over my shoulder. He looked more amused than annoyed, though both expressions were clear on his face.

Two pleasant surprises greeted us upon entering the house. One: No dogs bum-rushed us at the door. And two: There was a new houseguest sitting in the living room.

Mateo's book bag slid from his shoulder and hit the floor with a loud thud. "Mom?"

"Hi, *mijo*!" Swaddled in an old quilt, Mrs. Alvarez sat on the couch, watching daytime soaps with Grandma Trina. The woman must have been no more than five feet tall, with long black hair that reached her waist. Her honey complexion looked gray from lack of sun. Her feet, both in casts, were propped on the coffee table.

Her stay here had been a foregone conclusion. We'd cleared

out the extra room and prepared comfortable bedding, but we hadn't expected her early arrival. Mateo certainly hadn't, and he all but knocked me down at the door on his way to reach his mother's side.

He bent low for a hug. "Why didn't you tell me you checked out?"

"I wanted it to be a surprise." Her chubby arms wrapped around her son's waist.

"Yeah, it is," he said. "I'm so glad you're here."

Chuckling, she patted his broad back. "I'm glad I'm here, too."

"Well, Mateo, I'm doubly glad you're here, so you can carry her rusty tail upstairs." Grandma Trina pointed to the wheelchair by the sofa. "She's gotta use that thing to get around for a while, but this house ain't all that accessible. I'm not about to break my back takin' nobody up them stairs, so you do it. You're young. You've got less to lose."

Mateo stooped to gather his mom's legs, but she shooed him away. "No, no, not yet, *mijo*. I want to stay and see if that woman died in that fire." She craned her neck over his shoulder to see the TV.

We all turned, then winced at some shirtless dude covered in soot roaming a burnt mansion, shouting, "No! Maria! Nooo!" in the worst performance to ever hit the small screen.

"Child, please. You know they're gonna have her come back as a lost twin or somethin'," Grandma Trina told Mateo's mom.

"Now, go on up there and get some rest. It's time for your medication. There's a TV up in the room anyway."

The shirtless guy had nothing on Mateo, and watching him carry his mom to the second floor had me planning our wedding. When he reached the top of the stairs, his eyes met mine. A coy smile curled his lips before he vanished around the corner.

I'd need help getting up the stairs myself because my legs were too weak to move. I found myself wondering: What would it be like to have Mateo carry me over the threshold? Preferably shirtless. Or better yet, he'd carry me through the church doors, where guests would toss rose petals and confetti. We weren't allowed to throw rice anymore because it killed the birds and—

"Janelle!" Grandma Trina clapped her hands an inch from my face. Eyeing me askance, she asked, "Girl, what is your problem? You act like you never seen a boy before."

"Nothing." I scooped up my bag, raced upstairs, and hid inside my room.

I paced the rug at the foot of my bed, mouth dry, hands shaking, as red-hot electrodes surged through my system. A drunken giddiness I hadn't felt in years had me laughing at nothing and bursting to share the experience. The words had to be spoken aloud or else it never happened. More important, I needed to know what that smile had meant. Was I reading too much into it?

Needing an expert opinion, I dug into my bag, grabbed my phone, and dialed Alyssa. She had a creepy sixth sense about these things and could interpret all hidden guy signals. Every detail was crucial to what my next move should be, so she—

It was around the second ring when the realization hit me like a bucket of ice water. My thumb punched the END button before her voice mail could pick up. I dropped the phone on my desk and backed away until my legs hit the bed.

Once again, just as had happened in Alyssa's room, I'd gotten sucked in a strange loop in time. It took a few seconds to remember where we were and what we weren't anymore.

It then dawned on me that I had no one to share this moment with. Alyssa hated me, I couldn't even look at Sera right now, and Sheree was out of the country, which left me 100 percent bestie-free. For the first time in ages, I was sans buddy. I was minus one. Sheree was right. I'd need stamina and stiff principles to get through the rough parts. They couldn't get any rougher than this.

POLICY 15.2: CONFLICT OF INTEREST

TWO YEARS AGO

Stars covered the entire ceiling. Not just stars, but constellations, planets, and meteors named after celebrities. From wall to wall, an LED galaxy glowed in the semidarkness. The Air and Space Museum had a number of exhibits on each floor, but this one had me both speechless and jealous at first sight. Jealous because my ceiling at home looked bargain-bin busted by comparison. And speechless at how the creative team fit the entire Milky Way in a gym-size room.

But I was past all that now and had reached a whole new level of pissed off at what I'd witnessed in the hallway.

Five minutes ago, I was walking around, enjoying the sights, minding my own business. Now I was questioning my own sanity and racing through the exhibits in need of a second opinion.

I zigzagged through the crowd, my neck straining in the search for a sophomore with wavy hair. Under the monster rings of Saturn stood Alyssa in a bubble jacket, leggings, and Ugg boots. She'd given up her staple glittery gold costume pieces for a look that was a bit more . . . *basic*. It didn't fit her at all, but that was what her "new friends" were wearing.

"Come with me," I said. Before she could protest, I grabbed her by the wrist and pulled her toward the entrance.

We stepped out of the observatory and into the blinding sunlight of the main corridor. The museum resembled an aircraft hangar, with glass taking up the front side of the building. Our classmates wandered the open hall, pointing and taking pictures on their phones while teachers and chaperones micromanaged the tour group.

Alyssa squirmed and pulled at me, but I only let go of her hand when we reached the side balcony.

I pointed to the scene below. "You mind telling me what that is?"

She peeked over the railing toward the bottom floor, then noted the capsule suspended in air by wires. "A large model of the *Apollo* space shuttle."

"Not that. The two people standing under it."

Her eyes moved to where I pointed. Then she frowned. I'd hoped for shock, outrage, and maybe a quick plan of attack, but all she offered was a shrug. "Oh. That would be Mateo Alvarez and Destiny Howell holding hands. They made it official this weekend."

My mouth fell open and all the blood in my body drained to my feet.

"What?" I cried out, then held up my hand when she

opened her mouth to repeat herself. Her words were clear the first time. But I wanted to deny this new reality.

Laughter steered my attention back to the first floor. Destiny giggled while Mateo palmed a giant plasma lightning ball. His curly hair shot straight up from the electric static of the glass. Those two coexisting in any capacity felt not only profane but scientifically impossible. One of the museum guides could probably prove it.

"Why didn't you tell me?" I asked Alyssa.

Arms folded, she rested her back against the railing. "I figured you wouldn't care either way."

"Of course I care!" I lowered my voice. "You know how I feel about him."

"Feel or felt?" she asked. "Because you haven't done anything about it in the past three years. What, you expected him to wait for you on the off chance you'd turn brave enough to approach him? That's not how life works. When I first told you I liked Ryon, I didn't wait for the stars to align. I planned out a five-step system on how I was gonna get him down the aisle. And yes, my methods might be devious—"

"You locked him in the janitor's closet with you—"

"—but my methods got results." She spoke over me. "I have a doctor's note to excuse my weaknesses, you don't. Yet you'll sit back and let a girl take the guy you want. I say more power to her."

"Really? Destiny, the klepto?" I pointed to the bottom

floor. "I can't believe you're defending her. She's faker than Monopoly money and keeps stealing my stuff in class."

"Mateo is not *your stuff*, and that's your fault, not hers," Alyssa shot back. "She's my friend, too. And I'll support anyone who shows backbone. In fact, I'll help them along."

Help them? It took me a second for the words to click. "You set them up?" I whispered.

She didn't bother to deny it. If anything, she looked proud of her betrayal. "I may have mentioned something to Mateo about a love letter in his locker. I didn't name names, but I didn't debunk his theory that Destiny sent it, either."

I leaned back and gave her a once- and twice-over to make sure I was talking to the same person. Was this the Alyssa Weaver I knew? Had she been hypnotized and trapped in the *Gossip Girl* version of the sunken place?

Come to think of it, this personality swap hadn't happened overnight. It had been a slow, gradual creep within the past year. Never mind her clothes—her whole attitude had changed. Her tone got colder, her visits to my house got shorter, and her banter got more hostile.

I shook my head slowly. "What *are* you?"

She held out her hands and shrugged. "I don't know. Effective? Ambitious?"

"Manipulative? Two-faced?" I offered instead. "Did you figure getting in good with Destiny would help you climb the social ladder? So you do your friends dirty just to sit at the cool kids' table? And you call me weak? Girl, bye." I walked away, not knowing where I was going nor caring if I broke the rules by straying from our group.

Alyssa was right on my heels as I marched past the astronaut suit display, the model figurines, and moon rocks sealed behind glass. Heads turned in our direction, feet scooted aside to give us room, whispers hummed in the air as we passed. The tension was pudding-thick, so people were bound to sense it. Yet my pace didn't slow until I reached the IMAX theater at the far end of the hall.

"See, that's my biggest problem with you, Janelle," Alyssa began, her short legs struggling to keep up with my long ones. "You get mad when stuff doesn't go your way, but you didn't put in any effort. I'm always stuck doing the legwork for every money-making scheme while your head's in the clouds. None of your protests and petitions make any lasting impact—it's just noise. You know why? Because you don't really care."

I stopped and glanced back at her like she was crazy. "That's not true."

"Sure it is. If you did care, you wouldn't let your crush slip away. You didn't even try. You're a spectator, a sports fan who tries to coach from the couch. You don't sacrifice or risk anything. There's nothing meaningful to you, not enough to *heat your seat*. Isn't that what your grandpa used to say?"

That was a low blow, even for her, but the disappointment on her face was what knocked the wind out of me. Or was that pity in her eyes? I couldn't believe she saw me as weak, like she was better than me, like things were all peaches and cream in her life. Oh, no, I couldn't let that slide, so I squared my shoulders and let her know a few things.

"Where do you get off calling somebody weak? You're the one who gets tired all the time and can't eat without getting sick. How about you check your glucose and leave me alone. And try not to pass out on the bus ride back to school. We wouldn't want your *new bestie* to find out about you." Those words were pure poison, and I regretted them the moment they left my mouth. But she'd pushed me to the edge, and there was no better person to share my misery with. If this ship was sinking, then we were going down together.

Alyssa just stared at me in silence, her body locked tight as if braced for a beating. Her chin quivered, her eyes watered, yet she stayed so still for so long, I thought she'd zoned out. With a voice thick with phlegm, she whispered, "We're done here."

I nodded, knowing that *done* referred to more than this conversation. "Yeah. We are."

CHAPTER 16

Sheree had warned me that, once word of my maybe-donation got out, the backlash would come in multi-levels of cray. But I didn't think it would be this bad. Or that it would include a phone call from none other than Elijah Pruitt Jr., better known as Dad.

"Janelle, you need to stop this one-woman movement you're on," he commanded through the phone. "It's not up to you to be the savior of the world."

"That hasn't stopped you in twenty years." See, I could clap back because Daddy was sitting up the street from Liberia and Grandma Trina was taking a nap in her room. "How is this any different from you going to war-torn cities with rebels, refugees, gunfire, and bombs going off at random, and a hundred other ways to die?" I went on. "You let Sheree go off to a third-world country and you have no idea what's happening to her. There could be another earthquake and she could get crushed under a building. But oh no! Me donating a kidney to someone in need, someone I know, someone I actually care about—that's where you draw the line? Really, Daddy?"

"You sure got a mouth on you, little girl. You've been hanging with that old lady too long."

Don't get mad at me. She's your mama, not mine. "I thought that was the point of me living with her. To keep me civilized." I smiled even though he couldn't see it.

He harrumphed. "Yeah, a lot of good that's done. Janelle, you need to think really hard about what you're doin'."

"I have," I told him. "No one in her family has a match and if they are a match, they have too many antibodies. I've already been screened and I want to go through with it."

"But have you weighed all the options? Do you know what types of risks are involved?"

I answered his question with one of my own. "If it were me that was dying, would you feel the same way? Would you hesitate like you are now?"

The anger in his voice melted into something close to compassion. "No," he admitted. "I wouldn't think twice." He paused. "But of all the things to fight for, you choose this? If you feel this strongly 'bout helpin' people, there are other ways to give back."

True, there were all sorts of ways to show support without sticking your neck out. Anyone could write a check, pick up litter, or hand over banged-up canned goods and clothes that no longer fit. Plenty of people, including Alyssa, had played that hand—giving but not really, with a righteous smirk tacked on for good measure. But a person's true nature showed when the gift exceeded what was deemed comfortable or convenient. My last conversation with Sheree came to mind, and I recalled something she had said.

It helped me respond to Daddy now. "Anybody can be generous when the gift costs them nothing," I said. "I found my call to arms—that raging fire that heats my seat. Pop-Pop said all the Pruitts had it, but it's different for each of us."

The silence on the other end lasted for years. When my father finally spoke, he sounded resigned and tired. "I can't really stop you, can I? This is who we are. Pop would be proud of you for sticking to your guns."

A warm tingle moved across my back at his words. My eyes prickled and I needed to clear my throat a few times before saying, "Thanks, Daddy."

"Don't thank me yet, little girl. You still need to speak with your mama."

"Oh God!" I collapsed facedown on the bed. The woman was worse than Grandma Trina, and it took twice the effort to make her see reason. Maybe that's why Dad had married her; she reminded him of his mom.

That thought was more disturbing than the phone call, which amounted to an hour of screaming on Mama's end when it was her turn to speak.

• • •

Then there was school. After Ryon's big announcement in the student meeting, I was once again a person of interest. Only this time around, it had nothing to do with my supposed wedding to Mateo in Dubai. The newspaper editor hounded me all through lunch for a quote to put in this month's article. No comment. The Borg begged me to appear in an episode of *Active Beauty* and offered to give me a makeover. Not even if I was held at gunpoint.

The last stall in the upper commons bathroom was the only spot in school to catch a moment's privacy—and a decent signal. During lunch, I was working on two good bars and blocking half the people on my social media when some lowbrow trash talk invaded my headspace. I leaned closer to the stall door to hear clearly.

"You think she's doing it for money?" A squeaky voice bounced off the bathroom tiles.

"Has to be," came another voice. "You see how they fight all the time. I'm thinking serious cash. How much is a kidney anyway? Or maybe she's being blackmailed. Alyssa Weaver's got dirt on everyone, so I wouldn't put it past her."

Through the crack in the stall door, I spied three girls chatting in front of the sink. Sophomores. I was getting bashed by sophomores. What was the world coming to?

"Speaking of black, how can you donate organs to other races?" Gossiper One said while fixing her hair in the mirror. "Ooh, wait. Does that mean Alyssa's kids will be biracial?"

"I don't know. She already talks like a black girl, so she's half-way there." Gossiper Number Two snorted and cackled.

All the kee-keeing and giggling stopped when I stepped out of the stall. Mouths dropped open. Eyes bugged out of their heads and terror scented the air once they realized I was recording them on my phone.

"You three have got to be the dumbest broads I've come across today," I began. "Selling organs is a million percent illegal. An organ transplant does not change your ethnicity. And you do not make racist comments and not expect to get recorded and get posted online in an hour." Wagging the phone in my hand, I strolled past the girls toward the doors, then asked over my shoulder, "What'd we learn, ladies?"

Up until the final bell, people kept stopping me to ask random questions about kidneys and dialysis. Some were curious, others believed it was the start of a new trend, while most kept eyeing me like I stole their boyfriend. At the end of the day, I couldn't hop in my car fast enough. The only reason I didn't drag-race off the premises like I wanted to was due to the fear of vehicular homicide.

Home was the only place I felt anywhere close to normal. My house was crowded with Mrs. Alvarez stumbling about and I now had more people to share a bathroom with. But it was heaven on earth compared to the outside world.

• • •

Just before dinner, I was in the kitchen, feeding Peekaboo lunch meat, when my butt started vibrating. Recognizing the number, I set the phone on the table and backed away as if the caller would kill me in seven days.

Mateo's stare bounced from me to the phone and then back to me. "Really?" he asked.

By the fifth ring, he pulled off his oven mitts, reached over and pressed the ANSWER button, putting the call on speaker.

"Hello? Janelle?" Dr. Brighton always sounded uncertain on the phone.

"Yeah." I swallowed hard, then tried again. "Yes. It's me."

"Good evening, Janelle. This is Dr. Brighton. I'm glad I could catch you. I just wanted to let you know that you've been approved for our Living Donor Program. You have been accepted to donate a kidney to your chosen recipient. Congratulations!"

Approved. Accepted. Congratulations. Those were positive terms that implied some sort of win. Then where was my victory cheer and fist bump? Why hadn't that ten-ton weight been lifted from my shoulders? Why did it feel heavier than before?

I kept my tone as upbeat and sane as possible. "Oh my God! Yay! That's great!"

"I'm glad you're excited," he said. "Once we get confirmation from the recipient, we can go ahead and schedule a surgery time. Does that sound good?"

"Yup," I managed to get out as Dr. Brighton discussed dates, appointments, and more paperwork. By the end of the phone call, a head rush hit me so strong that I had to sit down.

I also seemed to have misplaced my puppy. She was in my arms a moment ago. But I had more pressing issues. How was I supposed to feel about this? Was I happy? Terrified? Queasy? Emotions were hard to identify when they spoke out of turn.

I should have been running laps around the block in triumph. Instead, I was getting the burps and looking for the nearest exit. There was no way out of this now. The donor situation was no longer a hypothetical maybe.

Mateo moved to my side of the kitchen table. "You okay?"

Between breaths, I answered, "Don't know. I really don't know."

"Oh, I get it. Reality is finally hitting home for you. I've seen your Instagram page." He knelt down in front of me and touched my hand.

I couldn't enjoy this small show of affection. Not with my thoughts racing a mile a minute. But he was right, though. It was times like these when you saw a person's true colors.

The internet was a cesspool of negativity and ignorance. Haters dragged me from one end of Twitter to the other, talking real greasy behind faceless avatars.

— Gurl u stupid. Why u throwing ur life away for some white trash!

— *Ur such a sellout. Ppl been waiting years for an organ*
   & u turn ur back on ur own.
— *Ha ha! What a sucker! Have fun getting hacked up. Do*
   u people blead watermelon?

All I could respond with was:

— *DELETE.*
— *BLOCK.*
— *The word is "bleed". Learn to spell.*

Alyssa and I had more similarities than differences, but all people worried about was race. If I heard "Relax, it was just a joke" one more time, I was going to snatch someone bald. If I heard another "I'm not racist, but . . ." followed by some really messed-up comment, I was gonna throw hands.

"A man offered me twenty grand for my kidney," I told Mateo in a voice so small and broken it hurt my own ears. "He sounded so desperate and scared—I couldn't finish reading the message. I wish I could help, but transplants don't work that way. It's not a pair of shoes you break in. Why can't people see that?"

Mateo squeezed my fingers. "You put up a good front, but it's getting to you. Maybe you should go see Alyssa and hash it out."

I pulled my hands away, then rubbed at the heat behind my eyes. "No. She's set in her ways and I don't feel like arguing with her. When she digs in her heels, there's no getting her to budge."

"Then why didn't you cancel your application?" he asked. "Why didn't you tell the doctor she refused the surgery?"

My eyes lifted from my lap and settled on his greenish-brown stare. "Because it's just a matter of time before things get real. Her health is getting worse, and her body will make the choice for her. I want to be ready when it happens."

My phone vibrated again. Speak of the Devil and she will text.

I showed Mateo the message. "Alyssa wants me to come to her house now."

Grinning, he got to his feet and returned to the center counter. "See? There's your sign right there. Go see her."

My gaze darted to the clock on the microwave. "At seven thirty at night?"

He slipped on a mitt, then bent to check the pizza in the oven. "Yeah. Better to see her at seven thirty than the eleventh hour."

Chef Yoda strikes again. Did he have a book of inspirational quotes lying around? And that pizza sure smelled good. But I felt it best to face the devil with an empty stomach, so I went upstairs to grab my shoes instead.

CHAPTER 17

One thing I did not miss was going to Alyssa's house at night. Behind the backyard fence was nothing but wilderness, insects, scavengers, and eight different ways to go missing.

Through the floating pepper cloud of gnats, the door opened and Alyssa materialized, wearing pajamas and a frown. She crossed her arms, which brought my attention to the bandaged fistula on her bicep. I could be wrong, but that thing got bigger every time I saw it. Or maybe she was getting smaller. Her clothes hung on her in a formless tent and her cheekbones were looking really sharp these days.

"So, I've been hearing some things," she said.

"Me too. Sounds like the possums found your trash bins again. Nature's really scary at night, so can I come in?"

In a huff, she walked back inside, toward her room. I closed the door behind me and followed her sluggish gait. If she kept with her usual schedule, then she'd had another dialysis treatment yesterday. Her fatigue had to either be from that nasty powder medicine she had to take or from sleeping all day.

From the door, I scoped out Her Majesty's boudoir. It was clear that the only time she left the bed was to shower, which she did twice, sometimes three times a day to wash off the urine smell on her skin. It leaked from her pores, soured her breath, soiled her hair and the bedding, and left a briny ammonia smell in her room. Scented candles and time-release air fresheners ran nonstop, and sugar-free mints sat in a fishbowl on her bedside table.

I found that out on the day I drove her home from her dialysis appointment. The first thing she wanted after her treatment was a shower and clean bedsheets. She could barely stand, all knock-kneed and woozy like a baby deer learning to walk. Even then, she didn't want my help.

"I got it, okay? I can make my own bed." She'd snatched the fallen pillowcase from the floor before I could pick it up. Eyes closed, she'd exhaled slowly, then asked with controlled calm, "Just be here, okay? I don't need help. Just . . . be here."

And that's what I did. That's what I'd been trying to do ever since. She wasn't asking for the moon; just the remains of her dignity. The trick to honoring that request was to . . .

First: Get all the crying done in the car.

Next: Ignore the elephant in the room, even if the elephant was her.

Last: Treat her like I normally would, i.e., ratchet and hostile, where she'd grant me the same courtesy.

I'd mastered all three of these dark arts, which was why I was the only person from school—aside from Ryon—who was allowed in her house.

Alyssa sat on the bed and collected her phone from the nightstand. "Like I said, I've been hearing some things. It's not like I really care, but have you seen the posts online?"

Hands tucked into my jeans pockets, I averted my gaze and rocked on the balls of my feet. "Yeah, they're pretty brutal."

"Brutal, you say?" She scrolled down the entries in her phone, then read, "*Princess Mayonnaise likes her fried chicken with a side of rice.* Hmm. They must be talking about Ryon. Then there's, *I wonder if she's gonna start twerking after the surgery.* Oh, then there's—"

"Okay, I get it." I sat on the foot of the bed. "My feed is just as bad."

"It's trash like this that I wanted to avoid, Janelle," Alyssa said. "But like always, you gotta wear the cape and try to save someone, even when no one asked you to."

"Yeah," I snapped. "But my hero complex came in handy when you nearly died at the pool sophomore year. So how about you show some gratitude, you hateful brat!"

"Oh come on!" Alyssa hissed back. "I wasn't gonna die and you were the main one freaking out. And let's not forget your *betrayal*."

"Are you still mad that I told Ryon you have diabetes?" I asked. "Funny, that fact clearly wasn't a deal-breaker for him. And you sneaking around, trying to keep it a secret reached new heights of stupid every week. Your own insecurity is what created all this drama in the first place." My finger swung between the two of us, indicating the history therein.

"Mine?" She pointed to her chest. "*My* insecurity? Have you heard of a boy named Mateo Alvarez? Tall, curly dark hair; kids in school think you two have an arranged marriage?"

She had me there.

"And I'll bet my entire wardrobe that you still haven't come forward about that stupid love letter, have you?" she went on. When I didn't reply, she let out a loud groan and rose from the bed. "Omigod! What is wrong with you? The guy lives in your house, sleeps twenty feet away from your room, and you still haven't told him you wrote it?"

"I wouldn't have to admit anything if you hadn't forced me to write that note in the first place," I said through gritted teeth.

"I was doing it for you!" she yelled. "I thought I was helping!"

"Yeah, you said that a few times. The thing is I didn't need your help. Just like you don't need mine."

Silence.

Finally, I asked, "Why did you call me here tonight?"

"I wanted to see how you were. It's been nice the past few weeks. You coming by to see me, taking me to my appointments, and helping me get around afterward. I missed us hanging out. I forgot how much I missed it."

"Then why didn't you say something? You know where I live. You obviously know my number." I wagged my phone in front of her. "We could've done this a long time ago and saved a bunch of needless drama and back talk."

"That would mean admitting I was wrong, that I was weak. I'm neither. I'm not a fragile, pearl-clutching damsel who needs her boyfriend, her daddy, or her best friend to come save her. I worked so hard to break away from that label. Every class trip, every stitch of clothing in that closet—I earned with my own money. The girls I followed freshman year were following me junior year. Me, the marketing genius that could sell *anything* to *anyone*. I was so good, I bought my own hype. I was popular and winning at life *on my terms*."

"And now?" I asked.

Her mouth opened but she paused. Then she wiped the whole issue away with a wave of her hand. "Anyway, I'm gonna channel my superpowers on something worthwhile, starting with these bangs." She crossed the room, took a seat in front of her vanity, picked up a pair of shears, and began snipping curly strands on a mannequin.

With everything going on, I hadn't noticed the faceless white dummy heads. Three of them sat on her vanity table, all with gray wigs styled in short pixie haircuts.

Those blank faces sparked a number of questions. Chief among them being, "What are you doing?"

She fluffed the top of the curly wig with a hair pick. "I'm styling these wigs for Lorraine. She likes the short look. Says it's more believable at her age, but the ones she ordered are all too long for her taste."

Okay, that made perfect sense, except for one thing. "Who's Lorraine?"

"The old lady at the dialysis center."

It took a moment for the identity to click. "The creepy wig lady? You had nothing but jokes the whole time and now you're making wigs for her?"

"She bought them; I'm just shaping them. But yeah, I couldn't just sit back and let an innocent lady look raggedy. Oh no. Not on my watch. I had to do something." She kept snipping. "She's a nice lady. You'd like her. She mentioned having a crush on some guy in her book club but didn't know how to approach him. I recommended she get that dead raccoon off her head and get an eyebrow wax. I also suggested a good skin cream that fades liver spots."

"You're giving dating and makeup tips to old dialysis patients?" I asked, deadpan.

"Janelle Lynn Pruitt, shame on you. Just because you're old, doesn't mean you can't be fabulous. I know I plan to be. Because an *Active Beauty* is always on duty." She gave me a salute in the mirror.

This was the softer side of Alyssa that few people saw. I rarely saw it, but when I did, I took the time to reflect on its rarity. I sat cross-legged on her bed and watched her work her magic for nearly an hour, twisting the Styrofoam head here and there for a better angle.

Though congeniality wasn't her strong suit, Alyssa had always been smart. She got straight As and Bs and earned a master's in the hustle and grind by the age of twelve. It was a real shame. That brain was trapped in that body. That body was killing her slowly and making her feel every minute of it. That body, mostly loose skin and retained water that settled to her feet, now weighed ninety pounds. Nobody needed Grandma Trina to say that the girl looked hungry. It was a given.

"Those better not be tears, Janelle." Alyssa glared at me through the mirror.

I wiped my face. "Nah, it—it's just, you know, my eyes are sweaty. It's hot up in this piece. What you got the thermostat set on? Armageddon?"

She snorted a laugh. Her real laugh. "You've never been afraid to cry in front of me."

Very true, but this was different. I usually cried about things that were already gone or were never with me in the first place. This was mourning in advance, and I thought it best to hold out until that deal was closed.

• • •

A week later, at two in the morning, Grandma Trina tapped on my bedroom door and told me to get dressed. Her request was stern but soft, with a grave note of urgency. For a woman who'd stretch a ten-minute event into an hour-long saga, her vagueness was wrong.

The time of night was wrong. The need to leave my bed in such a hurry was wrong. Could I at least get dressed? No. No time. My shushed questions and the insistence to come peacefully and not wake the rest of the house was wrong. Why did we have to whisper and tiptoe down the stairs? Why couldn't the others know? More commands bumbled in the dim light of the hallway.

Shh, hurry. Grab a coat and come. Everything will be okay.

But why wouldn't it be? I hadn't seen this worry on her face since the night Pop-Pop passed away. A night like this one.

That chill I'd felt in Alyssa's hospital room returned, and I knew without Grandma Trina saying anything that something bad had happened.

Her minivan was cold—no time to warm it up. There was no time for anything; we just had to get there. Everything was closed at this hour, including the eyes of our sleepy town, leaving us to navigate the roads alone with green streetlights ahead.

Thin pockets of shadows covered the hospital parking lot as we parked close to the door. Not in the front for visitations and appointments, but the side of the building, where bold red letters revealed the truth of the situation. EMERGENCY.

Dressed in my sweatpants and a holey Bob Marley T-shirt, I

rushed through the sliding doors. My pupils shrank at the lights and the sterilized white of the waiting room. Mrs. Weaver paced the floor in her pajamas and a winter coat, chewing her thumbnail down to the nub. Her hair was a fried nest of disrupted sleep, her face a wet spill on a painting, a sad clown with black mascara tears.

When she saw us, she raced into Grandma Trina's arms, like a child who needed a mother, and any mother would do. And Grandma Trina held the woman tightly.

"She had an attack. Her levels dropped again and she went into shock," Mrs. Weaver cried. "We were so careful. We did everything right."

Feeling empty-handed and useless, I watched her fall apart in my grandmother's arms. "Is she all right?" I asked.

Mrs. Weaver wiped her black tears on her coat sleeve. "I don't know. I don't know. I don't know! She's all I have; I can't lose her. She's just a baby. I can't!"

"It's okay, calm down, Leslie. We're here. You're not alone." Grandma Trina wrapped a thick arm around the woman's back. "We might be here all night. You want some coffee? Does that sound good to you?"

Mrs. Weaver nodded, then locked eyes on me. "I'll sign whatever you need. She's not eighteen yet and I'm still her legal guardian. I'll do whatever it takes to make her better, ya hear?"

"Yes, ma'am." I tipped my head to her, then looked at Grandma Trina, who was still on the fence about the donation idea.

I expected to see her usual annoyed expression. Instead I saw compassion and a bit of sadness, but it didn't seem aimed at Alyssa's mom. Grandma Trina was directing that look toward me. All that worry that creased her forehead and had seemingly aged her in the past week or so had pushed out of her body in a tired breath.

"The Lord gave us common sense for a reason," she said. "It ain't always about floods and burnin' bushes. Prayers can be answered in a number of ways, includin' at the end of a scalpel."

I nodded at her and let out a long breath. I couldn't have said it better myself.

"Call who you need to so we can get this done," Mrs. Weaver told us. Large, mascara-smudged eyes bore into me, wild with grief. "If there's a chance that she doesn't have to go through this again, I'm takin' it."

Using Grandma Trina for support, she left the waiting room, her slippered feet dragging along the brown carpet. I moved to one of the boxy wooden armchairs and allowed my weight and the weight of the world to land on the stiff cushions.

Three hours later, the doctor gave me the okay to visit Alyssa. Only relatives could stay in the unit for very long, but Mrs. Weaver vouched for me. I told myself I'd stay with her for a few minutes. That's all I could stand.

I stood over her sleeping form, noting the various mechanisms that I now knew by their proper names, thanks to all my doctor appointments. The clear hose taped to her hand: IV catheter. The plastic clamp on her index finger that read the oxygen in the blood: pulse oximeter. The face-hugging breathing tube that tunneled down her throat: endotracheal tube. The ventilator, the EKG wires, the ski-boot-looking braces on her legs that prevented blood clots. I could be a certified RN before it was all over. That would never be a career choice—I was about as sick of looking at blood as Alyssa.

Her hands felt soft and clammy in mine. If she was cold, she wouldn't say. Stubborn people never admitted defeat or asked for help. Waiting for her to swallow her pride would leave her six feet underground, where hot and cold made no difference.

At my touch, her eyeballs rolled left and right under the skin before the eyelids parted. She blinked a few times before her gaze settled on me.

I smiled down at her. "What was that you were saying about winning at life?"

She tried to smile back, but she was too weak to do anything but blink.

I'd expected something like this would happen. It was a hope and a fear, and my reason for not withdrawing from the Living Donor Program. My paperwork was still active, and I would see this through until the bitter end, with or without Alyssa's blessing.

"All right, Lyssa, we tried it your way. Now we're gonna do it my way." I squeezed her fingers to drive my point home. "I'm calling the transplant coordinator first thing, and we're doing the transplant. I don't care if I'm pulling rank and stepping on your toes. You'll have plenty of time to ignore me, talk trash, and get on my nerves later. Because I'd rather have you hate me for the rest of your life than to have you not have a life at all."

The space between her eyebrows quivered in her effort to frown, but then the skin fell smooth again. Her watery eyes held mine as she nodded slowly.

I released a long, exhausted breath. Enough of the fighting, enough of the hurt feelings and bruised egos. Going against someone's wishes was necessary if it was for a good cause. Right now that was reason enough.

CHAPTER 18

Rocking yoga pants, wool socks, and Dad's baggy college sweat-shirt with a hole in the arm, I stretched out on the living room couch and watched TV in the barest of terms. Looking super cute for Mateo no longer mattered and all my past efforts to turn his head had been in vain. Take now, for instance. He sat on the opposite end of the sofa, staring at the screen. That adorable head never turned my way, yet the corner of his eye caught my every move. Few words passed between us as he waited for that overdue melt-down to kick off at any minute. I waited, too.

In a huff, Mateo reached for the remote on the coffee table and turned the channel.

The sudden movement shattered my trance. "Hey, I was watching that!" *Whatever that was.*

"No you weren't. You were zoned out." On the screen, a pudgy chef flipped a pan of veggies over an open flame.

His silent show of support was sweet, but I had to keep the lie going. "No, I wasn't. It was getting good."

"Yeah, the season finale of *Pro Bass Fishing* is 'bout to be lit." His arm draped the back of the couch, Mateo shifted in the seat so his whole body faced me. "You've been moping around ever since that phone call. This was what you wanted, isn't it? You're helping out your friend. She finally agreed to go through with the transplant. What's the problem?"

I could name a couple of problems off the bat. Alyssa was all doom and gloom about the procedure. Sera completely ignored me in school and used Devon Shapiro to relay messages to me during student council meetings. I had to close my Facebook account because I kept getting hateful messages calling me a sellout and a freak. Top that off with the mandatory diet I had to endure for the surgery and I was fit to be tied.

But why burden Mateo with my issues?

"I don't wanna talk about it," I mumbled, and sank deeper into the couch cushions.

"Fine. You need something else to think about. Go change. We're going out." When he got nothing but dead eyes for a reply, he said, "Come on. Let's go."

Channeling my inner five-year-old, I folded my arms and poked out my bottom lip. "I don't wanna go out, either. I need to rest up for the surgery anyway."

"We won't be out long. The fresh air will do us both good." He leapt from the couch and held out his hand.

My stare swung from his open palm to the suspiciously upbeat boy standing over me and blocking the TV. He didn't look like he would move anytime soon, so I planted my feet on the floor and took his hand.

Though I expected a long drive, we only traveled a few blocks toward a new subdivision that was under construction. People lived in the finished houses in the front of the complex, but their backyard views contained stacked lumber, abandoned machinery, and mountains of dirt.

Three blocks deep into the neighborhood, Mateo parked in front of a powder-blue, two-story bungalow. No one seemed to live there, judging by the bare windows and the REALTOR sign on the grass.

He killed the engine, then opened his door. "You wanna come in?"

I pointed to the house. "There? Why? Who lives there?"

"I do," he replied. "Well, me and my mom. I'll show you around. *Vamos.*"

I tore off my seat belt and flew out of the truck. Mateo unlocked the door to the house, then waited for me to step onto the porch. His new keys twirled on a link around his finger.

The house was small, but roomy enough for Mateo and his mom to not trip over each other. The kitchen was top of the line, with stainless steel appliances and plenty of cabinet space to house Mateo's cooking ingredients. I could almost smell the spicy, decadent meals he would prepare. Thinking about it made me miss him already.

"Hey, at least you have your own bathroom." My voice made a hollow echo against the blank walls of the second floor.

He inspected the hall closet. "Yeah, no chance of someone walking in on me while I shower."

I slapped his back, shocked that he would bring that up now. "I told you it was an accident."

"If you say so." The sly grin he gave me from over his shoulder was both a warning and an invitation. I chose the former and backed away slowly.

Admiring the high ceiling and the skylight in the center of the hallway, I asked, "When did you get this place?"

"Earlier this week. Mrs. Trina had some people donate their furniture. Our insurance covers most of the expenses, and we have enough saved until my mom gets better. We're going to start moving some stuff tomorrow."

I spun in his direction. "Tomorrow?"

"Yeah." Keeping his eyes on the floor, he shoved his hands in his pockets and stepped closer. "I won't be able to come to the hospital for your surgery, but I'll be there afterward. I promise."

He sounded so sincere, but I couldn't hide my disappointment. "It's no big deal," I said quickly, trying to cover. "You'll just be sitting in a waiting room for hours. Might as well kill time doing something constructive."

"You're right. So let's go." He reached for my hand and guided me to the door.

"Where are we going?" I asked.

"Our last stop."

After he locked everything up, we hopped back in his big junkyard truck and headed to the middle of town, rolling up to Aberdeen Park around sunset. Mateo parked in front of the Brew-Ha-Ha Café across the street from the park. I didn't want to risk ruining the moment by grabbing coffee inside.

I climbed out and watched the orange-and-pink sky peek through the trees.

"You'd think we'd get sick of this place." I circled the rear of the truck and joined his side.

"I am, but I wanted us to experience this moment together." He took my hand again, checked for traffic, then led me across the street to the park.

That was the second time within the hour that Mateo held my hand. It felt nice, *oh so nice*, but what kind of "moment" were we having exactly? From all the smiling and touching from his end, a "moment" resembled a date. I rejected the theory outright. We were both in sneakers, jeans, and hoodies—not proper date attire. And he'd mentioned nothing about dinner.

Aside from a few scattered tree limbs, Aberdeen Park had been restored to its previous glory. The lampposts, benches, and wooden fences were repaired, the grass was trimmed, and all the trash and hurricane debris was gone. We'd accomplished a lot in just a few weeks and it was something to be proud of, but the victory came with a bitter aftertaste. This place would always remind me of Alyssa's collapse and all that had followed.

By the time we reached the main entrance of the park, Mateo went quiet. He strolled beside me, fingers threaded through mine while he kept checking his phone. That cost him some serious cool points. Even for a nonofficial, kinda-sorta date, constantly checking your phone was a surefire way to ruin any chance of a second date.

"You expecting a call?" I asked, my attitude spiking to a 7.5.

"Nope. I'm checking the time." He glanced at his screen once more. "The sun goes down at 5:42."

I searched my surroundings. Joggers and dog walkers roamed the smaller pathways. Grinding wheels on concrete alerted me of a few skaters nearby. Nothing seemed suspicious outside of Mateo's need for darkness.

"What happens then?" I asked.

"The fruits of our labor come to life." As if on cue, the air swelled in a soft yellow glow. I looked up at the trees and their twinkling branches. I turned to the left and then the right of the path, marveling at the canopy of Christmas lights we'd strung up.

"I almost forgot how pretty they were." The lights shone brighter than the stars in the purple sky. They floated within reach, spaced together so that the gaps in between never got cold. It was how the universe should be.

"What's the secret of the universe?" I asked to no one in particular, not expecting an answer.

Mateo supplied one anyway. "That there's more than one secret and more than one universe."

I eyed him warily. "You're just a fount of untapped wisdom, aren't you?"

He bowed his head. "I try. Any other questions?"

"Okay." I glanced around the park for inspiration. "What's the meaning of life?"

Not missing a beat, he answered, "Relationships and experiences. All kinds. Great or small."

Whoa! I hadn't expected that. For my next question, I considered something simple. "What's your middle name?"

With a sheepish grin, he stared at the lights above, his gaze averted. "Esteban."

I let the name play in my head and swirl around my tongue. Why did everything sound hotter in Spanish? "I like it."

Those greenish-brown eyes met mine again. "Any more questions?"

"All right." I took my time, sifting through the miscellaneous drawer of my mind for something meaningful. Then I found a question that had been popping up regularly in the past month. "Why do bad things happen to good people?"

His playful smile fell. His brows pinched together, his face taut in a pensive expression when he answered, "So you can better appreciate the good. The world is full of opposites and they all complement each other. Otherwise, you're miserable on either side of the scale."

I never thought of it that way. "Opposites?"

"Yeah, like how food tastes better on an empty stomach. Water tastes awesome when you're dying of thirst. To see clearly in bright light, you cover your eyes with dark shades. To be immortalized in history, you have to die. Opposites. They're everywhere. People say opposites attract, but that can also be true about life, you know?" He shrugged.

I lifted a fist toward my temple, opened the palm, and mimicked the sound of an explosion. "I don't know how true that is, but wow. Mind: blown. All right, last one."

He spread his legs and bent his knees slightly, rubbing his hands as if getting ready for a pitch. "Lay it on me."

My heart was racing as I pushed out the words. "How can you tell if someone's meant for you?"

"Ooh! That's a tough one." He scratched the stubble on his chin. "My dad taught me this one trick in third grade. See, in *The Matrix*, there's red pill versus blue pill. In relationships, there's red versus yellow Starburst. *No one* likes the yellow ones, so if a girl takes it anyway, she's a keeper. If she takes the *red* one, she's a selfish, spoiled brat and it'll only get worse from there. Dump her."

Was there an AMBER Alert for common sense? Because all the logic in that explanation had gone missing. Maybe I spoke too soon about the wisdom thing, but I could now understand why his parents weren't together anymore. "I'll make a note of that," I told him.

He smiled. "Speaking of notes, you have a history of good ones."

My brain stalled for a moment then sputtered to life again. "*What?*"

"You know, notes. Like the one you put in my locker in the eighth grade. I don't usually keep notes and cards, but I couldn't throw that one away. It spoke to me. I didn't understand it at the time, but I knew it was important."

As I had the day Mateo first showed up at my house, I underwent a near-death experience. My soul left my body for two seconds. How the heck did Mateo know that note was from me? Alyssa said he didn't know and she had no reason to lie. She had more reasons to gloat and spit the live acoustic version of "I Told You So." Maybe Mateo was fishing for clues now. None were coming from me.

I held up my hands and backed away. "I—I don't know what—"

"I kept it with me constantly, read the lines over and over, dying to know who wrote them." For every step he took closer, I took two back.

"At first, I thought someone else wrote it," he continued, his gaze on me, "but that was a dead end. Then I just gave up and totally forgot about it . . . until after the storm when I went back to my house and picked up my dad's old trunk. All my valuables were locked in there. So was that letter. I was surprised you didn't see it."

He'd kept my letter all this time? He thought it was something valuable to stow away in that musty trunk? I didn't know what to say. He'd gotten me alone, lowered my guard, put me on the spot. Then, before I could respond, Mateo began speaking again. He was reciting something, I realized. Words I'd written four years ago rolled off his tongue like a first language. On paper, they'd sounded awkward, a child's weak attempt to sound grown. But the cadence, the rise and fall of his voice, released a spell that pinned me still.

"*This is not an easy thing to say. I can't crack a joke like I normally do. My feelings are too strong, too heavy to take lightly. When I see your face in a crowd, I forget my name and think it's yours. I forget the places I've been and the things I've seen, and somehow know we're meant to be—*"

"Mateo, stop! Please, just stop." I pushed him back with my outstretched hands. Oh my God! The cringe was so real! What was I thinking when I wrote that? "I can't do this right now. I was fourteen and in a really weird place . . ."

He kept coming until my hands lay flat against his chest. The heat of his shirt warmed my fingers; his heartbeat pulsated under my palm.

"I get why you never told me this was from you," Mateo said, "but I really wish you had. It would've saved me a lot of detective work."

I dropped my hands. "What?"

"When I was cleaning out the spare room in your house for

my mom, I found school supplies: markers, scratch-and-sniff stickers, and colored paper. I found old essays and book reports in there, too. Your handwriting hadn't changed, and whaddaya know? A perfect match."

This was too much. He'd known all this time and he picked *now* to bring it up? The eve of my operation?

As if he knew what I was thinking, he said, "I was planning to tell you after the surgery, but I didn't want to waste any more time. I'm not saying it will, but if anything were to happen to you tomorrow, I . . . I needed to at least experience this once." He closed the gap between us and held my waist.

Too stunned to argue, I allowed him to pull me against him.

He began reciting again, his voice soft, his eyes on me.

"I'm not scared that you'll find out and reject me. I'm afraid that you might love me back. And being your girlfriend means loving the things you love, too. So I'll never tell you who I am, only how I feel. That's enough for me."

He finished reciting my letter, then lowered his gaze to my lips. "Now I've got a question for you, Janelle Pruitt. Now that I know how you feel, is it really enough?"

"It's a start," I whispered.

Mateo bent forward, placed a hand on my cheek, and touched his lips to mine. The kiss was gentle at first, then slowly gained pressure and urgency. My fingers threaded in his soft hair, playing with his curls.

This wasn't a kiss. This was years of daydreams and self-denial and wasted opportunities. It was a clash of emotions: gratitude that this was happening, and regret that we hadn't done this sooner.

If only I'd just told him how I felt before now, I would've had more moments like these: more kisses, more touches, and more freedom to stare at him without looking away. If something *did* happen to me tomorrow, this would be the happiest moment I'd ever had with Mateo. What a waste—all this drama born from insecurity and pride.

Everyone had secrets they worked overtime to keep hidden, and those fears gained pressure under the surface. The truth would eventually erupt, destroy all in its path, and once the smoke cleared, you'd realize it was just a crush. It was just a storm. It was just insulin. Those huge, world-ending issues all seemed small now.

I hadn't realized I was crying until Mateo wiped my tear with his thumb. Neither one of us said a word as we stood with our foreheads together until the sky grew totally dark. We both talked too much anyway.

CHAPTER 19

On the day of the surgery, Grandma Trina and I left the house at ten a.m. to arrive on time for the early check-in. The surgery had been scheduled for that afternoon, but we needed last-minute testing and a final dialysis treatment for Alyssa.

I'd hoped to say goodbye to Mateo, but he'd already left for school by the time I awoke that morning. The door to the room across the hall from mine was open, and looking inside the room proved painful. It had somehow developed an identity crisis. Technically, the room belonged to Sheree, but Mateo had been here for so long that I'd come to think of it as his. And it already felt empty without him—especially after what had happened between us in the park last night.

His absence had me feeling like I'd been stood up at prom. It stung a bit that he hadn't bothered to see me off, but I had to stay focused.

Grandma Trina drove us to the Atlantic Wellness Center. The

huge facility was made up of three buildings locked in a triangular formation with a courtyard in the center. Grandma Trina and I entered the pavilion at the rear of the second building. According to Dr. Brighton, that was where all the magic happened.

We found Alyssa and her mom in the waiting room outside the transplant unit. We had another four hours before we'd get called in for surgery, and the first few minutes were taken up by floor-gazing and awkward small talk.

"Is Ryon coming?" I asked Alyssa.

Her head lifted from her phone and she brushed the hair from her face. "Yeah. He's coming after school."

"Oh." I tapped my feet. "Are you nervous?"

"Yeah. I'm pretty freaked out, but I think things will go well." She glanced around the waiting room. "This place is state-of-the-art and top-notch. I don't think anything bad will happen to us."

"There's more to it than that," I told her. "There's also the aftereffects we'll have to deal with."

"Yeah, well, I'm sure there's a pill for that somewhere." She flashed a smarmy grin. It was her defense mechanism: giving attitude before showing fear. I couldn't knock her for it; I'd done the same thing in situations that were less terrifying.

A nurse in blue scrubs stepped into the room, chart in hand. "Alyssa Weaver?"

Alyssa got to her feet and collected her bag. "I'm off to dialysis. Hopefully my last one."

"I hope so, too." My smile fell as I watched her sluggish steps toward the nurse. She no longer had the energy or the coordination to strut.

Ten minutes later, I, too, was called to the back room for another round of tests. Urine, blood, tissue samples. Blood pressure, EKG, X-ray, and ultrasound. It was the speed round version of my donor evaluation, where everything was done in two hours.

"After assessing all of your test results, we've decided that your left kidney will be the one we'll remove," Dr. Foster said, looking more into his file than at me. He was the surgeon in charge of the transplant, the man behind the magic.

"Now, this could be done a few ways, but we will be using the keyhole method," he said. "It produces less scarring and a shorter recovery time."

"Uh-huh." I nodded out of reflex so we could speed things along. I'd gone through the rundown of the surgery before with the doctors, so I wasn't hearing anything new. The routine loses its luster once the trick has been explained in agonizing detail. Let's keep it real: Nobody wanted to know how the sausage was made, so to speak. And right now, I was more concerned over whether the butcher was missing any fingers.

Dr. Foster was a nice-looking guy, though. Olive skin, salt-and-pepper hair, trim physique, and a bit on the short side—roughly five six. He had all ten fingers, and he looked to be in his forties. So I wasn't dealing with some old, jittery dinosaur who should've retired a decade ago. That was comforting. Still, the whole thing was draining me, body and soul, and I would die happy to never see another lab coat or needle again after this.

"There will be three half-inch incisions in the front, one just under the left rib for the camera. The other two will be work ports, located on either side of the belly button." Dr. Foster indicated the points on my stomach with the tip of his pen.

"Uh-huh," I mumbled, chewing on my thumbnail to the meat. My stomach was gurgling, my right knee would not stop bouncing, and I observed all of this as if it was happening to someone else.

Scars weren't really an issue for me—that was more Alyssa's area of narcissism. I was all about simpler things, like not dying during the procedure. Every horror story that had been told—be it via email or word of mouth—flashed in my head. The guy who woke up in a tub of ice with his kidney missing. The guy who died from a staph infection because the surgeon sneezed in his open chest cavity. The nurse who tossed a healthy kidney in the trash by mistake. Shiny, happy thoughts.

"The final one will be a five-inch incision at the bikini line where the kidney, its artery, vein, and ureter will be removed and prepared for transplant. The abdominal area is a very compacted space of the body, so a small pouch will be inserted to inflate the area, similar to a car jack lifting the wheel off the ground." Dr. Foster continued his rundown of the procedure like he had somewhere else to be within the hour. It all sounded cut and dried. No muss, no fuss. The operation could be performed in his sleep, let him tell it.

"You'll lie on your side during the operation and be placed under general anesthetic. You'll have time to talk to the anesthesiologist before the surgery about whatever concerns you might have."

"I just wanna know if it will hurt," I said while my stare drifted to the stomach diagram hanging on the far wall.

"No. You'll be under general anesthetic, so you'll be completely unconscious. You'll feel discomfort afterward, as is to be expected, and we'll prescribe pain medication for you," he explained.

"How will they know I'll be totally under?" I asked. "I saw this one movie where this guy was awake during the whole thing and could feel the blade and hear the doctors talking smack and everything."

His wry smile implied that this was a common fear. "Yes, we are well aware of that condition and it is extremely rare. And the anesthesiologist will be available to treat you in case something goes wrong. The overall surgery will last three to four hours. You will be taken to recovery, where you'll be observed for any issues. After a few hours, you'll be sent to your hospital room. So, any questions?"

Tons, but sadly none that he could answer. Stuff like, *How bad will it hurt afterward? Will I feel the lost kidney like when amputees can still feel their missing limbs? Will I have to watch what I eat like Alyssa does? If the kidney fails to work for Alyssa, can I get it back?* But instead of sharing all that, I mumbled, "Uh-uh."

By the time I was sent back into the waiting room, I felt like

I'd just survived an alien abduction. I refused Grandma Trina's offer of food. The doctors had explicitly told me not to eat anything before the surgery. And anyway, I had no appetite. My nerves were all over the place and nothing entering my stomach would stay there for long.

While Grandma Trina discussed overnight accommodations with the nurses, I hung around the common room with Mrs. Weaver. We sat a seat apart, facing a TV with no sound on. I checked my phone for any new messages. There were a bunch of well wishes from my parents and Sheree, but I hadn't heard a word from Sera. I'd texted her before I left the house this morning. Her brother no doubt told her about the surgery today, so what was with the crickets on her end?

I glanced over at Mrs. Weaver, not entirely sure if she was awake. Her head tipped as far back as it could go, her hands covering her face from the overhead lights. She looked as though sleep hadn't crossed her path in years. It had been a pattern lately for people to lose sleep over Alyssa and that trend needed to die with the Jheri curl.

"Is Alyssa's dad coming?" I asked her.

Her arms dropped to her lap. The heavy sigh that pushed from her mouth told me all I needed to know.

"It's just as well he stays where he's at. He'll just be in the way, tryin' to run shop like he's been here the whole time. But he called her last night and wished her luck." Her head rolled in my direction. "Whadda champ."

"You mean chump?"

"That too. So how are you, Miss Janelle? You doing okay?" she asked.

"Freaking out a little," I replied honestly.

"That's natural. Look at it this way: You two will be a lot closer now. Best friends don't get no closer than this."

Best friends. I'd hoped for something a bit more traditional. You know, the stuff you see in commercials—girls prancing around at the mall arm in arm, checking out boys, and smiling because they have clear skin. To tell the truth, I never had that experience with Alyssa—or Sera.

My phone buzzed on my lap then, and I wondered if Sera was psychic.

SERA: Good luck today. I hope it goes well for both of you.
ME: Thanks.

Brief but effective. I wondered if she'd visit me after the surgery. It had been a lonely few weeks without her.

Smiling, I tucked my phone away, then asked Mrs. Weaver, "Is it possible to have more than one best friend at one time?"

"Sweetie, you can be in love with two men at one time with the same passion. So yeah. I s'pose it's possible."

For real? What had Mrs. Weaver been up to in her spare time? I pushed that thought away. "But how?"

She rubbed the back of her neck and thought it over. "The doctor said when they take your kidney out, the one left over will grow to make up for it. I reckon the heart works the same way. You think somebody's your one and only and can't nobody replace 'em. You ain't gotta replace 'em. The heart makes room for more folks to fit in."

That kinda made sense. If anybody knew anything about packed spaces, it was the queen hoarder herself.

Extending her arms, she bent back for a full body stretch. "I tell ya what, hon. People are the fun-house mirrors of your life. Some make you tall, some make you wide. Some make you see double or twist you into somethin' you can't recognize. Not even that one regular mirror will show your true self. The thing is, *all* of them images are your true self."

I guessed that was true. People do change you, for better or worse. After all, I was now surrounded by a lot of deep thinkers. Perhaps Mateo and Mrs. Weaver could swap philosophies over coffee.

"Best friend or not, y'all two got somethin' special," Mrs. Weaver continued. "I saw it soon as she first brought you over to the house when you were kids. You really are an angel for my Lyssa."

I wasn't looking for praise, but I nodded all the same. "Thanks."

"No, I mean it. That's what she calls you." She leaned in, her bony shoulder touching mine, and whispered, "You know how all the angels got E-L at the end of their name? Gabriel, Michael, Raphael, that sort of thing? She thought you were like that."

Janelle: the watcher of sick and angry gingers. And not to nit-pick the issue, but my name wasn't spelled that way, so my next question came from a place of concern. "Was she on any medication when she said that?"

"Always. But that's when you get the truth out of her, so get it while you can."

That didn't sound like such a bad idea.

I tapped on the door and poked my head inside the room. "Alyssa?"

"Yeah." She sounded drowsy and distracted.

I stepped inside and closed the door. She reclined in what looked like a leather padded barber's chair, magazine in hand, ear-buds in, and TV monitor on while the robo-kidney did its thing. According to the timer, she had another hour left on the spin cycle. Dialysis always left her drained and I wanted to catch her before she was too loopy to talk. There was no telling when I'd have the chance before surgery.

I grabbed the chair in the corner and dragged it closer to hers. "How are you?"

She pulled the bud out of one ear. "Nervous."

"Me too." My eyes panned across the room. Not much to see—everything was white, disinfected, and boring. No generic landscape paintings. No motivational posters, no gross diagram of human body parts. At least she had a television.

"Look, I don't know what's gonna happen today, but I just wanted you to know that I'm sorry," I said.

Her brows dipped into a frown. "For what?"

"For being a crappy friend. For babying you and treating you like a charity case. For always talking trash to you. All of it."

"I think I know that. I mean, I know you didn't mean to do any of it intentionally. It's so hard trying to be normal with *this* hanging over your head." She gestured at the dialysis machine. "It sucks having to explain to people why I can't eat certain things and why I get tired all the time and what this thing is sticking out of my arm. And the stares." She blinked away the moisture from her eyes. "Either they feel sorry for me or they don't look at me at all. Like I'm a freak."

I bent forward and propped my elbows on my knees. "You're not a freak."

"I'm not normal, either. I'm not . . . healthy." The words left her mouth in a wet, strangled sob. "Something's . . . wrong."

I placed my hand over hers, careful not to crush it. Her fingers felt like bones in a sheer casing of damp skin. "I know. But that's why we're here. We can make things right. This can be fixed."

Her chest heaved as more tears trickled down her cheek. "I'm sorry for ditching you and pushing you away. It was messed up and I'm so sorry, Janelle. I just want you to know that."

I nodded.

"Do you think that's why this happened to me?" she asked. "Because I hurt you and did all those mean things to other people? This is karma biting me in the butt, isn't it? It's a punishment for past sins? Do you think that's why I got sick?"

"No. Alyssa—"

"Look around. Look at them." Her eyes circled the room. "You see all the awesome show of support standing around? Neither do I. I just see you. And it hurts because you're the person I've trampled over the most and now you're the only one here."

Maintaining full eye contact, I scooted closer until our chairs touched. Her seat stood high off the ground, so I had to look up at her to get my point across. "You are not cursed. This is *not* your fault. It just happened. Bad things happen to good people *and* bad people. No one is exempt from that exam. No one is born absolutely perfect. Look at me. I'm pigeon-toed, I've got oily skin, and—"

"You're really comparing that to kidney failure—"

"And split ends galore," I finished. "That's why I keep my hair in braids, so I won't be bothered."

Eyes narrowed, she replied in a lazy monotone, "A true underdog story for the ages. How did you overcome such adversity?"

"A good moisturizer, mostly. But I take it day by day." I was about to say more when I realized that neither she nor the media had been notified of a certain cosmic event. "Hey, guess what? I kissed Mateo." This truth had to be spoken aloud, testified, or else it didn't happen. A tree-falling-in-the-woods-type deal, but with lips.

Alyssa's own lips formed a perfect circle before she shrieked, "What? Shut up!"

"I'm dead serious. I've seen the promised land. I've been to the mountaintop, and I'm still high from the altitude."

Her face lit up. "Really? How was it?"

I struggled to find a good description. "Highly emotional. Wasn't really expecting that."

She made a tsk-ing sound. "Let me guess. You cried for all the wasted years you spent pining over him when all this time you could've had all that Latin goodness and a free chef. And . . . this would be the part where I say, I told you so, and you laugh at your own stupidity. If you're not up to it, I'm happy to do it for you."

I found her observation unsettling. "How did you know that? Did you have someone spy on me?"

"Nope. No need to with you, Janelle." She pointed to her temple. "Twinsies, remember? I know you. I might even know you better than you know yourself."

CHAPTER 20

The call had come in forty minutes ago. Alyssa and I parted ways as a nurse escorted me to the opposite side of the hall in the transplant unit. The nurse led me into a small, private room where I'd stay for the next two nights. I was relieved; I'd never had a problem with sleeping in strange places, but the last thing I wanted was a hacking, coughing roommate.

The nurse did the usual tests: blood pressure, pulse, and last-minute samples, as if my vitals from four hours ago weren't accurate enough. They put an IV catheter in my arm, so they wouldn't have to keep pricking me whenever they needed to draw blood or inject me with fluids. Once she was all done, the nurse handed me a paper gown wrapped in plastic, then left me to change.

The next hour was a parade of doctors. First came Dr. Brighton and his floppy hair and Hollywood smile. "So are you having any anxiety or reluctance about the procedure?" he asked.

"A little," I admitted. Cold air glided over my skin like fingers as Grandma Trina helped me tie the back of my gown. She sat behind me on the bed and pulled my braids back into a bun and twisted it so it laid flat. A hundred memories of sitting at her kitchen table flashed in my head and helped thaw some of the chill of the room.

"Some hesitancy is to be expected. It's perfectly normal and again, you are under no obligation to continue," he warned.

After everything I'd gone through? Was he serious? Even Grandma Trina stopped braiding and looked at the man.

"I'm fine. Just got the jitters," I assured him.

"Good. Most of it is anticipation and buildup. The other half is the fear of the unknown. Just know you're in the care of one of the best surgeons in the country. You're in excellent hands." He wished me well and quit the room.

"You sure he's a doctor, baby?" Grandma Trina craned her neck to watch him leave, then shook her head. "That boy don't look real. He might be CG like that prince from them *Shrek* movies."

"I know, right?" The muscles in my face felt strained when I laughed, like I hadn't done so in a while.

Twenty minutes later, the last thing I wanted to do was smile. Humming a gospel tune, Grandma Trina sat in the chair next to my bed and fiddled with a piece of peppermint she always had stashed in her purse. The candy wrapper crinkled like TV static and shredded my concentration.

I closed my eyes and counted to ten, then twenty, and getting nowhere. Everything seemed amplified. The walls were too white; the furniture and sink area was too boxy, too sterile to be a real room. Medical equipment lay everywhere, complicated and impersonal.

My mouth was dry; my heart felt huge in my chest. Pop-Pop would say that you only noticed the heart when you're in trouble. Boy, did I notice it now! Its beat rolled thunder in my ears, the mother of all countdowns.

Two nurses came in with the stretcher that would transport me to the operating room. "Okay, Janelle, are you ready to go?" the first one asked, and sounded too cheery, too eager, too suspicious.

No. No. No! NO! "Yeah," I told her.

Was it too late to back out? There had to be someone else who could do this other than me. This wasn't like getting a tooth pulled. This was major surgery where I'd be knocked out for hours. I no longer had power over the situation.

It's not too late to change your mind. There's no obligation. You need to be certain this is what you want.

Dr. Brighton kept telling me that. So had an entire army of specialists. It was their catchphrase that never caught on, because I was too stubborn to see things for what they really were. But then that was always my problem.

Alyssa had mentioned karma. Well, maybe this was mine kicking in for being a smart-mouth, and a coward, and thinking I was better than everyone else because I gave more and cared more. Was I any different than Alyssa? Was there even such a thing as a good cause? None of this was feeling good right now. This was *not* what I ordered and I just wanted to go home.

I felt hands transfer me from one bed to another. Soon, I was being wheeled toward the elevator in the hallway. Blind terror rushed over me once the elevator doors opened and I was wheeled inside. When the car began to drop, so did my stomach. My breath released in shallow, labored pants.

It was happening, the eleventh-hour second-guessing they warned me would come right before surgery. After weeks, days, hours of waiting for calls and lab results, stares in school and the comments online, the highly anticipated freak-out was finally here, folks.

This was the *real* reality show—not that fake crap the Borg slapped together. I wasn't watching destruction, pain, and injustice on TV. It wasn't secondhand accounts of a hurricane ruining lives while only howling past my own. It was the phantom I felt in Alyssa's hospital room, the cold skin of Pop-Pop's cheek. It was death paying me a visit and I. Was. Not. Prepared.

On the sidelines of my panic, I heard Grandma Trina's voice.

"Baby, I'm right here. You're gonna be just fine."

A slight pressure forced me to glance down at my hand. Had she been holding it the whole time? My grandma had worker's hands: thick skin corded in raised veins, capped off with bright-red nail polish. I would need those strong hands to get through this.

The doors opened again and we rolled down a white corridor.

The overhead light sped across my vision like broken lines on a road. The bed stopped at some pre–operating room docking port where the anesthesiologist waited for me and began busying herself with my left arm.

"Okay, I'm injecting the anesthetic," she said.

"I thought it was a mask you put over my face," I said.

She smiled, her eyes studying the needle in her hand. "No. This will tunnel into your IV and in a few minutes, you'll feel a little woozy and then you'll drift off. I promise, you won't even realize you are under."

"Okay." I nodded as she leaned in with the needle. "Wait, you're doing it now?"

"Yes."

"Okay. Okay." I looked away, not for fear of pain, but in some vain attempt to delay the countdown that had already started.

Everything was hitting me at once. I was going under the knife. People with sharp, pointy things would dig into my skin, touching parts of me that I'd never even seen. And what if I did wake up and feel all of it? They said it wasn't likely, but I could be that 0.00001 percent that starred in that horror show. What if the surgeon left something inside me, like a scalpel or chewing gum? What if they took the wrong kidney and I'd be stuck with the smaller one? What if I died while under anesthetic? How would I know that I was dead? I wouldn't graduate or see my family or kiss Mateo again . . .

"We need to get started," the doctor announced, and the bed began to move again.

"Just breathe through it." Grandma Trina squeezed my hand. "I'm right here, baby."

My body clenched, my limbs stiff as petrified wood. I tried the breathing thing she suggested, but it came out in shallow hiccups. "I'm. Scared."

"I know. You're gonna be fine, you hear me? You are the bravest person I know," she said.

My head teetered along the pillow. "I'm not brave. I'm not brave. Grandma . . ."

At some point, she'd let go of my hand and we were moving again. I closed my eyes tight and envisioned the stars on my ceiling and wondered if Alyssa was going through the same thing. Was she scared, too? Was she cold? Or was it just me . . .

CHAPTER 21

"Janelle? Janelle!"

Someone was calling my name. They kept saying it over and over, trying to get my attention. Eventually, my eyes opened. My lids felt heavy and sticky. I strained to pull them apart, but then they snapped closed again.

Grandma Trina's voice whispered in the dark, warm and soft as the hand on my cheek. "How are you, baby?"

"Drugged." That was the only way I could describe this all-encompassing weirdness. I could sense that some significant amount of time had passed, but I couldn't get up to speed. Everything had happened in a blink. I was awake, freaking out over the anesthesia, death, and life. Then blink-blink. I lay in the recovery room. What had happened during the surgery? Why did my body feel so stiff? What was this thing up my nose? What was this thing sticking under my—

"It's a catheter. They need to test your urine and see if you're at full capacity," Grandma Trina supplied helpfully. "You won't be able to leave the hospital till you can do a full number one and two."

I cringed. "How's Alyssa?" I mumbled.

"She just came out of the OR. The surgery went well. The kidney's already workin'." Her smile eased what little anxiety I had left.

"That's good." My eyes rolled around, up to the hanging lights, searching for her in the room. "Is she here?"

"On the other side of the curtain." Grandma Trina scooted between our beds and pulled back the partition.

Alyssa was still unconscious, but even from this distance, she looked better, not so ashy and clammy. She had more color in her cheeks.

"Alyssa?" I whispered. "Alyssa?"

"What?" She sounded annoyed, which meant she'd recover quickly.

"Are you okay?"

Her eyes were closed and her face was mashed against her pillow. She mumbled, "I was fine before you started buzzing around my ear."

"I think the operation went well," I told her.

"Oh yeah? That's great, buddy. Yay, teamwork! Night-night."

Nothing but soft snores came from her side of the curtain for my next four hours in the recovery room. A nurse came in every few minutes to check on us between naps.

After I got the all-clear, the nurse rolled me back to my room on the third floor. The initial purpose for the move was for me to get sleep in a peaceful setting. However, the constant beeping of machines, the inflating and deflating blood pressure cuff on my arm, and the incredible throbbing in my back kept me up most of the night.

The nurse instructed me on how to use the painkiller button. The dosage was preset, only dispensing the prescribed amount every few minutes so I wouldn't OD. I wasn't used to sleeping on my back, and every shift and roll on the bed felt like being swaddled in a blanket of fire.

But the hard part was over. I'd done what I set out to do.

The next morning, I was forced by the on-duty nurse to eat. I ordered eggs and toast, and no food in the world could pack this much flavor. My taste buds felt brand-new. The nurse told me that it was a common side effect after surgery, but I suspected it had to do with me not eating for thirty-six hours. All the same, Mateo's theory about opposites came to mind and lingered after every bite.

The first few hours went as expected. Doctors and nurses poked at my bandages and took more tests, all the while refusing to remove the catheter.

"It needs to stay in a little while longer, sweetie. We'll take it out tomorrow and see if you can go to the potty on your own," the nurse told me in a cutesy voice suited for a Muppet.

Did she really say "potty"?

Soon, Grandma Trina returned from our house with more food, an extra blanket, and my laptop, as requested. I spent the next few hours on Skype with Sheree while Mama called in on speakerphone. I gave them both a detailed rundown of the surgery. Mama was making her feelings clear about me having a serious operation so young, but as always, big sis stood in my corner. It was hard to get a word in edgewise when talking to two opinionated women in the same room, let alone through two gadgets.

"I can't believe you donated a kidney!" Mama wailed.

"I told you weeks ago, Mama." My ears were still ringing from that last conversation with her. Rumor has it that the memory was the first thing to go in old age. Or maybe she was in shock or denial or both.

Now Mama's words came out shrill and panicked. "I still can't believe it! I just . . . How could . . . I didn't know you had it in you, baby."

"She had two in her, actually. They're a set. Like Twinkies," Sheree replied.

"Oh, you hush up, smart-mouth," Mama chastised. "What are you gonna do about school, Janelle? You'll need time to recover. How long will you be out? Will you be able to graduate on time?"

"Mama, she's still in the first semester of senior year—"

"Did I ask you, Sheree Claire?" Mama snapped. "I ain't make this long-distance phone call to talk to you about somebody else's medical problems. I wanna talk to my baby."

"I'm your baby, too!" Sheree cried.

"Girl, you got one more time to interrupt me and I'ma hop on a red-eye to Haiti and it's gonna be me and you."

There was something wickedly amusing about seeing your sibling getting chewed out by your folks. It created a balance in the cosmos and confirmed that you weren't the lone troublemaker in the family. Plus, the scrunched-up faces Sheree made through the screen gave me the giggles.

"Just know that Christmas break is in a few weeks, and I've got a long memory, Sheree. So make all the faces while you can." Trust Mama to issue a threat from another continent and still give me the chills.

Sheree and I froze. My eyes searched the room for cameras. How did parents do that? I think all moms have a bit of Professor X in them or they bug their kids with microchips at birth.

When the room got quiet, Mama redirected the conversation to me. "Go on, Janelle."

I pointed at the screen and made an Ooh-you're-gonna-get-it face at Sheree, who stuck her tongue out at me. Then I informed our life bearer, "As long as I pass all my exams, I should be okay. My teachers know what's up and all my assignments will be emailed to me. But I'll only be out of commission for two weeks and be at full capacity in six."

Though she sounded perturbed, Mama conceded. "Well, I guess that's something. I wished you'd done this after high school. You're just so young and haven't seen the world yet."

"I've seen more of the world than most. And I doubt Alyssa would've made it for that long," I explained.

Sheree watched me through the monitor and asked, "So how are you feeling?"

I twisted my shoulder left and right, then fell back onto the pillows. "I'm mad sore. They're gonna try and make me walk around, but they won't let me pee on my own."

"No. I meant in here?" She patted the space over her heart.

"I feel good. I feel more relieved than anything else. Alyssa will have a chance at life now. Let's hope she makes the most of it."

Day two was more of the same. Food, vitals, reflex test, and a bandage change. These guys had an unhealthy interest in my pee and kept checking the volume level in my catheter bag.

Today was visitation day, and everyone I knew rolled up to my room: kids from school, people from church, and the transplant team. Even Nurse Bambi swung by to check on me. By the time everyone left, my room looked like a flower shop. Grandma Trina had to take a few to her suite in the humanity house where she was staying on the Wellness Center campus.

Late in the afternoon, just when I was about to settle into a nap, someone tapped on the door.

"Come in," I called, then sat straight in my bed when I saw who stepped into the room. Holding a potted plant, Sera stood in the doorway, looking out of place.

"Hey," I managed.

"Hey." She held up the flowerpot and stepped up to my bed. "I brought you this. I wasn't sure what to get you."

"Thanks." I took the plant and set it on my meal tray. "You rode up here with Ryon?"

"Yeah, he's in Alyssa's room now. She looks great, by the way. Not so pale anymore."

I nodded. "That means stuff is working like it should. A very good sign."

"You haven't gone to see her yet?" she asked.

"Not yet. Maybe once I'm well enough to pee on my own, I'll go. I'm trying to hold food down and not pull anything."

Sera grimaced. "You can't pee on your own? Are you wearing a diaper?"

"No, that would be dignified. I'm wired to a bag."

Sera searched the floor, then flinched at something at the foot of the bed. "Omigod! Is that what that pouch is for?" She backed away a few steps.

I nodded, then moved on to a more important topic. "I'm glad you came."

"As if I'd stay home. I'm not that heartless." She shifted her feet, fumbled in her pockets, but eventually got the ball rolling. "Look, I'm really sorry for the way I've been acting. I was hurt that you kept me out of the loop and I blew things up and I handled things badly."

"Yup," I agreed. "But so did I. I'm sorry for not telling you about the donation, and for biting your head off all the time. It wasn't about you. Life was stressful enough and I didn't want to make things worse by getting you involved. I know you don't like Alyssa dating your brother—"

"You think Ryon's the reason Alyssa and I can't stand each other? Ryon?" She scoffed. "You never notice how she acts when I'm around? Her left eye gets all twitchy just seeing me stand next to you. That's some jealous ex craziness, and you're not even dating." Nervous hands unraveled one of her braided pigtails. "She was your best friend. You guys have a history that I don't even know about. And when I found out that you were gonna give her a kidney, it just added on to the whole thing. What if you guys become besties again and you get sucked into the Borg's mainframe and turn into one of them? I mean, Alyssa's tied to you for the rest of your life. You are literally a part of her. That's deep—on a whole other level, man. I can't compete with that."

It was comforting to know that I wasn't the only insecure person in the room. "Why do you need to?" I asked. "I can have more than one friend. And what's to say Alyssa and I are gonna be BFFs after this?"

Pursing her lips, she tossed me a looked that said: *Girl, please.*

"This is a life-changing event," Sera argued. "And think about it: All movies end the same way. The oddball cop duo who fought all through the movie, ride off into the sunset together. Happily ever after. You and Alyssa are like the super duo."

And here I thought I watched too much TV. "Um, maybe,"

I said, trying not to laugh. "But that still doesn't mean I can't have more than one friend," I told her. "I can use as many as I can get right now."

Her face brightened. "Oh yeah?"

"Yeah. I mean, I'm not allowed to lift anything over ten pounds for six weeks, so somebody's gotta carry my books." I gave her a cheeky grin.

With a sardonic smile, she placed a hand over her heart. "Aw, so sweet." She glanced around the monitors by my bed. "So which one of these buttons shuts off your oxygen?"

We talked for about an hour before the nurse came in with more food. Sera sat with me while I ate. After my meal of mushy meat and potatoes, Ryon dropped by. He was all misty-eyed and blubbering. Sera had to calm him down.

"Dude, get it together. You're embarrassing everyone on the floor." Sera handed him a box of tissues.

"I'm sorry, I just . . ." Ryon blew his nose. "Janelle, I just don't know how to thank you for what you've done."

"You just did. You're good, man. There's no need for the—oh boy! Here we go." He swooped in for a bear hug that lasted longer than anyone was comfortable with. I patted the top of his head. "Okay, thanks. I'm feeling the love, really. It's running all through me."

"Okay." He pulled away, wiped his face on his shirtsleeve, then turned to Sera. "You ready to go?"

"*Are you?*" she fired back. "I'll gladly drive home and leave you here if you need to get checked."

After they left, I lay back in bed and settled into a peace I hadn't felt in years. An overwhelming sense of accomplishment spiked my adrenaline. While I basked in the high, Sera's potted plant caught my attention, its purple flowers sprouting from dirt.

I didn't know much about plants. The poor thing would probably die within a week. I considered giving it to Alyssa since she loved the color, but regifting a get-well/let's-be-friends-again token was probably poor form. I thought about what Sera had said, about how movies ended. But the thing was, in movies, you never really saw what happened after "happily ever after." You never saw the collateral damage and cleanup after the alien invasion. You never got to see if the hero suffered nightmares or battled trauma once the dust had cleared. It's a shame, really. I would've appreciated the honesty.

CHAPTER 22

The next day, I passed all the basic requirements: I was able to keep food down, sit upright, walk on my own, and perform the necessary bathroom functions. I was allowed to go home the day after.

Alyssa would spend a week at the hospital, as her condition was way worse than mine, but she was expected to make a full recovery. Ryon and other members of the Borg would keep her company, so I didn't feel too guilty for leaving her there. My body craved a real bed, with all the comforts of home.

Later in the evening, I was encouraged to stretch my legs and do some more walking. Not much ground could be covered on a walker with an IV stand, but I made it down the hallway and back.

"You're doing great, Janelle. Good job!" A nurse cheered and clapped. I almost expected a doggy treat for my efforts.

I returned to my room, drained and wanting to pass out, but I didn't want to turn in just yet. It was time for me to make a visitation.

With the aid of the nurse and a wheelchair, I reached Alyssa's room and tapped the door.

"Come in."

The nurse rolled me inside and spoke to Alyssa in a goo-goo baby voice. "Hey there, sleepyhead! Guess who's here to see you!"

The nurse stood behind me so I couldn't see her face, but Alyssa's troubled expression said it all.

"Uh, hey there." Alyssa rolled her shoulders in a stretch and sat up on the bed. She had the worst case of bedhead I'd ever seen, but she looked well rested.

The nurse turned to go. "I'm sure you got a lot of catching up to do, so I'll leave you two to talk. Just page me and I'll take you back to your room. Buh-bye now!"

When she left, I rolled my wheelchair closer to her bed. "She is so weird!"

"I know, right? She brought me food earlier and called it din-din." Alyssa shuddered.

"How are you feeling?"

"Like I've been run over twice. But the doctors say I'm at thirty-five percent kidney function. They think it'll go up in a few weeks."

"That's great." I pointed to her arm. "You can get rid of that fistula thing."

"Maybe. It's too soon to tell." She shrugged.

She didn't seem as thrilled as I was. "Are you at least hopeful?"

"I'm too scared to be," she admitted. "I'm trying not to think about it too much. I have to take these antirejection pills for the rest of my life. Things might be good now, but the kidney might stop working out of nowhere and—"

"Yeah, it's best not to think about it too much," I cut her off. "I don't regret my decision and neither should you."

"But what if you do someday?" Alyssa asked. "What if a few months from now or even a year from now, the whole thing fails and you're stuck with one kidney, and I'm back on the machine, back on the waiting list, waiting to live or die?"

I offered a different scenario. "What if the kidney is so strong, it exceeds the doctors' expectations and makes medical history and you live to be a grandmother? I'd be Dorothy and you'd be Blanche and we'll be having the time of our lives in a retirement home in Florida. It's possible, too."

She reached out her hands as far as she could. "Thank you."

Mindful of the tubes, I squeezed her fingers. "No problem."

"I mean for everything. For being there even when I push you away. For not listening to me when I say I'm okay and going above and beyond what a normal person would."

"If you start singing *The Golden Girls* theme song, I'm going back to my room."

A pillow sailed past my face at my remark. Alyssa dropped back onto the bed, sapped of what little strength she had.

"Hey, watch out. You don't wanna pull out any of those tubes." I pointed to her taped arm and hand.

"I'm being serious and heartfelt here," Alyssa went on. "This is a rare event, so you sit right there and suck up the gratitude." She pushed the hair out of her face. "I am grateful. I'm scared and confused, but I'm truly grateful, Janelle. I don't know how to repay you."

My chest felt full and empty at the same time. This had been a gift, not a transaction. But I was dealing with a shrewd business-woman here, so I had to think on her level. Though the price might be too high for her, I gave her my fee anyway. "Start by being a good person. No rewards, no guilt trips, no trendsetting. Yes, it's true that every good deed might have a motive; I guess just make sure that motive is a good one."

"So I pass it on somehow, like a chain letter." She nibbled her bottom lip and considered her payment plan. "Do I get to choose the theme?"

What was this? Prom? But I'd learned early in my relation-ship with Alyssa to pick my battles. She had the right to pick hers. Pop-Pop said that each fight was different for everyone. The thought wrapped me in a cozy warmth that had been missing for so long. "Just go with whatever heats your seat."

When I returned to my room, I knew a non-staff person had been there. The air carried an oaky-sweet smell of sandalwood, and a brief message was written on a hospital notepad.

Sorry I missed you. I couldn't stay long. M.

Oh crap! Mateo was here and I missed him! And I'd left my phone here in the room so he couldn't call me. I wanted to cry and flood his inbox with texts or race him to his car. None of these were doable options with fresh stitches and a phone battery at 3 percent.

Then my eyes fell on the envelope propped on the meal tray. The color of the stationery gave me déjà vu and caused the hairs on my arms to stand straight. Purple-and-pink construction paper in the shape of a heart. Unease turned to curiosity when I unfolded the paper and found a handwritten letter boxed in with scratch-and-sniff stickers.

I read the letter over and over, trying to find hidden messages between the sentences, tiny scraps of information that could answer my questions. Why hadn't Mateo come to look for me? He'd left a note, so did that mean he wasn't coming back? And where was the rest of the candy?

A half-eaten pack of Starbursts hid behind the letter on the meal tray, the wrapper twisted closed at both ends. He must've bought it from the vending machine. I unraveled the foil and found four pieces and balled-up wrappers inside. All of the wrapped candy was red and all of the paper balls were yellow. The orange and pink Starbursts were still at large—their whereabouts remained unknown.

I got into bed and admired the smooth penmanship, elegant and unrushed, as if he'd planned the letter for weeks. For a guy,

Mateo had nice handwriting, and it blew me away that he would use those skills for lil ol' me.

> *Janelle,*
>
> *This would be my fourth attempt to write this letter. Every time I try, I either lose my nerve or lose my voice. Words can't express how proud I am of you, and your courage is a quality I admire beyond words. I wanted to thank you for sharing your home with me and my mother. You and your grandmother have expressed kindness that I've never experienced. You've given me hope and a new outlook on life. But that's not the reason I'm writing this letter. I want to pose another question to you. If a simple love letter can stand strong against four years and a storm, what are the odds of the real thing?*
>
> *I'll expect an answer when I see you tomorrow. I cooked something special for you.*
>
>

Siempre,

Mateo
>

I tucked the candy under my pillow and curled under the covers. My eyes grew heavy reading the note once more. I pondered the question he'd posed to me. There was no guarantee of anything, but the outcome looked good.

POLICY 23: RECOVERY

SIX MONTHS LATER

Rocking camo-print short-shorts, an army fatigue halter top, and a matching ball cap, Alyssa stood at attention and saluted the camera.

"Hey there, cadets! This is Alyssa of *Active Beauty*, reporting for civic duty. The daily forecast is balmy: tank top and sandal weather. So wear your sunscreen, guys. Anyway, I'm here with my very good friend . . ." She paused and nudged my elbow.

"What? Oh! We're filming now?" The mic and camera in my face made me jump into action. With an awkward salute, I slapped on my biggest and most manic smile. "Okay—hi. Hello, internet. I'm Janelle Pruitt. Um, I'm a senior at—"

"Okay—stop. You're giving us crazy eyes." Alyssa took back the mic. "We're here at the *fabulous* White Chapel High School to raise money and help loosen the stranglehold that threatens these hallowed halls. Thanks to that stupid hurricane, the city is low on funds, so they're threatening to cut crucial programs next year. The arts and after-school activities are essential to academia. They allow the youth to explore their creativity and social interests. And as seniors, it is our duty, our *civic duty*, to ensure that these programs are available for future generations." She paused for dramatic effect, tugging at the hearts of her viewers.

Balancing the camera on his shoulder, Joel Metcalf followed her toward the ballooned and bannered entrance of the student parking lot. I had to admit that his camera work was top-notch and his editing skills alone made *Active Beauty* stand out from other vlogs online. With half a million subscribers, he and the Borg could make this a full-time gig. Alyssa insisted that the ad cents go into the school's funding. But not even their growing viewer count could bankroll our recent crusade. That's where my fund-raising plan and the day's festivities came into play.

I moved with Alyssa through the maze of yellow-and-white tents, concession stands, and inflatable attractions. Banners flapped in the warm breeze. Posters hung at every station:

SAVE THE ARTS!
WE NEED OUR SCHOOL PROGRAMS!

Beyond the lot, caution tape and sawhorses blocked vehicles from the rear of the school. The parking area in front had reached full capacity about an hour ago, so the police redirected traffic to the stadium parking lot across the street. The turnout was ridiculous and it all had to do with the bubbly ginger by my side. Joel moved in stride with her smooth gait until she stopped in front of an inflatable boxing ring.

"As you can see, we have a number of activities happening this weekend. There are games and raffle tickets and goodies galore! Over here, we have fake sumo wrestling, where you can vote on your favorite fighter. My money's on Ryon Kimura. Those familiar with *Active Beauty* know him as 'The Bae.'" Alyssa waved to the ring. "Get 'em, Ryon! You can do it! Woo-hoo!"

Stuffed inside a fat suit, Ryon hopped in circles around his similarly suited opponent. At the sound of his name, he turned to Alyssa and waved back. "Hey, babe!"

"You can do it, Sugar Booger! Love you!"

"Love you too—*ahhh!*" was all he got out once the other fighter rammed him to the air-padded floor.

The crowd surrounding the ring winced at the brutal takedown and erupted with a loud, "*Oooh!*"

Ryon rolled and teetered along the floor, then gained enough momentum to waddle to his feet. "I'm okay! I'm okay!"

At the same time, Tabatha Morehouse grabbed hold of Alyssa's microphone. Sporting purple hair and a flower painted on her cheek, she ranted into the camera. "Not only is this racial appropriation, it's also a barbaric form of fat-shaming. In this social climate, it is *highly* problematic—"

Alyssa nudged Tabatha out of the shot and kept going. "And over here, we have a gallery of student artwork for sale and a portrait stand run by our very own Mr. Russo. I took his art class freshman year, and he's amazing . . ."

I watched, amused at Alyssa's peppy hair-tossing on camera. She was doing the most with the bouncy cheerleader routine, and it was nice to see her in good spirits. Since all contact sports were permanently off the table, she had to get her cardio somehow.

She was now at 55 percent kidney function and no longer needed dialysis. She had to take medication every day to keep everything up and running, and to prevent her body from rejecting the new kidney. Aside from that, it would take an elephant tranquilizer to slow her down.

We wandered over to the concession area, where every baked good you could think of was on display. The air was warm and thick with the scent of buttered popcorn, homemade pies, and honey-roasted everything. My mouth watered for a sample, but I had to pace myself. I hadn't been put on a strict diet, but I also had to hold off on rigorous exercise for a while.

I'd been sluggish and sore for the first two months after the surgery, as was to be expected. Aside from monthly checkups and the ugly scars on my stomach and back, though, I felt normal. Alyssa and I had identical scars, but she was more inclined to show them off than I was.

That morning, Grandma Trina had caught me examining my incision marks in the bathroom mirror.

"Girl, put some shea butter and ointment on that and call it a day. You'll be fine," my grandma had told me as she'd walked past.

She'd been clocking me nonstop since I came home from the hospital, asking about my feelings and peeking inside my room at night. At first, I thought she was afraid I'd die in my sleep. Turned out she'd been advised by Dr. Brighton to watch for signs of depression. He'd warned us that that was a common side effect after donation, but all I felt was relief. Alyssa and I had survived the school year. That was a celebration in itself. To be honest, I was more depressed that Dr. Brighton wouldn't share his hair regimen with me.

While Alyssa interviewed a stuffed animal vendor, I wandered over to the booth with the red-and-white-checkered tablecloth. Cookies, brownies, and tarts formed neat little pyramids inside glass cake stands. Mateo stood behind the counter, ringing up treats for customers.

After starring in a cooking segment on *Active Beauty*, word of Mateo's culinary skills had gained traction. Now a line for his famous cinnamon cookies ran ten heads deep and wrapped around the tent.

I moved behind the counter. "Sold out yet?"

Mateo grinned at me. "Almost. Ran out of white caramel brownies an hour ago and I'm getting low on frozen cookie dough. They seem to be the big sellers."

"I told you so. People are all about the cookie dough.

There's more in the back. I'll get it." I scooted farther into the tent to the freezer chest. As I attempted to lift the twenty-four-pack of bottled water sitting on top, I felt a tug on my arm. I looked up and found Mateo standing beside me, wearing a serious expression.

"Oh, no you don't! No heavy lifting, remember? Doctor's orders," Mateo admonished.

"It was just for six weeks. It's been six months. I'm good," I told him for the hundredth time.

And for the hundredth time, he ignored me and took the burden from my hands. His warm fingers slipped over mine, slow and deliberate, as he hefted the case of water and placed it on the ground. He was kind of overdoing it with the kid gloves and we both knew it. That hadn't stopped him from driving me to school and carrying my books everywhere. It was a complete role reversal to be catching rides from him, but it gave me the freedom to ogle him without fear of wrecking the car.

I bent over the opened freezer and pulled out four frozen pints of homemade cookie dough. "At some point, I'll have to do things on my own. You baby me too much."

I felt a pair of hands squeezing my hips, a solid chest pressing against my back, and warm breath tickling my neck as he said, "Maybe so, but isn't it a term of endearment to call you 'baby'?"

I considered it for a moment. All was good in my world,

just as long as he didn't call me Sugar Booger. That alone was grounds for divorce. "Meh. I like the other words you use."

He eased me around, sandwiching me between him and the edge of the freezer. "Words like, say . . . *querida*?"

The sound gave me the tingles. I shimmied my shoulders. "Ooh. That's a good one."

His head dipped lower, then he whispered, "*Bomboncita*."

My focus stayed on his advancing lips until I went cross-eyed and my lids grew heavy. Of all the tasty treats he allowed me to try, his lips were my favorite. "That one, too."

Sharing a breath, his lips moved against my own. "*Mi corazón—*"

"Would you two hurry up? We ain't got all day!" a customer griped.

We glanced up, startled by the sight of half a dozen people, including Alyssa and Joel, gawking at us at the counter. I buried my face into Mateo's neck.

Chuckling, he pecked my forehead and whispered, "We better get back to work."

A sudden commotion parted the crowd. Devon Shapiro approached the snack stand, looking sweaty and out of breath. "Janelle, come quick! You've gotta get your girl!"

I knew who he was referring to, and I smiled. "She's *your* girl," I told him.

"Yeah, but only you know how to handle her. She's out of

control, man. She's eliminating contestants at random. They're not getting a chance to finish the song."

Alyssa rolled her eyes. "And people say I create drama."

"Because you do." I scooted out of the tent. Devon hurried alongside me to the center of the lot. We reached the messiest competition I'd ever seen. The sudden-death round at this morning's pie-eating contest had nothing on this.

I glanced up at the makeshift stage set on a six-foot-tall platform. The trapdoor in the center of a stage reminded me of the gallows in old Western movies. There'd be no hanging here, and the only crime was bad vocals. The punished would fall through the trapdoor and tunnel through a series of tubes beneath the stage, similar to a water park ride. Then they'd shoot out to ground level onto a slip-and-slide tarp. It was like a talent show and a carnival water dunk tank had a baby.

To my absolute horror, Sera had been left in charge, with a microphone and an amp at her disposal. Thank God the sound equipment was waterproof.

"Do you think you've got the voice? You think you've got what it takes to be the next American pop sensation? Well, step on up and take a chance with the SUPER STAR SOAK karaoke challenge. The louder the applause, the longer you stay dry! The winner will win a prize of two hundred dollars!" Sera yelled into the microphone, effectively scaring the crowd. "We're looking for the best of the best. You've got a voice of a dying cat? You can't hit a high note on helium? Then stay right where you are."

"Give me that." I snatched the microphone from her. Its feedback shrilled in my ear. "You can't insult people before they get onstage, Sera! Let the crowd decide."

Hands on hips, she rounded on me to make her case. "Hey, this game is not for the faint of heart. They need to know that going in."

I groaned. Now that Sera and I were back on good footing, our battle had returned to the usual issues of volume control and being extra. Despite it all, we still made a good team. My heart swelled at the thought of what we could accomplish by joining together for a common goal. No need for rivalry and pettiness; *that* vital organ could expand to accommodate everyone.

Scanning the crowd, I spotted Alyssa standing by the food tent. Knowing smiles passed between us. We hadn't shared that look in ages.

I remembered how I'd told Sera that Alyssa and I were friends. But the truth was, we were more like sisters, bearing the same scars, both seen and unseen. It didn't matter if we never spoke again after graduation or if we fought every time we did. Our bond would keep us in two places at once. That was the weird twinsie connection we shared, molded and tried by fire. The threat of losing that connection was hot enough to heat my seat and fight to keep what was left between us alive.

If that didn't make for a good cause, I don't know what did.

ACKNOWLEDGMENTS

If I were to summarize the theme of *Sorry Not Sorry*, it would be: the act of giving and the motives behind it. This story holds a special place in my heart. Its creation has been full of emotional ups and downs that seemed to echo my personal life. Though I've never endured the issues of diabetes or organ failure myself, I've seen its impact on those close to me.

I've learned from this project that time is precious and it's the most valuable gift to give to others. My mother's victory over breast cancer taught me the value of quiet strength. Between treatments and checkups, I've seen more hospitals than I'd ever care to, yet she handled her recovery with a graceful dignity that I envy. I am extremely thankful for my sister's wisdom of the medical field, along with the nursing staff for answering all of my nitpicky questions.

I would like to give my sincere thanks to the doctors and medical experts who proofread the initial manuscript and made sure I used the proper terms and technical jargon. Special thanks to

Dr. Alyson Myers and Alana Webber for their helpful reads and feedback. I send thanks to my editor, Aimee Friedman. Her enthusiasm never wavered no matter how many times she combed through the manuscript. Her diligence knows no bounds.

Lastly, I'd like to give special mention to my cat, Casey, who passed away from organ failure while I was writing this story. From the outside, it seems strange to use an ailing cat as a muse, but artists find creativity in the strangest of places. Like life, inspiration can happen in a flash of lightning or in a slow crawl around your ankles while you write. A small, unassuming presence with nothing profound to offer but his company. If you ask me, that is one of the greatest gifts in the world.

JAIME REED is the author of the Cambion Chronicles series and *Keep Me in Mind*. She studied art at Virginia Commonwealth University and now lives in Virginia, where she works part-time as a line producer for a small independent film company. But mostly she watches '80s movies and writes. Learn more about her at jaimereedbooks.com.

Books about Love.
Books about Life.
Books about You.

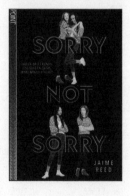